Noble Deeds

Melinda Byrde

Published by Stillwater Muse

ISBN 978-0-9977197-0-3

Chapter One

Then...

Molly grew up on venison when it was available and canned tomato soup, stored by the case under her mother's bed. Tomato soup was cheap; only 11 cents a can back then, and with crackers could officially be considered a meal. At least that's what her mother thought, for she bought cases of tomato soup whenever she had a few extra dollars. Her reasoning was that they may not have milk and they may not have bread, but the family could always have a nice dinner with tomato soup.

Many things were different back then. Television sets were like portholes into a black and white world that was, for the most part, alien to the residents of the small mountain town of Hickok. Computing was done with paper and pencil and maybe a slide rule, if you were lucky enough to have one and know how to use it. Mothers stayed home, whether they wanted to or not, and the American Dream perpetuated itself with row upon row of tiny rectangular houses.

The town, having nothing else going for it, was dedicated to fully exploiting the legend of Wild Bill Hickok, rumored to have spent at least a portion of his life there. Thanks to the wry humor of a local rancher, the original town, founded in the late 1860s, was given the improbable name of Sheep Dip. The government, however, had the last laugh, and Sheep Dip was washed away as part of a federal dam project at the turn of the century. The population picked itself up, moved to the other end of the canyon and reinvented itself as Hickok, "Wild Bill's Home Away from Home."

Happy to live the legend, Hickok worked hard to become a picturesque old west town. Over time, it was able to offer something for everyone. Tourists could wander down wooden sidewalks and through authentic cabins and sarsaparilla saloons, ending up at the rodeo grounds for a nightly display of cowboy macho. Others could peruse the trinket shops and souvenir stores for just the right thing to commemorate their western vacation. Local residents breathed a collective sigh of relief when the tourists arrived in the summer and again when they left in the fall.

There were always a few drunken brawls, an angry husband or two, and an occasional "hippy" bashing (way back then), but other than that life in Hickok was generally uneventful. Like any other small town, gossip was the local pastime. Even though what happened in the family usually stayed in the family, the occasional bona fide scandal kept the phones busy for days or even weeks.

When Molly was ten years old, something big and bad happened… something that left a black mark on her town from that point on. A young girl, Cathy Locke, was found brutally murdered in her own home. Cathy lived in an elegant house on a tree-lined street in the older and better part of town. She was thirteen when she died.

Everything changed then. The founding families were alarmed, because this kind of thing just didn't happen to the pampered elite -- especially to the children of the pampered elite. The working class was uneasy, because anything that unsettled the founding families

2

usually had dire consequences for the local economy. The town's poorest people avoided eye contact and stayed quiet, for they knew that whenever anything happened to the pampered elite or the working class, the poor were usually blamed.

Life went on, but it was different.

Now…

Molly was speeding through the dusty high plains in a black BMW, the result of her latest mid-life crisis. With the approach of middle age she seemed to be having a lot of mid-life crises. It was as if her ever vigilant "I need to be responsible" filter had somehow broken. Now it was more like, "I want a pedicure and I don't care if the deck needs painting." Part of her was horrified with her new attitude, but the new Molly was happier, more stylish, and had great toes.

She was listening to what her kids called the "Oldies and Moldies." They could tolerate Joe Cocker and Crosby, Stills, Nash and Young. They would even listen to Cat Stevens, but Bob Dylan almost made them cry. And sometimes she threw on Sinead (they called her Sinbad) O'Connor and Tracy Chapman just to spite them. Right now she was wailing away with Janis Joplin, trying very hard to forget that she was driving back to her old hometown of Hickok.

Of course, trying to forget about Hickok only made her think about it more, so she gave up and let both the pleasant and not-so-pleasant memories wander in. She was going back home to see her mother, whose most recent telephone conversations had seemed vague and distracted, as if she was only slightly attached to this world. Molly called her siblings, at least those who were speaking to her, and they agreed that someone should check on Mom. Molly turned out to be that special someone.

Just thinking about her mother gave Molly a twinge of guilt – no reason in particular, just this sense that she must be guilty of something.

Not her mother's fault, really, since she had been a child of the Great Depression and was raised to believe that it was wrong to want anything. Her mother told these wonderful stories about living in tents and eating canned fish and wearing clothes made from salvaged (stolen?) highway flagging material. But there was perhaps more truth in the stories she did not tell. To the world she always put on a happy face, but there was something fragile about the woman. Something breakable, that could not be easily repaired. Molly learned to be responsible at an early age. She also learned that guilt was the currency of that era, and that under no circumstances, should waves be made.

But thinking about her mother also made Molly smile. Here was a dynamic and intelligent woman who could make an adventure out of being poor. She wrote silly poetry, and sang sweet songs, and made sweet treats for all the neighborhood children. She kissed "boo-boos," made mud-pies, and never failed to quiet a fussy baby using her own special "bonk-a-butt" method.

She was a woman of many contradictions, eliciting mixed feelings from her eldest daughter.

Molly's father had died ten years earlier in a hunting accident. He was a hard man... hard working, hard drinking, and hard to be around. Molly had been afraid of him because he was loud and angry most of the time she was growing up. He, too, was the victim of his own upbringing, but every once in a while Molly could see a chink in his armor. She had feared him, yes, but she had also loved him. She knew that he was more than what he seemed and she deeply regretted not having the opportunity to know him better.

Startled from her reverie, Molly realized that she had begun her descent into the Clarks Fork River basin. If she squinted a bit, she could see a miniature Hickok in the distance. It had always surprised her that it looked so big from this vantage point. It could still be considered a small town, but it was much larger than she remembered growing up. It had easily doubled in size... maybe even tripled. And the outlying areas had become pricey housing developments, not readily affordable to the regular working stiff. In the past few years, Hickok had decided to change its image from "old west tourist trap" to "western cultural oasis." The main street became home to art galleries, theme restaurants, specialty leather shops, and high-ticket Western fashion (whatever that was). Those people who actually needed to buy groceries, or antacid or work socks were banished to the shopping centers on the outskirts.

As she approached the edge of town, Molly took a deep breath, steeled herself for return to a different life, and promptly pulled into the nearest specialty shop to buy chocolate.

Over the years she chipped away at all of her so-called vices, but she drew the line at the finest of confections. She loved silky dark ... no fruit, no nuts, maybe a truffle or even expensive fudge. In recent times (remember the mid-life crisis), Molly had taken to buying exotic and often expensive candy, rich in dark cocoa and she enjoyed it so much that sometimes she embarrassed herself in front of other people. She would occasionally share with like-minded connoisseurs, but she refused to share it with her children because there was no possible way they could give it the proper appreciation. At the store, she made her purchase and then sat in the car, eyes closed, until she had finished half of the

6

bar. Feeling better, Molly revved up the engine and headed to her mother's house.

Molly's mother still lived in the same white house, in the same non-descript neighborhood, not exactly on the wrong side of the tracks but pretty close. When Molly was small there were hardly any trees, because the neighborhood had been hastily constructed on scrub grass and pastureland. But trees were lovingly planted and the more stubborn ones grew until Molly and her siblings could actually climb one without it bending dangerously close to the ground.

Molly didn't knock. Nobody ever knocked. A visitor might rap on the door as they went in or call out, but knocking was unheard of. She found her mother sitting in her favorite chair watching the Jerry Springer Show. Red flag! First of all, her mother looked surprised that her eldest daughter had just walked into her living room. In fact, she said, "Honey, what a nice surprise. I was just thinking about you." Molly had called her mother that morning before she left and again on her cell phone only fifteen minutes earlier as she drove into town. The second red flag was the Jerry Springer Show. While Molly believed that anyone was constitutionally entitled to watch Jerry Springer, it just didn't fit with everything she knew about her mother. She was more of a "Murder She Wrote" or "Poirot" or "Nero Wolfe" kind of person. But the woman actually had tears in her eyes as she watched a large, bald, heavily tattooed man, whose pants rode so low that he was, in essence, mooning the audience. Molly was not sure why, but the man kept saying, "Ah loved that little gal liken she was my own flesh'n blood." She got the creepy feeling that this was not a good thing.

"Mom," said Molly. "I'll make you a cup of tea. Can I fix you anything to eat?"

Her mother turned off the TV set and asked, "Honey, did you come for lunch?" It was 4:00 p.m.

Becoming seriously alarmed, Molly busied herself in the kitchen, trying to formulate a plan. After a few minutes, her mother wandered in, but seemed to be completely bewildered as to why she was suddenly in the kitchen. A few years ago, one of Molly's dogs had a close encounter with a porcupine and had to be sedated in order to remove all the quills from his face. Still high on sedatives when she picked him up, he would stand in one place for a while, listing slowly to one side. Then he would perk up and trot with obvious purpose into another room only to forget why he was there. He entertained the whole family for hours until the sedative wore off. But this wasn't funny. Her mother was behaving the same way and Molly was pretty sure she had not had a run-in with a porcupine.

Abandoning the tea idea (her mother had forgotten all about it anyway), Molly said, "Mom, I think we need to go for a ride. Maybe go see the doctor." Her mother promptly got up, grabbed a candle from the table next to her chair and headed for the door. After a brief struggle to get her mother out of her bedroom slippers and into shoes, and drape a jacket over her tiny frame, they were both headed to the new walk-in clinic on the edge of town.

Two hours later, Molly was filling out paperwork and calling family members with the news that Mom was in the hospital, had walking pneumonia, and that her blood oxygen level was dangerously low. As she plumped her mother's hospital pillows, Molly realized how very pale and fragile she looked… and frightened. It was going to be a long night.

Startled out of an uneasy dream, in which a huge porcupine with tattoos was chasing her and her only weapon was a candle, it took Molly a moment to realize that she had fallen asleep in the recliner next to her mother's hospital bed. It took her another moment to realize that she had been awakened by laughter. She thought at first that the nurses were sharing some off-color joke at the duty desk down the hall, but then she realized that it was coming from the other occupant in the room. The privacy curtain had been closed and, with worrying about her mother, she had barely realized there was another occupant in the room. From the sound of the laughter, Molly guessed that it was a young girl… maybe having a funny dream like her kids sometimes did. She leaned around the back of the chair and pulled the curtain aside so she could get a peek.

But it wasn't a child at all. It was a woman at least her mother's age, if not older, and gravely ill, judging from the dark circles under her eyes and the gray pallor of her skin. She had an I-V drip, as well as what Molly guessed was a pain medication (morphine?) drip that was set up for self-administration. She was giggling like a naughty child and looking right at Molly.

Molly began to apologize, but the woman held up a finger and shook her head, warning her to be quiet. Looking furtively around the room, she whispered, "I knew you would come back to me. But I won't tell… I promise." She laughed again, her childlike conspiratorial laugh, and said, "I fooled them this time. They think I'm crazy, but I fooled them all." A spasm of pain crossed the woman's fragile features and she hit the pain button at the side of her bed. As consciousness faded away, she looked sadly at Molly and said, "I have missed you so much." Molly let the curtain fall and sat thinking in the dim light until she drifted back into a fitful sleep.

Early the next morning, after checking on her mother, who was somewhat more coherent thanks to an oxygen mask, she asked the nurse about her mother's roommate. The nurse, Cheryl, a shy girl Molly remembered from high school another lifetime ago, shook her head sadly and said, "Poor soul. That's Lucinda Locke. Even though she can afford one, she refuses a private room. I think she's lonely... she doesn't get many visitors."

Molly's mother, on the other hand, had a handful of concerned friends gathered around her bed before breakfast was over. Her breathing had become labored and she was coughing a lot (a good sign according to her doctor), but the oxygen had helped clear her mind and she was obviously enjoying the attention.

Feeling outnumbered, Molly escaped to book herself a hotel room, find something that looked more edible than the hospital breakfast (probably not difficult), and pick up a few crossword puzzle books, in case her mother's social calendar cleared up and she had some time to kill.

Even if she had considered staying at her mother's house, that was not on offer. Her mother had become increasingly protective of her space, almost to the point of paranoia. And, to be honest, even the thought of tossing and turning in her old twin bed made her tired. Besides the creepy clown wall hanging that had terrified her as a child was still somewhere in the house. And even now, after all these years, she still didn't trust it… not one bit. So, a short time later she found herself sitting in the Wild Bill Suite at the historic Calamity Jane Hotel, eating a bagel and sipping a very nice hot cocoa. She knew she should get back to the hospital, but decided to finish her drink first. To ward off the guilt, she set her mind to the task of reconciling the picture she had of Lucinda Locke with the sick, sad creature she had seen last night at the hospital.

The thing that Molly remembered best about Lucinda Locke was that she was the mother of Cathy Locke, the young victim of Hickok's only unsolved murder. But even before the tragic murder of her daughter, Molly had known of the woman. She was always present at charitable events, social gatherings and celebrations of note. She was tall, and elegant, and seemed perfect in every way. Her hair was dark and lovely, and always swept into an understated chignon. Her makeup was tasteful and her clothes were expensive. Molly used to pretend that one of her Barbie dolls was Lucinda Locke, and the doll was aloof and powerful and mysterious.

Lucinda's husband, Calvin Theodore Locke, was very rich. The story was that he came from old money back east, but had somehow embarrassed his family to the point that they had shipped him out to the wild and woolly west, and continued to give him lots of financial incentive to stay there. "Remittance Man" was the term that came to mind. He was the acknowledged moneyman – sometimes a silent partner, sometimes not – for most of the huge land development schemes around Hickok, and had the reputation for turning a nice profit. He was also known to be arrogant, sarcastic and generally mean-spirited. Local merchants would cringe when he walked through the door because, more likely than not, he would find some way to humiliate them before he walked out.

Calvin met Lucinda, who called herself Lucy, when she was working at her father's ranch supply store in the neighboring town of Fremont. Calvin was used to getting what he wanted, and the pretty dark-haired girl was no exception. They were married six months later and set up house in Hickok. It was then, at least for Hickok's middle class population, that Lucinda ceased to be one of "us" and became one of "them."

Shortly after the wedding Calvin surprised Lucinda with a stepson; three-year-old Preston, from a previous relationship back east. Lucinda gave birth to two more children. The first, a son, died in infancy... a tragic crib death. Catherine Elizabeth, known to Molly as Cathy, was born two years later.

Cathy was a beautiful child, with lovely dark hair like her mother and bright green eyes like her father. She was raised like a princess.

After Cathy's death, and the resulting media frenzy, Lucinda Locke seemed to fade into the shadows and soon disappeared altogether. Molly was surprised to realize that she had not actually seen Lucinda since that terrible time, not even in a photograph. Until last night, that is.

Molly visited with her mother, checked on the house, ran errands and kept generally busy until mid-afternoon. Everyone was working hard to maintain a cheerful appearance, but Nurse Cheryl had taken Molly aside and told her that her mother was not immediately responding to antibiotics and they were beginning to get concerned. "Not to panic," she said, adding, "But you might plan to stay in town for a few days." Of course, Molly did panic, but she tried very hard to sound confident and calm when she called her sister. Ginny saw right through it, though, and was ready to hop a plane and be there by morning. Molly assured her that she would stay as long as she needed to stay and that if things got worse, she would call right away. Somewhat mollified, Ginny said she would call the brothers and give them an update.

"Close call," thought Molly, as she hung up. She loved her sister dearly, but what had happened to Molly so long ago had affected all of her siblings in one way or another, and her relationships with them were uneasy in the best of times. This was definitely not the best of times.

She sat for a while with her mother and watched an old rerun of "Murder, She Wrote." About halfway into the plot, her mother fell asleep. Molly turned off the TV and settled into the big recliner with a newly purchased book, supposedly about a pre-menopausal woman coming to terms with her life, by way of a wild and crazy mid-life crisis. Molly thought she could relate.

Lulled by her mother's snoring (her mother was always adamant that she had never, ever snored in her life and never would because it was very unladylike), it took Molly a while to become aware that Lucinda Locke was softly humming what sounded like a lullaby.

As she listened, Lucinda added words, and Molly soon recognized "Mockingbird," sung sweet and low. When she ran out of objects that "momma was gonna buy," she added nonsensical things, just silly rhyming words, and Molly was enchanted. After a round of "elephant trunks" and "stinky skunks," Lucinda suddenly stopped. There was silence for a moment and then she whispered, "Are you there?"

Molly quietly got up from the chair and walked around to the other side of the curtain. As Molly neared the bed, Lucinda grabbed her arm and drew her close. She was smiling, as she whispered, "That was your favorite song when you were small. Do you remember?"

Molly knew, of course, that Lucinda Locke had mistaken her for someone else. They had never met, as far as Molly could remember. Rich families from elegant houses didn't usually socialize with poor families from tiny rectangular houses. Molly had never even met Cathy since she had gone to a better school and was three grades ahead. She had seen them both, of course, but from afar. She wasn't sure how to deal with this case of mistaken identity. To pretend she was someone from Lucinda's past felt dishonest, but she also believed that the woman wasn't long for this world and if it made her happy to think she was talking to a loved one, what could be the harm? Given a choice between "right" and "kind," Molly liked to go with kind. She had wasted too much of her life being "right" and it had left her feeling lonely and distant from the people she loved.

Leaning close to the old woman, Molly said softly, "I remember. I remember the stinky skunks."

Lucinda drew Molly closer, and whispered in her ear. "I'm starting to figure it out," she breathed. "You must be very careful," she continued, pausing to glance around the room. "I found the words and then I knew it wasn't over… You need to go away, now. Go away and be safe," she said softly. There were tears in her eyes.

Molly stroked her hand and said, "But I wanted to see you. I wanted you to know that everything was okay."

"But it's not okay," hissed Lucinda. "It was never okay and I couldn't bear to lose you again, Cathy. Now, go!" she said as loudly as she could. Suddenly, Lucinda's grip on Molly's hand tightened and she

14

began singing Mockingbird again. Molly realized that something had changed and as she turned around, she realized that there was a man standing in the doorway. "You'll have to forgive my mother," he said. "She's a bit out of it because of the pain and the medication."

Molly eased her hand out of Lucinda's grip and stepped away from the bed. "Please forgive me," she said. "I didn't mean to intrude, but I thought she could use some company."

"No," he said. "I'm happy you spent time with her. I don't see her as often as I should and I'm glad that she had someone to talk to."

He stepped forward and offered his hand. "I'm Preston Locke, by the way, and you look familiar to me."

"My name is Molly... Molly Noble. I used to live in Hickok," she said, taking his hand. Feeling suddenly self-conscious under his intense gaze, she said, "I'm here to look after my mother," pointing to the other bed, "and I had better get back to it." Rather gracelessly, she disengaged her hand and took a couple of steps toward the other side of the room.

As she returned to her mother's bedside, Molly glanced back at Lucinda Locke and realized that, although she was singing about "doggy bones" and "ice cream cones," tears were running down her face.

Lucinda Locke was floating. She allowed herself that, especially after the difficult visit from her stepson, Preston. It was a welcome reprieve from the pain, both mental and physical. She found it necessary to push the button more often these days, and that was okay. People around her thought she was just another crazy old woman, lost in a morphine induced fog, and that was okay, too. It was easier for her that way, and safer. Lucinda knew she was dying. How could she not know? Nobody had actually told her as much, but she could read it in their eyes and their fixed smiles and their encouragement that she use all the pain medication she wanted. They treated her like a child and she played the part when necessary.

But deep inside, she was still Lucy – a one-time Rodeo Queen, aspiring blues singer, and her Daddy's little girl. That Lucy was always 20 years old and it startled her when she looked into a mirror and saw a sad-looking old woman with her eyes. That Lucy was feisty, and fearless, and strong. That Lucy hadn't been defeated by a carelessly cruel husband. That Lucy hadn't been destroyed by the loss of two children.

Lucinda wasn't altogether unhappy about dying. Most of her life had been a struggle and she was so very tired. But Lucy was still mad as hell and had a thing or two to set right before she checked out

Molly sat for a long time on her side of the privacy curtain and thought about her brief exchange with Preston Locke. He was several years older than she was, but was still a handsome man, and she was pretty sure he knew it. Tanned, trim, and perfectly groomed, he seemed strangely at odds with the cowboy casual attire he wore. Her version of cowboy casual consisted of well-worn and comfortable blue jeans, a baggy sweater, and a pair of sloppy leather boots. His look was just a tad too coordinated, a bit too on purpose, to be real.

And, on top of everything, Molly felt just ever-so-slightly put in her place. *Nothing new, there*, she sighed to herself, then shrugged her shoulders and settled back into the cadence of her mother's snoring.

Chapter Two

After two days things began to settle into a routine for Molly. Her mother was still in the hospital, but was improving, according to Nurse Cheryl. Molly began her day by checking her email and putting out any immediate fires for her consulting clients. Most of what she was doing right now was maintenance, though, and she had no big projects scheduled in the immediate future. For most of her working life, Molly had drifted into jobs almost aimlessly, but would soon find herself tethered to a computer or some other piece of high-tech equipment. About computers, there were two things that Molly knew absolutely: 1) She had a gift when it came to working with computers… especially in helping others learn what they needed to know in order to do their jobs; and 2) She hated computers… hated the lingo, and the arrogance, and the impersonal nature of them. She even hated the television remote, and her kids laughed at her, saying that every time she picked up the remote it was as if she had never seen one before. The truth was, that she had trouble seeing the buttons on the remote, but was way too vain to admit that she might need reading glasses as much as she did.

Her most recent job, eight long years with a construction company as a database analyst, had ended abruptly with a layoff. At first, it threw her for a loop, probably because she had slowly fallen into the trap of identifying with her job. She would meet people for the first time and they would say, "Oh, yeah... you're the database analyst." They wouldn't remember her name, but they knew she was a high-tech guru. Molly jokingly called herself the All-Powerful Goddess of IT, but she was beginning to like the sound of that too much.

So, with the help of a global financial crisis, she became one of the masses of bewildered white-collard workers suddenly out of work. For a few weeks, she moped around in her sweats, watching way too many old episodes of *Law & Order*. She slept late, ate badly, and cried at inappropriate times. At first her behavior frightened her kids, but it wasn't until she realized that she was embarrassing them that she decided to pull herself together.

Since what she did was somewhat specialized she searched the internet for jobs, and actually had a number of phone interviews. The high-tech world is all about outsourcing and she spoke to employment consultants, with unlikely names like Brendan and Eric and Debbie, who worked from India and Pakistan and Malaysia. Of course, these jobs all required that she move to some exotic place like New Brunswick and, with one son in college at the time and the other still a senior in high school that was something she could not do.

Finally, one day when she was beginning to feel desperate, she had the idea to start up her own consulting business. She made a few phone calls, and the next thing she knew, she was a business owner. That was two years ago, and business was booming!

After taking care of her clients, Molly would then wander down to her favorite coffee shop on Main Street. It was called "Strange Brew," and Molly found the name appropriate. The place was new enough that no one cared about Molly's scandalous past life in Hickok, yet old enough that the owner remembered Molly from some of her previous home visits and always made her feel welcome. The owner was a big cheerful woman named Lissy, who liked to decide what Molly should have for breakfast and have it ready and waiting for her. Today it was a yogurt, fruit, and granola parfait, along with the world's most beautiful mocha latte. Perfection. Absolute perfection.

"Honey, how's your momma doin?" Lissy asked, as she was foaming milk for a cappuccino. Molly gave her the latest on her mother's progress, and then sat back for a few minutes to watch a master at work. Lissy had designed her work area so that she never had to climb off her stool. She could spin around, making specialty coffees, popping pastries into the toaster oven, and running the cash register in the most amazing and graceful way. Sometimes when it was busy, onlookers would come in off the street just to watch her. Molly had once heard Lissy respond to a tourist who had muttered under her breath about how lazy she was. "Lazy," she said. "Sugar, I'm the polar opposite of lazy. I'm efficient. And if you want me to get up off this stool, I will… but it will be to kick your sorry ass out of my café!" The poor tourist almost choked on a donut and trotted out of the shop as fast as her orthopedic sandals could carry her. From that moment on, Lissy had Molly's undying admiration.

After breakfast (and sometimes a show at Strange Brew), Molly would head up to the hospital to look in on her mother and try to catch a visit with her attending physician. Managing to pin down the elusive doctor at the nurse's station, Molly learned that her mother was slowly getting better but he was worried that many years of smoking had finally caught up with her and he wanted to run a few tests. Not great news, really, but Molly was going to think positive.

Her mother was cheerful, almost perky, when Molly walked into the room. She was wearing an old fashioned bed jacket that she insisted Molly bring from the house a day earlier, and she had made an effort to tame her fluffy flyaway hair. She looked almost girlish, in spite of the oxygen tubes in her nose. *This is something new,* thought Molly, suddenly alarmed that oxygen deprivation may have caused some type of brain damage.

She was about to go find a doctor, when she saw that an elderly man had entered the room. He looked surprised to see her there and her mother looked, well, busted. After an awkward silence, Molly offered her hand to the man, who shook it sheepishly, and introduced himself.

It turned out that he knew Molly's mother through their mutual interest in Thursday night bingo. According to him, they sort of sat together and he had been worried when Shirley (Molly's mother) had not shown up. He insisted they were just friends, but her mother's coy look told Molly otherwise. He said his name was Dick, and Molly managed to keep a straight face, but when her mother said, "Molly, honey, you might really like Dick if you give it a chance," she had to leave the room.

Molly escaped to the hospital cafeteria to try and sort out her conflicting emotions. On the one hand, it had been ten years since her dad had passed away and she had always encouraged her mother to get a social life. On the other hand, she found it difficult to get past the "yuck" factor that involved the idea of her parents having sex, now or ever. She actually choked on her coffee when she found herself wondering just how much her mother liked Dick.

Fortunately for her, Molly was startled out of her reverie by an out-of-breath Nurse Cheryl. "Molly," she huffed, "I was supposed to give this to you yesterday, but I forgot and I didn't want to miss you again today." She handed Molly an envelope from a card of some type. In fact, the front of it said "Lucinda," but there was a line through the name. Below it, in a spidery scrawl, was written "Shirley Noble's girl."

Cheryl, who obviously was not used to running up and down stairs, pulled out a chair and collapsed into it. "Phew," she said, still catching her breath. "Lucinda is such a sweetie. I didn't want to disappoint her. She seems to have taken a real liking to you and she stayed off her pain meds way too long yesterday so she could write this. It was all very secret... I had to get her some paper and then stand guard at the door. Between you and me, it's probably the morphine, but I don't mind helping the old gal."

Feeling confused, Molly took the envelope and was about to open it, when Cheryl said, "Oh, yeah, Lucinda said that you should only read it when you're alone, and she also said you should be careful. Again... probably the morphine talking, but whatever. Oh, and by the way, Preston Locke asked about you yesterday. Looks like you're the most popular girl at the dance." With that, Cheryl sighed and pushed herself up from the table. "Gotta go," she said, and headed back towards the door.

"Thanks, Cheryl," Molly said. "Maybe when you get off shift we can go do something... lunch or coffee or something?" Molly was out of her comfort zone in Hickok and was, to be completely honest, bored out of her skull.

"Wow! Sounds great," Cheryl beamed. "Gotta run, but I'll call your cell." Molly watched her bop up the stairs and smiled. She had never really gotten to know Cheryl in high school, but she realized she really liked this open and guileless woman. *Better late than never...* At that moment, the elevator opened and Preston Locke stepped out. He was talking on the phone and he didn't look happy. Molly watched him punctuate the air with his free hand and couldn't help but notice that by the end of the call he was punching the air with a closed fist. When he put his phone away and headed toward the door, he noticed that Molly had been watching him. He stopped and held her gaze for a few seconds too long, before smiling and strolling out the door. It wasn't a nice smile, though, and Molly found herself feeling anxious for no good reason. She slid the envelope off the table and casually tucked it into her coat pocket.

Chapter Three

Lucinda had a sense of swaying, gently rocking, as if on the water. It was pleasant and she was not frightened. Not like the other time.

When she and Calvin had first married, they took an extended honeymoon, going first to New York to meet his family and then sailing to Europe on a luxury cruise ship. She had never been outside her landlocked state, never even been to a big city, but suddenly she found herself in New York. Lucy was a girl who rose at dawn to ride her horses and could find her way in the dead of night by the position of the stars. In New York she was completely lost and it seemed to close in on her and make it hard to breathe. It might have been exciting, but Cal was not patient and seemed dismissive of her distress. When she met her in-laws in New York, they made it abundantly clear that they were not pleased with their son's choice of a bride. Honestly, she was not impressed with them either. Cal's mother was a well-dressed prune of a woman, who treated servants badly and family members even worse. His father was a ruthless business man, blessed with the winning combination of old money and political connections. He was cold and arrogant and manipulative. Too late, Lucy learned that her Calvin took after his dear old dad.

Lucy remembered breathing a sigh of relief when they boarded the cruise ship and left the New York harbor. But as soon as they hit the open sea, she began to feel something she had never felt before. Fear. She had never been afraid of the water, but there really wasn't much of that where she came from, and the typical body of water there could be crossed with an old rowboat in an hour, maybe two. But suddenly there was nothing but sky and ocean. The immensity of it, the endless motion, and the brooding sense of violence panicked her and made her tremble. It was a rough crossing, even for an experienced traveler, and she was sick most of the way over. Calvin was disgusted with her and preferred the action at the poker table or bar. There were some nights he didn't return to their suite at all.

Europe was grand and beautiful, but they spent most of their time in the company of people like Calvin and his family. These were bored, wealthy people that chose to live abroad, yet they spent much of their time finding fault with their hosts. Lucy stayed outside the circle and was sometimes able to wander off and explore these exotic places on her own. She loved the narrow streets and the raucous market places and the spicy foods. Eventually, though, she was found and dragged to a museum or art gallery or opera… for her own good, of course.

When they returned to New York on the same luxury liner three months later, Lucy was a changed woman. She was beginning to understand how much it would cost her to be Lucinda Locke and she realized the price was too high. But she also understood that it was too late. The weather had been mild and the crossing gentle, but she had been ill for entire voyage. This time, however, it was morning sickness.

When they arrived in New York on a wet and chilly afternoon, it was all she could do not to run down the gangplank and fall to her knees on dry land. Instead, she dressed carefully, applied rouge to her cheeks, and walked slowly off the ship like royalty. She was pale and cold and very, very beautiful.

Chapter Four

Molly spent the rest of the afternoon working with her consulting clients, running errands, and staying out of the way of her mother's budding romance. She called her sister for a quick update and then went in search of a few essentials and a new book to read.

As she strolled through the Super Save-Mart, throwing this or that into her cart, she realized that she had been away from Hickok for so long that she didn't know many people. There were a few that she recognized, though. For instance, she had gone to elementary school with the guy working the evening shift at the hardware department. His name was Mark and he had been a shy boy who cried if he missed a word while reading aloud. Molly had heard that he was now a high school teacher in Hickok and that he had a huge family and was well-liked. *Way to go, Mark!*

The woman behind the Jewelry counter was the sister of one of Molly's junior high friends. Back then she had been a perky, pretty thing… very thin and very popular. But she had made some bad choices and now had a hard edge to her that couldn't be hidden by too much makeup.

Junior high… How did any of us survive? She had been smart, awkward, and had no self-esteem whatsoever – an unfortunate combination in junior high. She knew nothing about fashion or make-up, and had no idea that failure to shave one's legs was punishable by death. Those were the days of go-go boots and fishnet stockings and Twiggy. Molly wore home-made clothes, saggy knee socks, and had breasts.

No one can be prepared for the cruelty of adolescent girls, and for some strange reason, Molly became the target of a girl who had more social standing. This girl wasn't pretty, wasn't particularly smart, and wasn't rich, but she had "mean" down to a science. Her name was Barbette. Really… Barbette, and Molly couldn't think of a more appropriate name, because after every encounter with the girl, Molly felt that she had been poked in the eye with a sharp stick.

Just then, because the universe has a wry sense of humor, as Molly turned the corner into the paperback book section, she saw Barbette browsing the wrapping paper.

Molly was an adult woman who was assertive, efficient, and well respected in her community. She owned her own business. She had raised two wonderful boys and was putting them both through college. She owned her own house and drove a BMW. But the shy, Junior High Molly said, "Crap," backed up and whipped the cart around before she could be seen by her nemesis.

As she turned, high speed, into the candle aisle, running away from her past, she ran right into… *Her future?* And with that odd thought in her head, she ran head-on into a man with her shopping cart.

"Crap," she said again, before she could stop herself.

"Ouch," he replied. "But I get the crap thing a lot from women."

Molly just looked at him. He was tall, really tall. Not exactly thin, but maybe lanky would be a good word for him. He had reddish-blond hair that was graying nicely at the temples, and he had the most wonderful eyes. They were bluish, greenish, grayish, and they were focused on her with a look of pure puzzlement.

"Well, I suppose, then, that I should apologize for being directly in the path of your racing cart," he said. "Here, I'll just move aside so you can make it to the finish line." He had the hint of a nice accent, maybe Scottish. "Oh crap," she said again. "I mean, I am so sorry. I was just trying to avoid… and anyway… I mean… I'm sorry," she babbled, feeling like an absolute idiot. *Talk about Junior High*!

She took a deep breath and slowed down. "Completely my fault," she said, "the racing track is actually past cookware and through towels and shower curtains. Just took a wrong turn." He smiled and she continued, "Actually I was just trying to avoid talking to someone I don't care for. I really am sorry. Hope you'll someday be able to walk again."

"The name is Quinn," he laughed, "and I'm afraid you might have to help me limp over to the lunch counter for a wee coffee."

She smiled back. "Thanks, I'm Molly, but I don't have coffee with men I run into, or over, for the first time," she said. "Maybe the next time I injure you."

Molly was turning to leave, when he leaned over and whispered, "I think the person you were avoiding has spied you and wants to have a nice chat." Molly turned and, sure enough, Barbette was shooting towards her like a poison arrow. Molly's heart sank. Quinn had moved away, but he was still within earshot. *Not now, not in front of this beautiful man.* She sighed and put on her game face.

"Moldy," said Barbette, licking her lips and baring her sharp little teeth. Moldy was the nickname that Barbette and her band of evil cheerleaders had given Molly, and it had stuck. Barbette was tall and thin. Her style had not changed much since junior high, with her cat-eye glasses and her short spiky haircut, but she had not aged well. "Mean" usually doesn't.

"Hello, Barbette," Molly said. "How's Don?" Don had been Molly's secret crush in school, but when Barbette had somehow found out about it, she pursued Don and actually married him. Molly felt very sorry for Don.

"So, Moldy," said Barbette, ignoring Molly's question. "I'm surprised to see you in town. What could possibly be important enough to bring you back?"

Torn between being a coward and trying to answer the question, or telling Barbette where she could shove it, she hesitated for a moment. Right then, she felt a hand on her shoulder and looked up to see Quinn.

He spun her around, gave her a light kiss on the forehead, and said, "Molly, Darlin, it's so grand to see you!"

Molly almost said, "Crap," but managed to stop herself. "Quinn," she said. "It's been, a…"

"I insist you come to dinner with me as soon as you're done here. But first, be a love and introduce me to your Mum," he continued, smiling innocently at Barbette.

Barbette's face froze, and Molly quickly said, "Oh, Quinn, this isn't my… ah… Mum; this is an old friend from school. Her name is Barbette."

Quinn looked genuinely horrified, and said, "Ach, that's me putting me foot in muh mouth. Pleased to meet you, Miss Babette, is it? Any friend of my lovely Molly is a friend of mine." His accent had thickened considerably. Quinn held out his hand to Barbette, but she shot Molly an arch look and stormed off.

Molly was stunned. She gaped at Quinn, who looked like he had just eaten the canary, and laughed. She laughed until her sides hurt and she had tears in her eyes. When she could breathe again, she said, "You have no idea what that stunt is going to cost me, but I'll fondly remember the look on her face until the day I die! Damn, man, you just earned yourself a coffee!"

Quinn followed her through the checkout line and made a big show of not noticing that her shopping consisted of panty liners, a Dove bar, and dental floss. She made a big show of not noticing that he was buying toilet paper, extra-large sport socks, and Granny Smith apples. It was all very civilized. They were to meet at Strange Brew, but Molly wanted to get there first so that she could give Lissy a head's up.

Lissy looked up as she arrived and said, "Hey, girl, right on time! I'm thinking a mocha latte with a hint of mint."

Molly, looking a bit sheepish, said, "Actually, Liss, I'm meeting someone here… a guy I ran over with my cart at Save-Mart. He'll be here any minute and I'm so nervous. I'm not sure I remember how to talk to a man."

Lissy laughed and said, "Oh honey, it comes back to you, just like riding a bike…"

At that moment, Quinn walked in. Lissy gave him the once over, raised her eyebrows and said, "Whoa, make that riding a Harley! Okay, I'm thinking Mexican mocha with a dash of cayenne pepper for you both." Without bothering to wait for a response she proceeded to make them.

Quinn looked puzzled, but Molly said, "Sorry, Lissy makes the rules here and we really have no choice. It's her way or the highway." Soon, hot drinks in hand, they made their way to a corner table and settled into a mismatched pair of well-worn chairs.

After some polite sipping and an awkward silence, Molly blurted, "You know, I'm not really sure what to say to a man whose foot I've crushed with my shopping cart."

"Crushed, no," he replied. "Bruised, maybe… agonizingly painful, but not crushed, and the limp will always remind me of you." He laughed at the horrified look on her face. "Just kidding… it would take more than a wee shopping cart to damage a foot this size," he said as he lifted it to show her. "Actually, the cayenne pepper in this drink has taken my mind off my injury completely. It wouldn't have been my choice, but I think I could get used to a spot of fire in my life." He raised his cup to Molly.

Molly felt her face flush, and it wasn't the cayenne pepper. "Well," she stammered, "except for the size of your feet – and they really are impressive – I really don't know anything about you. I mean, you could be a serial killer, or a terrorist, or even an attorney. Oh crap, you're not an attorney are you?"

"Alas, no," he said. "Nothing as dark and dangerous as all that. I was sent out here by a British oil and gas company to look at some drilling prospects. I decided to use Hickok as my home base, and that's my story. What about you?"

"Well," began Molly, trying to decide how much to tell him. "I grew up here but moved away right after high school. Put myself through college, did some traveling, got married, had two kids, got divorced, worked for the "man" but hated it, created my own business, and I'm here right now looking after my sick mother… and that's about it for me."

"Molly, love," he said. "You just raced through your whole life, but I'm afraid I must insist on the walking tour. So let's take our time over dinner. Besides, your friend has been trying to make eye contact for several minutes and she keeps pointing to the "Sorry we're closed" sign that now hangs in the window."

Molly jumped up and headed towards the door. "Oh geez, Lissy, I'm sorry!" But when she glanced at the clock, she stopped and said, "Hold on there. It's not closing time yet and, even if it was, you never, ever close on time. What's the deal?"

Lissy, the picture of innocence, said, "Well, Honey, I'm suddenly feeling tired and I thought that you two kids might want to run off and do something fun." She actually winked at the end of the sentence and then she got up off her stool and held the door open for them. There was no arguing with Lissy.

"Traitor," whispered Molly as she walked out, but Lissy just laughed and shoed them out the door.

Standing on the sidewalk in the crisp fall air, Molly wanted more than anything to go out to dinner with this beautiful stranger, but she still had a hospital visit to make, some fires to put out for her clients, and her weekly phone calls to her boys. And, the truth be told, she was beyond flustered and wanted some time to sort out her feelings. So, with a sigh of regret, she said, "Thanks, Quinn, but now I need to be the good daughter and the good business consultant and the good mother, and say no for tonight. I don't know how long I'll be in town, but maybe I'll run into you again… just not with my shopping cart."

On impulse she stood on her tiptoes and planted a light, sweet kiss, on his cheek. "And, thanks for the Barbette thing. I'll cherish that forever.' She looked at him a moment and then she climbed into her car and drove off.

Chapter Five

Quinn stood on the sidewalk for a long time and watched the black car disappear down the road. *What is it about this woman that makes me behave like a fool?* Normally, he thought of himself as reserved, maybe even dour. In his field he was well-known as a sharp businessman, and his boardroom persona was legendary. But, even though he covered it well, he was uncomfortable in social settings, especially around women. Women confused him. Women were not logical. Women had this mysterious power that frightened him. It may have had something to do with his one serious relationship that had ended in disaster. But it also stemmed from the fact that he was innately shy. Being over five feet tall at the age of eight tends to push a child into situations that he is not ready for. Quinn matured quickly, though he had never lost the sense of running to catch up.

But this woman, with her wild dark curls and surprising green eyes… and a figure a man could really hold on to. There was something about her that unlocked a door inside him, and he wanted to swing the door wide open and step through. He was pretty sure his stern Scottish ancestors would not approve, but that was just fine by him.

Lucinda became aware that Shirley Noble's girl had arrived and was fussing around her mother's bed. With an effort, she brought herself back into the world of pain and waited for an opportunity to speak to the girl. She wanted her to know that she wasn't crazy, and that she knew, deep down, that her Cathy had been laid to rest a lifetime ago. They did look alike, though, and that tugged at her heart a bit. Cathy would have been about the same age now, and she liked to think that she would have been as kind to her as Shirley's girl, Molly, was to her mother. With an effort she changed the direction of her thoughts. As tempting as it was to retreat to the "what if" world in which Cathy grew up, blossomed, and became a beautiful woman, Lucinda had to focus on the "what is" world, at least for a while longer.

She wondered if the sweet nurse had delivered the note to the girl, and she wondered if she had read it. She wouldn't understand, though, not without some background, and that is what kept Lucinda from pushing the red button. For a moment, Lucinda felt a pang of regret for involving this nice girl in the mess that had been her life. But she had to tell someone, and she sensed a kind of strength in Shirley Noble's daughter, even if the girl herself was unaware of it.

Eventually the chitchat on the other side of the curtain diminished and soon, Lucinda could hear the familiar sound of Shirley's snoring. She glanced longingly at the red button but, instead, whispered, "Are you there?"

The girl pulled back the curtain and then quietly stepped to Lucinda's bedside. "Your name is Molly. I remember seeing you around town when you were a child," said Lucinda, in a soft voice. "Could you get me a sip of water, please?"

"Yes, I'm Molly," the girl answered, and she held the water glass and straw for Lucinda. "I grew up here, but moved away a long time ago. That's my mother in the next bed."

"Your mother is a bit of a character," said Lucinda. "But I like her. And I like that you are taking care of her. She's a lucky woman."

"I don't know about lucky," laughed Molly. "She's had her turn at taking care of me... all of us kids have been high-maintenance at one time or another. It's just what you do," she added. "You take care of the people you love."

"Like I said... lucky," repeated Lucinda. A wave of pain shook her frail body, and she grabbed Molly's arm. "I don't have a lot of time," she said. Molly began to say something comforting, but the older woman silenced her. "Read the note," she whispered. The girl looked surprised and pulled the envelope out of her coat pocket. Lucinda grew agitated. "Not here. Put it back and wait until you're alone. Read it and then burn it. Promise me you'll burn it."

Lucinda's expression must have alarmed the girl, because Molly quickly put the note back into her coat pocket and promised.

Lucinda let go of Molly's arm and sank back into her bed. "Read it and think about it and then maybe tomorrow, if we're alone, we can talk. Just think about it..." she said weakly. She finally allowed herself the red button, and was only faintly aware that the Noble girl waited with her until she drifted off to sleep.

Chapter Six

Feeling strangely unsettled, Molly decided to grab a light dinner to take back to her hotel room. As she stood waiting at the elevator, she was surprised to see Cheryl.

"Don't you ever go home?" asked Molly.

"I pulled a double shift," she answered, although she didn't seem too upset about it. Molly knew that Cheryl had planned to become a nurse, even back in high school, and obviously loved her job. "I meant to call you but, duh, spaced it. Our girl's night might have to wait a couple of days."

"No problem, just give me a call whenever it works for you. Right now I'm very flexible!" Molly stepped into the elevator and gave Cheryl a cheerful wave. As she walked out of the hospital and into the cool evening air, she noticed that the street was empty, except for a lone man sitting in a non-descript car across the street. He made eye contact with her briefly, then looked quickly away and picked up a magazine.

Molly's cell rang just as she was fumbling with her room key. As usual she had an armload of paperwork, a take-home salad in one bag, her recent Save-Mart purchases in another one, and a cup of tea that was so hot that she had to switch it back and forth from one hand to the other to keep from scalding her fingers. She finally got the door open and raced to put down her baggage before she missed the call.

It was her oldest son, Alex and her heart did a cartwheel, as it always did when her boys called her without being coerced into it. "Hi, son," she said. "You beat me to the weekly phone call. You okay?"

"Great, Mom. I was just thinking about you and wanted to hear your voice," he answered.

The kid is good... thought Molly. *He knows exactly how to melt my heart.* They talked for a while, and before she hung up Molly found herself once again wishing he wasn't so far away. Then Molly called her younger son, Jack, and they had a somewhat one-sided conversation as he tried to pretend that he wasn't in the middle of a video game challenge match with a room full of dorm-mates.

Alex was both a dreamer and an intellectual, so much like her in personality that it worried her. In appearance, though, the boy took after her ex-husband's side of the family and had the look of a charming, but somewhat tragic, 18th century hero. Jack, on the other hand looked more like Molly, with his dark curly hair and strong bone structure. But he was the spitting image of her ex-husband as far as temperament was concerned. She sighed. Nature doesn't play fair, but she had to admit that they had turned into very interesting people.

Both boys were now in college, only a few hours away from their hometown. Just two years apart in age, they had chosen completely different fields of study. Alex preferred the brooding and angst-filled world of theatre and fine art, while Jack was more likely to get his hands dirty and have way too much fun in the study of Forestry.

She used to laugh when people talked about the empty nest syndrome. She would snort and say, "Are you kidding? I can't wait until my kids are out of the house." But now she understood, and she had it bad.

With a sigh, she picked up the bags she had tossed on the bed, grabbed her salad, and fired up her computer so she could check her email and complete some maintenance work she was doing for one of her clients. As she waited for it to boot up, she pulled the envelope out of her pocket and opened it carefully. It was obvious that the envelope had been recycled from some type of get-well card. She slipped out a folded sheet of paper. As she opened it, she noted that it had the logo from a pharmaceutical company at the top... a promotional giveaway she guessed. Molly remembered that Cheryl had supplied Lucinda Locke with paper.

It's a poem… what a strange surprise. When she took a second look she realized that it was actually in the format of the Mockingbird lullaby. The writing was thin and spidery, but quite legible. It read:

Now with all her babies gone,
Momma needs a way to right the wrong.
Momma knows a secret no one knows.
Momma needs to tell before she goes.
Momma says look where bluebirds fly,
Momma says the mirror doesn't lie.
Momma says remember Cathy's song,
And find the words that don't belong.

Puzzled, Molly read it again. It was more than just a children's rhyme, and it almost sounded sinister. Lucinda was definitely trying to tell her something. She sat with her cooling tea and spoke the words aloud; even tried singing them to the Mockingbird melody, but that didn't quite work either. Finally, she gave up and turned to her computer.

No rest for the weary. Right at that moment, she realized with a shock that her laptop was plugged straight into the wall. *Oh, this is not good.* She always carried her own power strip, not trusting the ups and downs of wiring, especially in older buildings. And, even though it bordered on paranoid, she usually unplugged her computer when she left it for any length of time… just for good measure. She had learned her lesson from a very bad experience with lightning, one that had cost her a new mother board. She could have sworn she remembered unplugging it that morning. Feeling shaky, she moved the plug from the wall to the power strip. *Okay, just had a brain cramp… just spaced out a bit… could happen to anyone… and it has absolutely nothing to do with my age…*

With some effort, Molly forced herself to focus on work. When she was finished she took a hot bath, and hopped into bed. She still felt vaguely uneasy, though, and had trouble drifting off. Finally, she felt herself letting go…

In Molly's dream she was driving down an empty road, which was surrounded by open prairie, and it was beginning to get dark. She was pretty sure that she was going to Hickok, but it didn't look familiar to her. She was nervous because she knew that there was a storm coming and she had to find shelter, but there was nothing in sight. She was very worried about lightening. All of a sudden, in the distance, she could see a large building, a really large building and she realized it was a Super Save-Mart. She was relieved because the storm was closer and she could see the lightening and hear the thunder. But she was headed straight for the building, and she was unable to slow down. Curiously, it turned out that the road went right through the store. As she drove through the store, passing the towels and bath curtains, she could see people she knew, but they didn't pay her any attention. The "muzak" was Elton John's, "*Goodbye, Yellow Brick Road*," and it became louder as she headed towards the back of the store. As she passed through a dark corridor, she realized that she was in a part of the store she had never seen. Everything seemed old there, and dusty, and the building had become dark. With a jolt of fear, she realized that she shouldn't be there and that she had to get out right away, but for some reason her car had slowed to a stop. She looked down and realized that she was no longer in a car, but a shopping cart, and there was a scratching noise right behind her…

Molly woke with a jolt, "*Goodbye, Yellow Brick Road*," still ringing in her ears. It took her a moment to realize she had been dreaming, and then she sheepishly turned on her light to check her room. She listened to the sounds of the old building. Somewhere a toilet flushed. The ancient heating system was gurgling. Someone was going down the creaky old staircase that led to the lobby. Nothing was out of the ordinary. *Big sissy baby… no more spicy Mexican drinks for you!* She stared at the ceiling for a long time, but soon noticed that her thoughts kept returning to the mighty Quinn, and she drifted back to sleep with a smile on her face.

Chapter Seven

"Hush little baby, hush little baby"... the words played over and over in Lucinda's head. Her babies...

The day that her Teddy was born was a day of hope and happiness for Lucinda. It had been a difficult birth, twenty-two hours of labor. They wanted to knock her out for the birth, because that was the way things were done back then, but she refused. She argued hotly with Calvin about it and stood her ground. When the baby finally arrived, her body was trembling with exhaustion, but her heart almost overflowed with joy. He was this beautiful, perfect creature, and she knew she would be the best mother ever.

Not like Preston. She was so sad about Preston. She had been about five months pregnant with Teddy, when Calvin had announced, "He had a son from a former relationship and that, since the low-life mother (Calvin's words) had apparently done a runner, we were stuck with the kid." The boy showed up, with a nanny hired by Calvin's family, two days later. There was no question about the boy's parentage; he was the spitting image of Calvin. She, of course, had been shocked and upset... not so much about the arrival of the child, but about the fact that Calvin had not told her about it. She wondered what else he chose not to tell her. But Lucinda loved children and she was determined to care for the child as if he had been her own. The boy was three years old, and he was quiet and withdrawn. But Lucinda had a way with wounded birds and skittish colts, and she gave him plenty of space, enough attention, and let him know she would be there when he was ready. After a few days, she could sense that he was ready to come around. She took him to a nice store in town and helped him pick out some clothes that would help him fit in. They stopped at the bakery afterwards and had warm donuts. As they walked home, he reached up and took her hand. "This is going to work out just fine," she thought.

But Calvin was waiting for them when they walked through the door and he was furious. He sent the boy to his room, and told Lucinda in no uncertain terms that she was not the boy's mother and that she was to spend her time preparing for the birth of their own child. The boy was only there because he had no other place to go and, while his immediate needs would be met, he was not a legitimate Locke and would not be treated as such.

Lucinda could not believe what she heard and vowed to love the child anyway. But Calvin had also spoken with his family, and together they transferred responsibility for Preston to the nanny. Her name was Helene, and Lucinda supposed she was nice enough, but she was quiet and kept the child away from the rest of the family whenever possible. It was a train wreck, Lucinda knew even then, but one she was unable to stop.

But Teddy was her own sweet baby, and she loved him with her whole heart. He was such a good-natured little fellow. He was considerate enough to sleep through the night almost right away and he used to stroke Lucinda's face as she nursed him. That was another argument she had with Calvin... He insisted that nursing was inappropriate and undignified in this day and age. She said it was the most natural thing in the world and, again, stuck to her guns.

The morning she found her baby cold and still, something inside her died.

Chapter Eight

Molly woke up early, still thinking about Quinn. She couldn't seem to get *"Beyond the Yellow Brick Road"* out of her head, though. *It could be worse. It could be 'Cat Scratch Fever'.* Her first order of business today was to have a chat with her friend, Lissy, about her blatant attempts at matchmaking. Later in the morning, she had managed to finagle a meeting with her Mother's doctor, so she could get at update and outline her game plan.

Lissy smiled her big innocent smile when Molly walked in.

"So, get lucky last night?" she asked. She managed to use the casual, what's the big deal, tone she would have used to find out if Molly wanted 2% or skim.

"No, missy," replied Molly in her sternest voice. "For your information, I sent him packing. What kind of girl do you think I am anyway?"

"Horny?" replied Lissy, without missing a beat. "What's it been for you... months? Years?" She set a simple latte and plain bagel with cream cheese in front of Molly. "And here comes this gorgeous man, big enough to share with me, and you give him the boot?" She shook her head sadly, "How many kinds of stupid can a woman be?"

"Way stupid," agreed Molly, her false chagrin completely gone. She looked at her latte -- no special flavor, no whipped cream, not even a sprinkle – sitting next to the naked looking bagel and sighed. *Penance for being so uptight*, but she was hungry so she dug in.

"I don't know, Lissy," she said around a mouthful of bagel. "If I was back in my own house, 100 miles away, I would probably still be in bed." Her eyes glazed over at the thought. "But, it's being here in Hickok. I'm so afraid to make a mistake or call attention to myself."

"Come on, woman. Get real. You deserve a life and you know it, so don't give me that hang dog, I'm not worthy, look. Then I really will have to kick your sorry ass. You need some serious help in the love life department, whether you want it or not, and I'm the gal for the job."

"Thanks, Lissy," said Molly, as she finished her latte. "But I'm afraid that ship has sailed. Remember, I sent him packing?"

"Well, yeah," began Lissy, again with the innocent grin. "When you kicked the poor guy to the curb last night, I might have just happened to walk by before he left, and I might have told him that you usually stopped by here on the way to the hospital… around 9:00 or so… you're early, by the way... and that you also stopped by here on your way back to the hotel, maybe around 6:00 PM, and I think I mentioned that your hotel was the Calamity Jane. And I might have said that if that doesn't work, he could try hanging out in the hospital cafeteria. Oh, and I said that chocolate is your weakness and he should try to exploit that… Or something like that… I guess I was in a chatty mood."

Molly's jaw dropped. "Oh, Lissy… you're impossible!" she exclaimed, "But I love you. I have a meeting at the hospital right now, but I'll check my social calendar and see if I can fit in another visit later this evening… You really are evil, you know…"

"Why yes, yes I am," agreed Lissy, amiably, as she turned to serve the early morning customers that were beginning to trickle in.

Chapter Nine

Quinn spent his morning at the courthouse, reviewing oil and gas leases. Of course he could have hired someone else to do it for him. Actually, he already had an entire department of intelligent and able-bodied employees who specialized in just that very thing. But they were there and he was here and he liked to "keep his feet on the ground" as far as his company was concerned. To be honest, he had chosen to come out here specifically to find some space and some time to think… someplace away from all the distractions of running a large energy corporation. But suddenly, he's hit − literally − by the biggest possible distraction… with lovely green eyes, wild curly hair, and an air of happy chaos that seemed to surround her. *Molly,* he smiled to himself. *Who would have thought…?*

Forcing his thoughts back to the task at hand, he realized that the clerk was watching him again. She did that a lot, and he knew that if he gave her any encouragement at all his stay in Hickok might not be so solitary. She was a looker… he'd give her that… with her straight blond hair and eyes of blue. But Quinn was not interested in casual romance, and he wasn't looking for a fling. Even if he was, her type was exactly what he wanted to avoid. Too much like the very lovely and very cold Jessica, with whom he had invested far too many years of his life. *Never again;* and he concentrated again on the legal document in front of him.

But his thoughts kept straying to the whirlwind of a woman with the black BMW. *I think I might fancy a wee cup of tea later, maybe around 6:00 PM."* He shook his head at how lame that sounded, *but, hey, a man's got to drink, right?*

Molly's meeting with the doctor had been a good news/bad news affair. The good news was that Molly's mother was recovering nicely from the pneumonia, and that her blood oxygen level was also slowly improving. The bad news was that years of smoking and bronchitis had caused permanent damage to her lungs and that she would require some extensive respiratory therapy in the near future, as well as using oxygen for a several hours every day. He wanted to keep her in the hospital for a few more days and suggested that they begin the therapy right away and work to fine-tune the equipment for the optimum oxygen mix.

Okay, visualizing her game plan. She would stay until her mother got out of the hospital, and get her settled in at home. After returning to her own home to take care of a few things, she would then dash back to make arrangements for the respiratory therapy and home oxygen. She felt better having a plan, even though it meant a lot of driving for her. But, she had a BMW, and she knew how to use it!

She had lunch with her mother, sneaking in butterscotch milkshakes for each of them from the local ice cream shop. She told her mother about her meeting with the doctor, and about her plans for getting her to and from the therapy and taking care of all the details. Her mother protested, saying that she could take care of things herself, but Molly could tell that she was secretly relieved to have some help. After lunch, she told Molly that she needed a nap before her "afternoon company" arrived – her "afternoon company" meaning Dick.

At the sound of the soft, familiar snore, Molly opened the curtain to see if Lucinda was awake. The woman was curled up on her side, and Molly thought at first that she was asleep, but she opened her eyes and looked right at her. She gestured for Molly to come closer. When she was close, Lucinda, once again, reached out and grabbed Molly's arm.

"I read your poem," said Molly. "It was nice, but I'm not sure what it means."

"It's a puzzle," whispered the older woman. "But you need to solve it and you need to tell. It's time, and we all need to rest." Lucinda's voice sounded hoarse, and Molly offered her some water.

The grip on Molly's arm strengthened, and that surprised her, considering how frail Lucinda seemed. "I found out some, but the rest is up to you. Read the words and think about them," she said softly. "Think about the song; think about the words that don't belong. There were pictures of that time, that sad time, look at those, and be careful, little girl, be so careful. It's never what you expect..."

At that moment Lucinda's grip loosened and she looked past Molly, over her shoulder. Molly turned around to see a smallish woman, maybe around the same age as her mother, or even Lucinda, for that matter. But this woman was the picture of good health. She reminded Molly of Mrs. Claus, with her pink cheeks and white hair and short round body.

"Oh, dear," said the woman. "Lucinda, I didn't know you had company. I'll just come back later."

50

"Oh no, please," said Molly quickly. "Mrs. Locke is my mother's roommate and I was just paying my regards. My name is Molly Noble. I have to leave anyway."

The woman marched forward and held out her hand. "The name's Helene... Helene Blanchard. I'm an old friend of Lucinda's... we're almost family, we've known each other for so long."

Molly held out her hand and the woman grasped it with a surprisingly firm grip. "So, I'll be off then," she said, noticing that Lucinda was smiling strangely.

"Regards to your mother, Molly," the older woman whispered, and she waved Molly off.

"Goodbye, Dear. I'm sure we'll meet again," chirped Mrs. Clause as Molly headed out the door.

Chapter Ten

Lucinda's attention drifted in and out while Helene chattered on. She talked about the size of the pumpkins in her garden and the way this year's apple harvest was disappointing. She talked about the shocking behavior of one of the young characters in her favorite soap. "What is the world coming to," she said primly, "when a mother and daughter have a conversation about nipple rings, right there on TV." She made Lucinda smile.

Over the years, she and Helene had become good friends. In the beginning, there had been some awkwardness. How could it have been any different? She had shown up one day on Lucinda's doorstep with virtually no warning, and with her husband's out-of-wedlock child in tow. To Helene, Lucinda was the beautiful, aloof, lady of the manor. And to Lucinda, Helene was the other woman in the house, charged with raising her stepson. They were wary in the beginning, and gave each other a wide berth. But the needs of the quiet boy drew them together, and soon each woman learned that there was more to the other than either realized. Of course, Lucinda never did get over the loss of baby Teddy. A crib death, they called it... such a simple name for an event that had knocked a permanent hole in her life. But even in her darkest times, she worried about Preston and was glad that Helene was there for him. Eventually she brought herself back to the world of the living. She was young, then, and resilient. When Calvin wasn't around, Lucinda played with Preston and spoiled him… maybe a bit too much as far as Helene was concerned. But she made sure that Preston knew he was loved and cared for.

And Helene, who was a young paid servant thousands of miles away from her family, stepped right up to the plate and, in essence, became a mother to the boy. She came from a big farm family and might have been stern and overly fussy, but she made sure she was always there for the boy. She had sacrificed another type of life to raise this child, who was not her own. And she had never once, as far as Lucinda knew, voiced any regret.

"A young couple moved in next door," continued Helene. "They looked so nice and normal. But when I walked by I heard music coming from the house and I'd swear it was rap. Rap! Can you believe it?" She pursed her lips and frowned. "Now that I think about it, I don't remember seeing any wedding rings… what IS the world coming to?"

Lucinda touched her friend's hand. "Helene," she said, "I need you to do something for me."

"Well, of course, dear," said Helene, "Anything at all."

"I want you to arrange for Molly Noble to get Cathy's old toy chest," she said. "I want her to have it right now."

"Well, Lucinda, don't you be giving your things away… you know this is just a bad spell and you'll be up and kicking before you know it…" But Helene didn't sound all that convinced.

Lucinda wasn't convinced either, and said, "Just do it for me, Helene… please. You have the key to the house. It's just an old toy chest and I want her to have it. I emptied it out a long time ago, but it's still sitting in Cathy's old room. You can have the neighbor boys help you with it, but I want it delivered to Molly Noble's hotel room at the Calamity Jane."

Helene looked puzzled. "Well, okay dear, if that's what you want..." and she began to reach for her purse.

But Lucinda patted her friend's hand. "I don't mean right this minute, Helene, but soon. Just stay with me a while longer. Maybe you could watch your program here..."

Later, when the same young character with the "nipple ring" issue announced to her perfectly-coifed June Cleaver of a mother that she was pregnant, Helene actually moaned in dismay. "Lordy, Lordy, Lordy," she intoned, "what IS the world coming to!"

Lucinda smiled again. It was good to smile.

Molly went back to the hotel and worked on the computer, not wanting to be around when her mother's "afternoon company" showed up. She finished up some maintenance work for one of her steady clients and then worked on a bid package for a prospective client. That one would keep her kids in college at least for another semester. All in all, business was good for Molly, but it was "you cruise, you lose," when it came to the world of technology and Molly made it part of her daily routine to keep current in the field.

Soon, though, having nothing else to do, she began to think about her recent encounters with Lucinda. The song she kept referring to was obviously the Mockingbird song, but which were the words that don't belong? And what did she mean about the pictures of the bad times? Maybe she meant around the time when her daughter,

Cathy, had been killed. On a whim, she did a search on Cathy Locke… Of course, there were so many Cathy Lockes in the world that she had thousands of hits. But when she narrowed it down to "Cathy Locke murder Hickok" she found quite a few references to what must have been very bad times, indeed, for Lucinda Locke.

Much of the information covered things that Molly already knew. She had been ten years old at the time and it was all anyone talked about for weeks. It was near the end of the school year, she remembered, and she had been in Mrs. Wayne's fifth grade class. It had happened on a Saturday night, so she heard about it on the bus Monday morning. At first she thought it was a joke or some TV show, but finally she understood that Cathy Locke had really been murdered.

"Somebody chopped her head off," Paula White had said, and Molly was horrified. Things like that just didn't happen in real life, especially not in Hickok. The truth was that her throat had been cut. It had happened in her own kitchen on Saturday evening while her parents were attending a charity event. Versions she heard varied, but all agreed that there was a lot of blood and that someone had tried to clean it up. It was Lucinda that had found her. People close to the family indicated that she remained calm long enough to call for the police and an ambulance, but that soon after she lapsed into a silence that was almost catatonic.

Molly looked through several articles, and found nothing new, but one name kept coming up… Eric Lentz. She remembered that he had been on the police force when it happened, but left soon afterward. Larger agencies had become involved, because of the nature of the crime and political connections of the girl's father, and they made the Hickok police force a laughing stock. The investigation had been completely bungled, according to them, and because of this the murderer would walk free. Eric Lentz, though, told everyone it was personal and vowed to solve the crime if it took him the rest of his life.

Part of her wanted to walk away and rack Lucinda's behavior up to too much morphine. *But, what could it hurt to ask a few questions,* the more responsible part of her answered, getting a *ditto* from the more curious part. *So, Mr. Lentz, let's see what you know.*

Shutting down her computer, she glanced at her travel alarm and realized it was almost 6:00. *I think I'll just grab a quick mocha,* as if she hadn't been watching the clock all afternoon. *After all, a girl's gotta drink.* She pinned up her unruly hair, added a hint of color to her lips, and headed nervously out the door.

When she got to Strange Brew, Molly had an anxiety attack. It really had been a long time and what she wanted more than anything was to run back to the hotel, get in her car and drive around until she found some courage. But she was a big girl and she could do this. She took a deep breath and… then walked right past the door, glancing up long enough to see Lissy shake her head and roll her eyes through the window. Feeling like an idiot she turned around, marched back and briskly opened the door… right into Quinn.

"Oh… Oh…" Molly was at a loss for words. "Crap?" offered Quinn, helpfully.

He looked undamaged, but Molly couldn't say the same about her dignity. Lissy was laughing so hard that she was in real danger of falling off her stool. Molly hoped she did.

"You know what?" Molly said, miserably. "I think this relationship is completely doomed and I think you need to stay away from me for your own protection. You're just lucky that I didn't run into you with my car! But, hey, the night's still young!"

"No damage, Miss Molly. All the vital parts... foot, nose, door... seem to be just fine. But let's go back to that part about us having a relationship. I quite like the sound of that... and also the 'night's still young' part" Quinn flashed a killer smile and gently led her back to the table they had before. Drinks were already there, thanks to Lissy – a Wild Cherry Mocha (no hidden message there) and an extra tall Latte flavored with Amaretto for Quinn.

"My fault really, Lass. I saw you race past the shop and thought you might be having a wee spot of bother with your brakes." He said.

"You must think I'm this huge idiot... not huge, but an idiot... at least I hope not huge... Anyway, what I'm trying to say is that I'm not usually like this. It's just that I haven't... I mean I don't normally... I really like you, and... it's just been a long time," she finished lamely.

Quinn was quiet for a moment, and then he leaned forward and said softly, "Just so you know, it's been a long time for me as well, so I'm perfectly happy just to spend time with you and see what happens. But I may need to spring for some body armor in case you decide to like me a lot."

Molly laughed. She suddenly felt better. "Okay," she said. "No pressure, we just see what happens."

Quinn really liked this woman. He liked her a lot, and he knew it was far too late for body armor. They had their coffees and then stayed until Lissy actually threw them out for real. "Come on, guys," she had whined. "I have a hot date with Ryan Seacrest and a Lean

Cuisine." According to Molly she was a diehard American Idol fan and she didn't care who knew it.

"Why don't you two get a room," she added, one eyebrow arched meaningfully.

Of course, part of him would like nothing better than to get a room. That part had a mind of its own. But the rest of him wanted to take this nice and slow. He felt at ease with this woman. She made him laugh, and he thought that if she never wanted to take it past the friendship stage, he would be okay with that.

He wanted to know everything about her and she was happy to oblige, for the most part. She told him about her work and her house and her taste in music. She bragged about her kids and she complained about them. He could see in her a fierce love and he knew that if anyone dared threaten her boys, she would be a force to be reckoned with. He was surprised at her intellect and found himself out of his depth when she began to wax on about database analysis... but she caught the glazed look on his face and quickly changed the subject. What he liked most about her, though, was the fact that she didn't seem to take herself too seriously.

The only subject she tended to avoid, he noticed, was her upbringing in Hickok. In fact, he would go so far as to say she was evasive. *A woman with a secret.* Quinn was intrigued.

Of course, he was one to talk about secrets... While he had not actually lied to her, he had been somewhat economical with the truth. He had led her to believe that he was a mid-level employee with an oil and gas company. He had failed to mention that he actually owned the company, as well as a few others scattered around the globe. She seemed anxious to learn about his life, but he was careful to give her just enough information. He told her his father was a government worker, when in fact he had been the Scottish First Chancellor in Parliament. He told her his mother had been a housewife, when in fact she had been a rather famous British actress, before her celebrated marriage to his father. Shortly thereafter, she retired from acting in order to "devote her full attention to her husband." Not her idea, Quinn thought, but he never heard her complain.

The voice in his head told him it wasn't a good idea to keep secrets from this woman, but he was so enjoying the fact that someone liked him for who he was rather than for what he was worth, that he couldn't seem to help himself.

Chapter Eleven

Molly sighed as she parked her car and headed for the entrance to her hotel. She couldn't remember when she had had a nicer time with a man. Maybe never and that, she knew, was a very sad commentary on her love life. *But, hey, now is good. In fact now is great!* She let herself imagine all kinds of interesting scenarios starring her and the very charming Scotsman. She was in such a fog, that she almost walked right past the desk clerk who was calling her name and waving to get her attention.

The clerk, a dapper old gentleman, who was a forty-year veteran of the hotel night desk and had seen it all, finally whistled impressively and Molly stopped, looking dazed.

"Oops... sorry," said Molly. "Guess I was daydreaming." "Guess you were, Miss," he said, looking at her strangely.

Molly suspected he was trying to decide if she was drunk or just ditzy. Apparently, he decided upon the latter, because he went on.

"You had something delivered here this afternoon and they went ahead and put it in your room... just wanted to give you a heads-up. They're not used to getting stuff like that so we didn't know what else to do with it. Can't rightly store it down here," he added, still eying her suspiciously.

"Okay. I wasn't expecting anything. It wasn't ticking, was it?" asked Molly, with a nervous laugh.

The clerk had apparently left his sense of humor in his other pants, because he just looked her in the eye and said, "No, ma'am, it wasn't ticking." Molly decided to cut her losses and escape up the stairs, thanking the clerk too cheerfully. As she glanced back, she saw him shaking his head ever so slightly.

Not used to getting stuff like that... What on earth? Her mind immediately conjured up images of her hotel room stacked to the ceiling with leather underwear, automatic weapons, and bags of fertilizer.

She unlocked her door, flicked on the light, and was relieved to see no bags of fertilizer or automatic weapons. She was slightly disappointed about the leather underwear, but that was another matter. What she did see, however, made no sense at all. It appeared to be a child's toy chest. It was smallish and brightly painted, but even from the doorway she could see that it had been well-used. Puzzled, she closed the door behind her and walked over to kneel in front of it. Taped to the top of it was a plain white envelope with her name on it. The envelope was sealed with wax and looked very old-fashioned. She broke the seal and read the note inside. The handwriting was no-nonsense and very precise. It read,

Molly Dear,

Lucinda Locke asked me to have this sent over to you. It is a toy chest that belonged to her daughter, Cathy, and she was insistent that you have it right away. Lucinda is my oldest and dearest friend and I couldn't say no.

She seems to be very taken with you, Molly. Perhaps you remind her of her daughter. But, whatever the reason, I know you have been kind to her and I wanted to thank you for making that choice. I often wonder what the world is coming to, but behavior such as yours helps restore my faith in human nature. I hope we meet again. (Signed) Helene Blanchard

Well, what do you know? She ran her hand over the top of the chest. It was obviously an old piece, handmade for sure. And in spite of a few scratches and a couple of nicks, it appeared to be in great shape. The top was curved and there was a bronze handle on either side. The front had an old-fashioned bronze latch that was warn smooth from usage. It was painted a delicate shade of pink, and all around the outside, frolicked whimsical animals. Molly saw roller skating elephants, and tap-dancing tigers, and monkeys with parachutes. There was a family of skunks eating ice cream cones next to a panda on a bicycle. Each vignette was an absolute work of art. It had been finished with several coats of varnish and then sanded until the wood felt like silk.

Molly flipped up the latch and carefully opened the box. It was empty, but the inside was just as sweet as the outside. It was lined in quilted satin, a shade or two darker than the paint on the outside. There were water stains here and there at the bottom, and Molly remembered the leaks in her old toy chest... a Betsy-Wetsy doll that had been thrown in the box before she had "done her business, a forgotten squirt gun, or broken snow globe from Christmas. There was also the time that her brother had... oh, well, but she didn't want to go there...

On the inside of the lid, there was painted a beautiful rainbow, and beneath it a small rectangular mirror in a gilded frame had been attached. Written in ornate golden script beneath it was, "The Little Princess." Even though it had belonged to a child, Molly thought it was one of the most beautiful pieces of furniture she had ever seen. She had certainly never owned anything like it.

Molly loved getting presents, and this one was wonderful and most unexpected. But she also knew that it had something to do with Lucinda's poem and she sensed that this gift came with a price. *So now, I have two pieces of the puzzle.* She took the poem out of her jacket pocket and reread it once more. She felt guilty that she had not yet kept her promise to Lucinda to burn the note. But after her encounter with the night clerk, she thought a fire alarm might just get her thrown out into the street, so it would have to wait until tomorrow. After a while she sighed and booted up her computer to do some database maintenance work. She glanced out the window, and had a moment of unease when she saw the same non-descript car she had seen at the hospital parked across the street. The man inside glanced up at her and then picked up a cell phone. She watched for a bit longer, then shook her head and jumped into her work. When she glanced out later, he was gone, and she thought no more of it.

Well, well, well... some naughty Nelly is poking her nose into someone else's business... my business. How disappointing to have complications, after all   this time. The killer sighed heavily. *But life is complicated... always having to clean up after other people... always having to take care of the weaker ones. But it does prove one's superiority; it certainly does. Now it's time to wait and see if the girl accidently stumbles into something that might cause me problems. She doesn't seem all that bright, but people are helping her!* In   a slow calculated movement, the killer flicked the side of the wine glass, causing it to topple over as if in slow motion. The glass did not break, but   the red wine soaked the white tablecloth with deep crimson, and it evoked a memory that made the killer smile. It was not a nice smile.

Just have to wait and see. If she can figure it out... she'll get what she deserves. If she doesn't figure it out, well maybe she'll get what she deserves anyway. It's all about patience, all about being smart, smarter than the others.   But that shouldn't be too hard. The killer picked up the wine glass, poured a   generous serving and made a silent toast to the stupidity of others.

Chapter Twelve

Lucinda felt unsettled. Helene had called earlier in the evening to say that she had delivered the chest to the Noble girl, and that was good. But Lucinda had the feeling that she had started something that could cause a lot of grief before it was finished. All these years, she had watched and wondered. All these long years… and then, just before her illness began to take its toll, she found something. But she had no idea what she should do with it. She didn't know exactly what the new information meant, just that it was more than they had before… one step closer to finding out who had taken her beautiful Cathy from her. She asked a few casual questions, but for the first time, she didn't know who to trust so she waited… almost too long. Now she had to rely on the kindness and resourcefulness of strangers. Maybe that was the best way, after all. Everyone else was too close to the tragic event and too damaged by it. She hoped and prayed, though, that nothing would happen to Molly Noble. And part of her was afraid that she wouldn't want to know what the girl might find out.

As she drifted to sleep, she allowed herself to remember her beautiful daughter. Lucinda had held her breath throughout the pregnancy, afraid to hope. But on the day Cathy was born, she was able to breathe again. She looked at the tiny girl, took a full, joyous breath, and vowed that from that moment on, she would breathe deeply, live fully, and enjoy every second she had with this angel. Unlike Teddy, the new baby girl did things her way from the very beginning. She was fussy and she was particular and if she was unhappy, she wasn't afraid to let the world know. When she gazed up at her mother, it was as if the baby knew that Lucinda was there to fulfill her every need, and that was the way it should be. But when she looked at Calvin, Lucinda could swear that there was an element of calculation... even then... as if she was already thinking of ways to wrap this cold, arrogant man around her finger. And she did just that, from the very beginning. She was a princess, and it was her birthright.

There was no malice in the child, though. As she grew older, she was very gentle with animals and other children. One day, Lucinda realized with surprise that the child was lonely. One would think that a beautiful child from an influential family would have lots of playmates, but that was not the case here in Hickok. She didn't get invited to other children's houses often. Lucinda could only speculate that it was because other parents were intimidated by their wealth or that they were afraid to expose themselves to Calvin's temper in any way. It was probably the latter, in all honesty. Because of this, Cathy fixated on her stepbrother Preston and followed him around like a puppy. Preston had been five when Cathy was born. Lucinda was afraid that he might be jealous, but the boy seemed overjoyed to have a new sister. She still had fond memories of a chubby Cathy and a very serious Preston in the back yard pretending they were Peter Pan's lost boys. He had woven a garland out of leafy twigs and put it on Cathy's head. Lucinda's favorite photo of Cathy was one she had captured on that day, with her garland, wild corkscrew curls, and a dab of muddy war paint on each cheek. Preston had loved his sister. There was no doubt in Lucinda's mind about that.

It was 10:00 in the morning and Quinn found himself folded into Molly's BMW, which was shooting like a rocket down a winding canyon road. When she took a corner faster than he would have liked, he casually reached up and took hold of the handle above the door so he could brace himself. He hoped she wouldn't notice.

They had met again that morning for coffee, and when she told him she had to cut it short to meet a man who lived up the canyon, he had insisted on going with her. She had tried to talk him out of it, but he had been persistent. Right now, his queasy stomach was upset with him about that. But the phrase, "meet a man" had stirred up something in him and he suddenly found himself wanting to protect his claim. *Protect my claim?* That wasn't like him at all, and he was shocked at the inference. *Now would be the time to book a flight and go back to a world that is safe and normal.* But he smiled to himself, and shook his head. He had spent years and years building a world that was safe and normal, but right now that was the last thing on earth he wanted. And strangely, in spite of his mutinous stomach, he couldn't have been happier.

Molly had explained that she was doing some sort of favor for her mother's hospital roommate. The woman had asked her to take a look at an old unsolved crime in Hickok and, through research, Molly had learned that Eric Lentz was something of the resident expert.

Okay, maybe I won't need to rough the fella up, especially since he must be an old geezer, though I could probably take him for sure. Quinn loved a mystery almost as much as he loved a challenge, and if the fair Molly needed information, he thought he just might be able to help.

Eric Lentz lived in a modest cabin a mile or so off the main road. It wasn't much to look at from the outside, but it was well-maintained and tidy. Lentz came out and stood on the porch as they drove up.

Quinn casually sized up the man and immediately had second thoughts about whether or not he could take him. The man could be described as old, but geezer, not so much. He had the look of an ex-boxer, obviously worked to stay fit, and looked much younger than his age. Lentz was neatly dressed in a flannel shirt and jeans, had an impressive silver crew cut, and sported a look that meant no-nonsense. There was a shotgun leaning casually on the deck railing, but easily within reach, and it definitely said no-nonsense.

Molly bounded up the steps and enthusiastically introduced herself. Quinn saw the man's expression soften. When she began to introduce Quinn, she realized to everyone's embarrassment, that she didn't know his last name. Quinn stepped forward and offered the man his hand. "Quinn Drummond," he said.

Lentz looked shocked. "Quinn Drummond?" he asked. "The oil and gas Quinn Drummond?"

"That, I am," answered Quinn lightly, glancing nervously at Molly. Although Lentz narrowed his gaze, he said no more and invited them into the cabin. Quinn breathed a sigh of relief.

The inside of the cabin was a pleasant surprise. It was neat and sparsely furnished, but the opposite wall was all glass, offering a breathtaking view of the river valley. On the end wall, there was a massive stone fireplace, and a wrought iron spiral staircase leading to a small loft area. The kitchen was natural pine, and Quinn suspected that Lentz had built the cabinetry himself. Molly oohed and aahed over the house and Quinn nodded approvingly.

Lentz gestured them toward a well-used sofa, facing the windows, and they sat down. He had just made coffee, he said, and offered them some. They, of course, said yes, and Lentz busied himself in the kitchen for a few minutes. As he was doing that, the largest German shepherd that Quinn had ever seen wandered out of a side room and stood a few feet from them. The dog didn't move, but looked first at Molly and then at Quinn. He growled when he looked at Quinn. Lentz stepped around the counter to calm the dog, but suddenly, the animal seemed to make a decision and trotted over to Molly, sniffing her gently and then butting her hand with his head... obviously looking for affection. Molly seemed oblivious to the size of the dog (or to the size of its teeth, Quinn added mentally), and brought her face right down to the dog, rubbing its ears and scratching its head with enthusiasm. Lentz looked shocked, and Quinn discretely scooted over a bit.

"Well, I'll be damned," said Lentz, with a note of awe. "I've never seen Jasper do that with anybody. I guess I'll have to trust you, Ms. Noble. My Jasper's a pretty good judge of character."

Quinn didn't miss the slightly raised eyebrow that Lentz aimed his way, meaning that he wasn't so sure about him.

Shaking his head, Lentz finished in the kitchen and brought out a tray with mugs of robust coffee and what looked like homemade oatmeal raisin cookies.

"So, Ms. Noble," he began, cautiously. "I take it from your phone call that you want to talk about the Cathy Locke case. You're not a reporter, are you?"

"No, not a reporter... and please call me Molly," she answered, still gently scratching the dog's head, which was nuzzling her lap. Quinn was jealous. "Lucinda Locke shares a hospital room with my mother, and we sort of developed a friendship. It's all kind of mysterious, but I think she wants me to see what I can find out about her daughter's murder. She probably thinks it's her last chance."

"Lucinda Locke," said Lentz with a sad smile. "I remember Lucy from way back. We were all in love with her then. She was really something in those days, still is I hear tell, but no one saw much of her after it happened. When she married that idiot, everybody thought she'd turn into one of them, but she never did. That husband of hers and his family, were always hinting around that she wasn't really good enough for them, but I'm here to tell ya that they were never good enough for her!" Lentz stopped, took a deep breath, and a couple of sips of coffee before he went on. "Anyway, when it happened, Lucy was the one that called it in. She was crying, sure, but she never lost it, at least not in front of us. Her husband was stomping around, yelling 'why me, why me.' But she was a real lady."

Quinn got the feeling that what Lentz felt for Lucinda Locke went deeper than mere infatuation. He was moved by the emotion in the man's voice.

There was a moment of silence, and then Molly said, "I was only ten when it happened, but I remember hearing that there were some odd things at the house... things that made no sense."

"The whole thing was a cluster... I mean a mess, the moment we walked through that door," Lentz said. "Sure we were inexperienced and it's true that we had never seen a murder before in Hickok. But, damn, we weren't stupid! At first we thought it was a prank call. I mean it was Hickok, and nothing ever happened in Hickok. But the sound of Lucy's voice on the phone told us it was the real thing. When we got there, we took pictures of everything and we wore gloves. We did not contaminate that crime scene, that's the honest truth. Somebody had already done that before we got there."

Lentz paused for a moment. Quinn could tell that it was still fresh in his mind and that his feelings were raw. It really was personal for him.

"You mean about the clean-up?" Molly asked gently. "I remember hearing about that."

"Well, yeah," he answered. "The poor girl was lying in a pool of blood on the kitchen floor, throat cut. There was a paring knife on the counter, but it had been washed. Wooden handle was still damp. We assumed that had been the weapon, but could never say for sure." He paused for a few moments. "The thing about the floor, too... I mean, a cut throat is messy... blood everywhere. But there was one place where the blood had been cleaned up. It was like somebody had mopped up the floor from the edge of the blood pool to the back door. You could still smell the bleach. We never found the rag that was used, either."

"No fingerprints?" asked Quinn.

"Well, that was a weird thing," answered Lentz "The front door hadn't been touched, but both the inside and outside handles of the back door had been wiped clean. There was this big stone patio out back and then the swimming pool and tennis court. The pool area was kinda wet, and that was strange. Never did figure that one out. We didn't find any shoeprints, so we assumed that whoever had done it had kept mostly to the paved areas."

"So, any suspects?" asked Quinn.

"We had been there about fifteen minutes when Locke's son, Preston, came wandering in, looking high as a kite. He really freaked out. I think they had to have him tranquilized. I never really trusted the kid, but he said he had been partying over at some friends' house and they vouched for him. They lived a couple of blocks away... the Golden boys. You probably remember them if you're from here," he said to Molly.

"Sure," said Molly. "Jeff and Curt... I knew of them, but they were quite a bit older and we never traveled in the same circles. Didn't the older one get killed in a car crash shortly after the murder?"

"Yeah," answered Lentz. "Jeff... he was a real piece of work. Got suspended from school for fighting. Almost killed another kid... stabbed him. But with their dad being a doctor and a pillar of the community, everything got hushed up and smoothed over. That's one thing I don't miss about police work... the politics. Actually, I wouldn't have put the killing past him. It was just his style, but there were other people up at their house who said he had never left."

"So anyway," he continued. "A few minutes after the kid shows up, in walks the housekeeper or nanny or whatever she was. Helene Blanchard was her name and she had been with the family since before Cathy was born. She'd been at some kind of function up at the Lutheran Church. She was pretty upset, too, but held it together better than the kid. In fact, she went right to the kid and tried to calm him down."

"So, we had a ruined crime scene, everybody accounted for, and a dead girl. In other words, we had nothing. The feds had a field day with us, and nothing ever got solved. What I remember most about that night is Calvin Locke storming around the house, knocking things over and shouting, while his wife sat on the sofa, still as a statue, with tears streaming down her face." They finished their coffee and cookies in silence. Molly asked about any photographs he could share and he said he would photocopy what he had and get them to her. He warned her that they weren't a pretty sight. When they left, Molly, a woman who feared neither gigantic dogs nor men with crew cuts, gave both dog and man a big hug. Lentz said he would be happy to answer any more questions and waved them off, the shotgun seemingly forgotten in the corner.

As Quinn looked back at the cabin before Molly shot around the corner, he saw Lentz drop his shoulders and put his face in his hands. There was so much sadness there, and so much anger.

Chapter Thirteen

Molly dropped Quinn off at his car in front of Strange Brew. He told her he was staying at a friend's cabin a few miles out of town while he was in the area, and invited her to come out for lunch, but she reluctantly declined. Her mother was being discharged the next day and she had a few things to take care of. As she pulled into the supermarket parking lot, her cell rang and it was Nurse Cheryl.

"Hey girl," chirped Cheryl. She even sounded perky over the phone. "How bout we catch the early movie tonight. I forget the name, but it's a chick flick, guaranteed to make us laugh, cry, and end up feeling better about ourselves."

"Wow," said Molly. "Just what I need. Want to grab a bite before the show?"

"Sorry, I'm on shift till 7:00, but I'll meet you there at 7:30. I'm already fantasizing about Malted Milk Balls and lots and lots of popcorn, swimming in butter. Yikes… gotta go." Molly could hear Cheryl's pager beeping in the background.

"Okay," thought Molly with a smile. "Girl's night it is!"

Molly spent a big part of her afternoon in the hospital business office going through piles of paperwork, in anticipation of her mother's release the next day. When she finally nailed down every "miscellaneous item" on the bill, she had to walk outside for a few minutes to uncross her eyes and get her blood pressure back to normal. She had learned after her mother's prior hospital stays that hospitals don't count on patients, or their families going over every line item. Molly found no less than twelve "miscellaneous items" on the itemized bill and demanded that each be clearly identified or she would contact the insurance company. Finally, after the usual display of posturing and bluster, they ended up removing each of those items from the bill, and the result was a savings of over two thousand dollars. It wasn't her money, but it was the principle!

After a discreet happy dance and a celebratory handful of M & M s, Molly made her way to her mother's room, but even before she walked through the door, she could hear the soft snoring that signaled an afternoon nap in progress. Quietly, she tiptoed in and took a moment to watch her mother sleeping. The older woman's color was so much better and some of the deep lines around her mouth seemed to have eased. Molly had always assumed they were permanent worry lines, but maybe they had been "lonely" lines. "You go, girl," Molly whispered to her sleeping mother.

At that moment, she heard Lucinda softly humming, and made her way around the curtain to the other woman's bedside.

Molly took Lucinda's hand. "Thank you so much for the toy chest. I've never seen anything like it. It's absolutely beautiful!" said Molly. "But I'm not sure you should be giving me things like that... things that have so much sentimental value."

Lucinda smiled, "No dear, I wanted you to have it... but I'll admit that I have my own agenda. Just remember what I wrote and what I talked about and you'll find the puzzle pieces. I guessed some, but I know there has to be more. Just promise me you'll be careful!" and she gave Molly's hand a healthy squeeze.

Molly suddenly realized that Lucinda's appearance had also changed. There was color in her cheeks, her eyes looked alive, and she was completely present. What a change from the pale, frightened, lost soul she had first met just a few days earlier. *They must be doing something right, here...*

"Did you burn it?" Lucinda asked, looking at Molly shrewdly.

"Oops," said Molly, and plucked the note out of her coat pocket, but Lucinda stopped her and then pulled her closer so she could whisper in her ear.

"Learn it and then get rid of it right away... not in a public place though and don't let anyone see it."

Conspiratorially, Molly whispered back. "I promise, Lucinda. It just never seemed like the right time... but I'll do it as soon as I can."

That seemed to satisfy Lucinda because she relaxed a bit. She patted Molly's hand fondly and they visited about Molly's mother and the fact that she was being discharged in the morning. Molly promised to continue her visits to Lucinda, though.

"Oh, and by the way," added Molly, "I went out to visit Eric Lentz and he is going to get me copies of pictures."

"Eric, oh my... Eric," said Lucinda, softly, and Molly could swear that her color had deepened. "I haven't seen him in years. He was always such a gentleman... always so kind to me."

"Well, he certainly thinks the world of you... he made that pretty obvious," Molly answered, noting the ghost of a sad smile on Lucinda's face. "That's nice, that's so very nice..." Lucinda looked like she was having a fond memory but, with a sigh, shook her head and went on, "well, anyway, remember what I told you to…"

"Mother, you must be feeling better if you are bossing Ms. Noble around!" Preston Locke sauntered into the room, looking perfectly put together, but he wasn't alone. There was another man with him, and Lucinda's eyes widened with recognition.

"Curt, I can't believe that my rude son dragged you up here," she said with a laugh. "It's good to see you, though. This is Molly Noble. Her mother is in the next bed, but she's been kind enough to spend time with an old woman and share some girl talk."

Molly couldn't believe that she was about to meet Curt Golden, especially given her earlier conversation with Eric Lentz, but there he was as big as life. He seemed to be waiting for her to say something, but when she didn't he stepped around Preston and came forward with his hand out. He was about six feet tall, fairly trim despite some extra girth around the waist, and was dressed conservatively. He had light blond hair, which was beginning to look thin on top, and a slightly crooked smile. His eyes were light blue, cool blue. Molly noticed that he walked leaning forward on his toes, and it made him look slightly goofy, for lack of a better word. The handshake was brief, hearty and businesslike, but he didn't immediately let go of Molly's hand.

There was an awkward silence, and then Molly disengaged and stepped backward towards her mother's side of the room. "Well, places to go, things to do…" she said too brightly. "Lame," she muttered to herself. "I'll see you later Lucinda. Bye Preston… and uh, nice to meet you, Curt." She checked once more on her mother and then escaped down the hall.

I've just met a real golden boy, she thought to herself, as she headed for the stairs. She was a bit surprised at how unimpressed she was. Nurse Cheryl flew by in a big rush, slowing down just long enough to mouth the word "later" and pantomime eating from a bucket of popcorn. Molly laughed to herself. She was really looking forward to their girl's night.

Finally, having run out of other things to do, Molly drove up to the house on the hill to make sure it was well-stocked and ready for her mother's return. She had such mixed feelings about that house.

Her memories of growing up there were a jumble... lots of people in a very small space... lots of personalities... lots of emotions... one bathroom. She had been the oldest of four, supposedly the responsible one. *Yeah, that really worked out well.* Shaking her head, she shifted a bag of groceries, unlocked the door, and walked in.

Molly was, pretty much, a neat freak. Her upbringing had been full of chaos and she found, at an early age that she needed to create her own order. Her room, at least her half of the room she had shared with her sister, was always spotless. It was her sanctuary and she used to escape there on a regular basis to get away from the constant upheaval of her childhood. Later, when she had children of her own, she worked very hard to lighten up and give them their own space. She was even able to let the housework go a bit, and after the initial discomfort, had found it liberating.

Unlike Molly, her mother had never been too bothered by clutter and housework was not high on her priority list. Molly rolled up her sleeves and sighed. She had a lot of work to do.

As she cleaned and tidied her way from room to room, memories came flooding back. She remembered the cold mornings when she and her siblings would vie for the closest spot in front of the old wall heater in the living room. She remembered watching the Beverly Hillbillies as a family, her dad making a huge batch of popcorn every Wednesday night. They would each grab a bowl and then huddle in front of the old TV.

In her old bedroom, which had been turned into a storage room, she remembered hours of playing with troll dolls and Barbie, and reading lots and lots of books. She bought herself a stereo with her babysitting money and played the only five albums she had over and over, much to the annoyance of everyone else in the house... Simon and Garfunkel, the Beatles, Ed Ames, and Herb Alpert and the Tijuana Brass. Looking back, she couldn't imagine a more bizarre mix of music.

Her brothers' bedroom, which was now a guest room, had been the site of any number of knock-down drag-outs. It was also the site of any number of fun times. She remembered building forts there out of giant boxes, and an old cardboard space capsule that one of her brothers had gotten for Christmas. She remembered her brother waking her up when he heard noises in the house at night, and together in the dark they would check against intruders, armed with a tennis racquet and scissors.

Her mother's room had been the original garage, but was converted into an extra bedroom when the family continued to grow. Although the entire house was poorly insulated, this room had no insulation at all and Molly remembered being able to see her breath in the winter, when she went in to kiss her mother goodnight. There was always a "take one/leave one" lending library of books in her mother's closet. It was a huge box that the entire neighborhood utilized. Molly learned a lot from some of the more risqué romance novels she found in that box.

The kitchen was where all the world's problems were solved, with a glass of iced tea and a cigarette. Her mother and her many friends and relatives gathered there, and it was where Molly learned all the latest gossip, while casually hovering just outside the doorway. The kitchen was an oddly shaped, awkward room, but her mother insisted upon brightening it up by painting it in ghastly hues of shocking pink or neon green.

And then there was the tiny bathroom… *Well…* Molly shuddered. *Not gonna go there!*

Surveying her work, she couldn't help but remember the last year she had lived in that house. That had been the year from hell, no doubt about it. But she had spent most of her adult life working to get beyond that year and turn it into something positive that helped to mold her into becoming the person she was right now. Sometimes that worked, sometimes it didn't. She took a deep cleansing breath, looked around once more, and decided she had done enough. With a shiver of relief, she closed the door and locked it. She didn't look back.

Chapter Fourteen

Quinn caught himself checking his watch, again. It was 6:10 and Molly still hadn't arrived at Strange Brew. The cool, calm part of him realized that this was a recognized business strategy. Keep them waiting and you have the upper hand. You also establish the ground rules for the business relationship. Who has more power... the person who is waiting, or the person he is waiting for? But he knew that Molly wasn't like that. She didn't seem to have a manipulative bone in her lovely body. She had probably just lost track of time, or maybe she had car trouble, or maybe she had been abducted... *Oh, lad.* He nervously ran his hand through his unruly hair. *You're drowning in a sea of Molly.* Again, the businessman in him said it was time to cut and run, but Quinn knew he wouldn't do that... couldn't do that.

With a jingling of bells, the door opened and Molly walked in, looking harried, slightly flushed, and very beautiful. She scooted around the counter and gave Lissy a big sloppy hug. Then she turned the full intensity of her smile on him.

Now, I know what a deer feels like, caught in the headlights. Quinn stood up awkwardly and stepped forward to meet her halfway.

They picked up their drinks, dark chocolate mochas with a hint of coconut. "I just made up a new combination in your honor," said

Lissy. "I'm thinking of calling the new drink 'Sex on the Beach.'" She added, her eyebrows moving meaningfully.

Molly blushed, but Quinn laughed out loud and said, "Well, then we had better make that a double."

When they had settled at their usual table, Molly leaned back and sighed, visibly relaxing. "It's been such a day," she said. "With my mom being discharged tomorrow and there were so many details I had to take care of! Sorry I'm late, by the way, but I had to check with her doctor one more time to make sure we're still on schedule. Pinning him down is like shooting at a moving target. I actually followed him to the men's room and then pounced when he… but anyway, I got everything done."

"No worries," smiled Quinn, just glad that she was finally there. "I amused myself watching the Java Queen over there deal with half a dozen Japanese tourists. She got everything right and didn't break a sweat. She even managed to explain, using some interesting body language, the difference between a café au lait and a latte." He gallantly saluted Lissy, who acknowledged the gesture with a haughty look and the Queen's wave.

Quinn then turned to Molly. "You know, Molly dear, I think it's about time we took this so-called relationship to the next level." He noted that Molly looked nervous. "How about I take you out tonight and buy you a proper meal?"

Molly looked a bit flustered. "Oh, I like to eat a lot. I mean, I like to eat, but not a lot. Well, maybe sometimes a lot. But eating is good."

Quinn laughed and decided to rescue her. "So tonight it is, and I'll take you anywhere you want to go."

Molly took a deep breath, feeling like an idiot. "What I meant to say was that I would love to go out to dinner with you, but I can't tonight because I have a hot date." Quinn was afraid that the look on his face could have stopped time, but Molly continued. "My friend, Cheryl, and I are going to the new chick flick at the old theater down the street... actually I have to meet her there in about an hour. I went to high school with Cheryl, but never really got to know her. She's a nurse at the hospital, so we sort of reacquainted. Anyway, she's a real sweetie."

Quinn exhaled in relief. "Well, woe be to the man who gets between a woman and her chick flick. What about tomorrow night?"

Molly thought for a moment and then answered. "You know, tomorrow night might just work. My mom gets out of the hospital in the morning and I need to get her settled in back at her place. I was going to spend the night here so I'd be close if she needed me, and then I was going to go back home for a couple of days to make sure my house is still standing."

Quinn blinked in surprise. "You're leaving?" He felt a flutter of panic. "Just for a couple of days," she answered. "I have to come back down and stay while Mom is signed up for respiratory therapy. She hasn't driven in years so I'll take her to her appointments until she gets used to it and then I'll make arrangements with the Senior Bus to take over when she's ready. Uh... you okay?" She had finally noticed the look of shock on his face.

"Fine. Fit as a fiddle," he croaked. He wasn't used to being at a loss for words. *Fit as a fiddle?* He mentally groaned. *Damn, but this woman makes me crazy.*

Molly reached over the table and gently touched his hand. "You know, you make me feel a little crazy," she said, looking into his eyes.

Blast... Quinn was stunned. *The woman can read my mind!*

"But I know that you won't be here forever," she continued, "what with your job and everything, and I already feel sad about that. Maybe we should just have the best time we can, in whatever time we have."

Later, when she left for her hot movie date, Quinn sat alone at Lissy's and had a good think.

The wee lass had captured his heart. It wasn't something he could change and he didn't want to. What he really wanted to do was stay in Hickok and see what happened. Truth be told, he had been distancing himself from his business connections for some time. Over the last two years he had sold all of his interests in a number of corporations, making a killing, incidentally. But his reasons were not financial, they were personal. Quinn was not a happy man. He knew he had to keep the oil and gas company, because that was his father's legacy, but one by one he was disentangling himself from all other business ties. He felt, deep down, that there had to be more to life than business.

Most people, especially those on the outside looking in, assumed that since he was enormously rich and relatively good looking (or so he had been told), he was happy. But that just wasn't how it worked. He was tired of things... they gave no joy. He knew that happiness had to come from inside, but somehow this spitfire of a woman had unlocked something in him... something he had not felt in a very long time. He found himself smiling at the very thought of Molly. *Maybe it's time for me to bow out... let the people I pay to run the company actually do their jobs.* Living more and working less, he smiled at the novel idea.

He looked at his watch, mentally calculating the time difference in London. The ever-so-proper Valerie would right now be screening his phone calls, checking his emails, and enjoying the added level of authority this gave her. But she would be doing it with just a hint of disdain, as if it was a great inconvenience and something of a personal affront. Yes, Valerie was lovely. She was petite, slender, and never a hair out of place. Ironically, in Quinn's mind, she was 'aboot as sexy as the queen'.

But even though she intimidated him, she was a good secretary. *No more stalling.* He winced in anticipation of her reaction. *Might as well just make the call and tell her my trip will be prolonged indefinitely.* Acknowledging Lissy's not so subtle hint that it was time for him to leave… it sounded something like, "Get your lazy butt outa here, Big Guy"… he stepped outside, flipped open his phone, and hit speed dial.

Chapter Fifteen

Lucinda had learned to take it one day at a time and, all things considered, this had been a good one. She felt better. The autumn sun had been warm; the changing leaves so golden that she could feel the color on her skin, and the sunset had been wonderfully slow. Best of all, she remembered Eric. He had been her first love, although she was pretty sure he never knew it. A year older than Lucy, he ran deliveries from her Daddy's store after school. She used to make silly excuses to be around when he was there. After a while she stopped making excuses. Around him Lucy was awkward and tongue-tied, which struck her as peculiar because usually she wasn't shy at all. His brown hair was streaked with the sun and he was tanned from working on his family's ranch. Every once in a while he would catch her looking at him and give her this crooked smile that made her heart skip a beat or two. His eyes were the color of warm honey.

One summer night, soon after he graduated from high school, Lucy finally got the courage to ask him for a ride home from the store. He didn't say a word, but just smiled and nodded. She climbed into his old truck and they headed towards her farm. The night was warm and the windows were down. It had just rained and she could smell the wet fields as they drove past. "Little Runaway" was playing on the tinny old radio and she wanted to sing along, but was too shy. She imagined scooting close to him and taking his hand. She imagined him pulling over and giving her the most wonderful and life changing kiss. It may not have been her first kiss, but she knew it would have been her best. She imagined him professing his love for her and asking for her hand. But none of that happened. She just sat there and he just sat there.

When he pulled up to her house, he looked like he wanted to say something, but then shook his head and reached across her to open the door from the inside. He brushed her bare arm as he fumbled with the handle and Lucy trembled. He said, "Night, Miss Lucy." She didn't say anything, couldn't, because suddenly she was very embarrassed. She just hopped out of the truck and ran to her house. But she watched from the window. He sat there in his truck for a very long time. Eventually he banged his head on the steering wheel a couple of times, then fired up the engine and took off. To this day, Lucinda believed with her whole heart that they had both missed something very important. How different her life could have been!

And then he was gone. She heard that he had joined the Navy or maybe the Marines, saw some action overseas, and then stayed on as MP. When he came back he joined the Police Department in Hickok. He had never married, although she had heard he was a bit of a ladies' man. She wasn't surprised... after all these years, her heart still skipped a beat when she thought of him. She drifted off to sleep humming "Little Runaway."

Molly found the chick flick monumental in that it covered all the bases. The cast of characters included: girl who pines for boy; boy who pines for someone else; long-legged blond man-eater; nice guy who happens to be rich; and monopoly man. After innumerable madcap situations involving love, lust, jealousy, slapstick comedy, misdirection, misinformation, bitch-slapping, and sitting on a park bench looking miserable, the final scene resolves all issues. The girl, dripping wet with pieces of someone's wedding cake in her hair, finally realizes she loves the nice guy, and tells the boy where to sling his hook, nicely of course. She and nice guy take off in a limo that just happens to be waiting at the curb, and catch a private jet to Bora Bora. The boy, also dripping wet and a bit cakey, finally realizes he just lost the love of his life and tells man-eater where she can sling her hook. Man-eater, who has big gobs of frosting in her hair, does not take it gracefully and knees him in the groin. He doubles over and falls to the ground, groaning. A bridesmaid runs over to help the boy, they look at each other and sparks fly. Man-eater strides away, looking like a runway model topped with frosting. As she leaves, an elderly gent, dressed not unlike the monopoly man, scampers after her, obviously hoping for a chance. As the credits roll we see the bikini clad girl and surprisingly hunky nice guy on a deserted beach. We see vignettes of boy getting kneed in the groin again and again. Apparently he has some issues with monogamy. We see man-eater striding down Rodeo Drive in Beverly Hills, followed by monopoly man who is staggering under the weight of her purchases. They both look happy. The end... or is it?

Molly and Cheryl sat in the theater until the lights came up, then looked at each other laughed... hooted, actually.

"What a stinker," hooted Cheryl, still licking butter off of her fingers. "But I really needed a girl's night and a chick flick. Sorry to drag you in…"

"Are you kidding?" answered Molly, still laughing. Her sides were beginning to hurt. "I haven't had this much fun in years! You know that part where they have the food fight in the Italian restaurant and everyone gets covered in tiramisu and fettuccini Alfredo… Brilliant… I'm thinking Oscar!" That brought on another wave of laughter.

Finally, when the theater had emptied completely and the manager's teenaged kids looked at them curiously as they cleaned up for the next showing; they took that as their cue to leave. They stepped out into the cool night air and chatted, then Cheryl headed towards her car and Molly, who was on foot, took off across the street to the hotel.

What happened next was a blur. Molly was about halfway across the street, jaywalking since it was almost 10:00 pm and there wasn't a soul in sight. All of a sudden, out of nowhere, a car came screeching around the corner. Molly quickly stepped back into the other lane to give the driver plenty of room, but the vehicle seemed to follow her movement and swerved into the wrong lane! She ran towards the curb, but the car kept coming straight at her. Finally, her heart pounding, she threw herself between two parked cars and then rolled up onto the sidewalk. She heard the squeal of brakes, but the car still sideswiped one of the parked cars that had shielded Molly, before racing off down the street.

In a daze, it took Molly a moment to realize that she was lying on the sidewalk in an undignified heap. She sat up, wincing as she put weight on her palm. The first thing she did was a quick inventory of all her important parts. Scraped palm that was oozing blood, one knee of her jeans was torn and she was pretty sure she would find the same type of scrape there. She had hit her hip on the curb and was already anticipating a whopper of a bruise. Her head had also hit the pavement, but, for once, Molly was grateful for her big hair, which had cushioned the blow and prevented anything worse than a goose egg. *So, no bones broken, all in one piece...* Molly breathed a sigh of relief. The second thing she did was look around to see if anyone else had seen her embarrassing fall… not logical she knew, but she couldn't help it.

The theater manager came running towards her. "You okay, ma'am? You coulda been killed! I was in the ticket office so I pretty much saw the whole thing. Had my boy call the police and they should be here any minute. Almost looked like that fella was trying to hit you!"

Molly could tell that he wanted to check her for an injury, or at least help her up, but was unsure of what to do, so he just hovered over her. She felt sorry for him.

"Molly, I can't leave you alone for five minutes," huffed Cheryl, having run down the street in her clogs. "Cripes, that guy musta been drunk or nuts or both!" Cheryl then went into nurse mode and gently checked Molly's injuries. "Okay, nothing serious. We're gonna get you up off the sidewalk now," and she helped Molly to her feet.

The police arrived and they all answered a few questions. Molly didn't have many details to give them. She did remember, right before leaping between the cars, thinking that the car had been an old beater. Odd thought, considering she had been literally running for her life. She thought the car had been a light color, like maybe light blue or silver. As a matter of fact, it reminded her of another vehicle she had seen recently, but she couldn't seem to remember when or where. Cheryl agreed about the color and also about the fact that it was an older car. Kind of "square" she thought, or boxy.

The theater manager had the best description. He said it had passed right under a streetlamp and that he was pretty sure it was a light blue Chrysler "K" car, like the ones the government workers all drove several years ago. He remembered that it had a dent or two and maybe some rust. No license plate number, though... it had happened too fast and he had been more focused on Molly. He said he saw the driver and was positively a man... maybe an older man, definitely not a kid... but was too far away for any other details. The manager also said that the only time the driver used his brakes was after Molly had "hit the deck" so to speak. In fact, he thought the guy had speeded up when she was still in the street.

Cheryl ran back to her car for her first aid kit, and then walked Molly to her hotel room and tended her scrapes and bruises. She stayed until Molly shooed her out, knowing that she was working the morning shift. Finally alone with her thoughts, Molly shivered, partly from shock and partly from that fact that she could have been killed and that it wasn't necessarily an accident.

It took her a long time to come down from the adrenaline, even with the pain killers Cheryl had insisted she take. She thought briefly about calling Quinn, but nixed that idea. She had fantasized that their first romantic encounter would involve more than the kissing of "boo-boos," and wanted to keep it that way. But, the scene kept replaying itself over and over in her head and she felt edgy and vulnerable. Eventually, after drinking a cup of chamomile tea and checking the door lock twice, she was able to drift into an uneasy sleep.

The killer laughed. It was a dry, hollow sound. *The car would be disposed of, and maybe even the driver if he threatened to make trouble. There would always be another down-and-out drifter who would be happy to take on a messy job if the price was right. Tongues would be wagging... a poor girl almost run down right on Main Street... Oh, dear me!* The killer smiled, imagining the look on Molly's face as the car headed straight at her. *Now let's see how smart she really is... she can walk away or, more likely, run, or she can keep poking her nose into the past and pay the price.*

Excited by the prospect of teaching Miss Molly a lesson she would never forget, the killer thought of all the other people who needed to be taught a lesson. *There were so many... Every betrayal recorded and every slight remembered. Maybe the whole town needed a lesson, but once the lessons began it would be very difficult to stop... very difficult indeed.*

Chapter Sixteen

In the dream, Molly heard a noise coming from Cathy Locke's toy chest. It was a squeaking sound, but not like an animal. It was more like a machine or a tool. She was in her old bedroom at her mother's house, but the room was much bigger than it should have been. It was dusk and she could see the sunset through the west window and the shadows in the room were beginning to lengthen. The chest was in the far corner of the room and she walked over and carefully lifted the lid. She wasn't afraid… well, maybe a little, but more curious really. It was empty. Suddenly someone pushed her from behind and she fell into the box, which seemed to be changing in size. Now it was more like a coffin, and she found herself lying there, in a bed of quilted pink satin. She noticed that the satin was stained, but she realized that it wasn't water… it was blood. She tried to lift herself out of the box, but she couldn't move… she could only lie there and watch as someone slowly closed the lid. She was struggling wildly, but couldn't seem to break free, and she was trying to scream but she couldn't make a sound. Just as the latch snapped closed, she managed something more like a moan than a scream, but it woke her up.

Even after Molly untangled herself from her sheets and switched on the bedside lamp, it took a long time for her heart to stop pounding. "Just a dream, just a dream," she kept repeating to herself like a mantra. Finally she got out of bed and limped to the bathroom to splash her face with cold water and, since it had been over four hours since the last one, take another pain pill. On her way back she glanced over at the old toy chest in the corner. Despite a shiver of fear, or maybe because of it, she went over, bent down and lifted the lid. Pink quilted satin, a couple of water stains… no blood. As she closed it, she caught her reflection in the small mirror that was mounted in the lid. *Little Princess… right! More like Miss Fraidy Cat!* She gently closed the lid and climbed back into bed.

Molly did some of her best thinking when she couldn't sleep. In her opinion, if you couldn't stop your mind, you might as well put it to work. She thought about her upbringing and the person she had become. She had made mistakes in her life, big mistakes, but she had done her best to make things right and learn from those mistakes. She had changed. She was a better person and a stronger person and she was tired of living with guilt. She thought of all the times she had avoided confrontation, all the times she had just accepted someone else's bad opinion and walked away. This encounter with mortality should probably have her running away as fast as her Beemer could carry her but, instead, it made her want to dig in and fight. Slowly, she felt her fear being replaced by anger. She was tired of backing down and she was tired of doing what others thought was best for her. Whatever was going on, she was going to get to the bottom of it and if it required butt-kicking, well, she had the blue snakeskin cowboy boots for the job! Finally, thinking about boots, she drifted off.

Chapter Seventeen

Quinn knew something was wrong the minute Molly walked through the doorway of Strange Brew, but he couldn't quite put his finger on it. She was pale, she was moving slowly, and her smile was just too fixed. As she walked past the counter she whispered, "caffeine, stat... and keep it coming."

Quinn could tell from Lissy's look of alarm that she sensed something, too. When he stood up to greet her, he noticed the bandage on her hand that she was attempting to conceal with a long-sleeved baggy sweater.

"Lass, what have ye done to yourself?" he asked. It came out sharper than he had intended and Molly jumped at the tone.

"Just a mishap after the movie last night... nothing serious," she answered brightly.

"So, it was you! Just a mishap, my ass! Hickok's finest are in here every morning for coffee and donuts and today they were talking about some woman almost getting run down last night in front of the theater. Geez Louise!" Lissy hopped off her stool and strode over to the table. "Molly, you coulda been killed... that sounds pretty serious to me!"

Quinn forced himself to stay calm. He gently took Molly's arm and guided her to her usual chair. "Now," he said evenly, "First of all, I want to know how badly you were hurt, and then I want you to take a deep breath and tell me everything you remember." If Molly had any objections, the look on his face changed her mind.

"Okay," said Molly. "No serious damage… just road rash on my palm and knee. Actually I'm more upset about the hole in my favorite jeans; a bruise on my hip that looks like a Rocky Mountain sunset and a good sized knot on my head… that's all" She looked hopefully from Quinn to Lissy but neither was going to let her off the hook that easily. "My friend Cheryl was there and she's a nurse. She checked me out and said there was nothing life-threatening. Honest!"

"Geez Louise," repeated Lissy. "Are you for real? Someone tries to run you down with a car and that's not life threatening? Earth calling Molly!"

"Let's hear it," said Quinn, in a tone that would have made his employees tremble.

Molly sighed. "Okay, okay, fine. I'll tell you everything, but not before I get some caffeine into my system."

When Lissy returned with a double cappuccino, Molly told them everything she could remember about the night before. When she had finished, Quinn sat back and shook his head. "Well, I could be wrong, but I suspect the driver was not some rival database analyst. Looks like you made someone nervous or angry or both."

Molly admitted that she had come to the same conclusion herself.

"So, my dear, seems that you looking into that old murder case stirred something up. Any chance you could just let it go and walk away?"

Molly finished her coffee and looked him right in the eye. "Not a chance. I need to make a stand and this is the right place and the right time."

Quinn was quiet for a moment. Then he nodded his head and answered, "That's what I was afraid of. In that case, you'll be wantin' a bit of help and I won't take no for an answer."

Lissy looked bewildered. "Old murder case? You mean the Cathy Locke case? That's just about the biggest mystery this town has ever seen. People still talk about it. Well, hell, count me in!" She looked positively excited, as she ran back to her stool to wait on a small group of customers that had been waiting patiently.

After Molly left to check her mother out of the hospital, Quinn sat for a while before he could trust himself to make the calls he needed to make. Schooled to carefully control his emotions, only a handful of people in his life would have been able to guess what was going on beneath the surface… one eye slightly narrowed; the hard set of his jaw. He couldn't remember ever feeling so angry. In a real way, whoever threatened Molly was threatening his newfound happiness and he was not going to let that happen. He had resources and he knew people. As he headed out the door, he hit speed dial on his cell. *If you want to play rough, let's play rough.* It was time to call in a favor or two.

When Molly arrived at the hospital, she found her mother sitting on the edge of the high hospital bed, fully dressed, with her overnight bag next to her, and clutching the large brown purse she had carried around for years. She smiled broadly as her daughter entered the room and hopped off the bed, ready to go that minute. Molly smiled to herself. The woman who not so long ago had given everyone a scare was now the picture of health. In fact, she was downright peppy and Molly had to stop her as she tried to get past her through the door. "Whoa, Nellie," laughed Molly. "You get a free limo ride, and here it comes right now."

As if on cue, Cheryl came around the corner with a wheelchair. As she came to a stop, she leaned over to Molly and whispered, "Not sure who needs the wheelchair more… you or your mother. You doin' okay?"

"I feel about 200 years old, but I'll probably survive. Thanks for the TLC last night; I was really glad you were there," Molly whispered back. Cheryl opened her mouth to respond, but Molly shushed her and nodded at her mother, who had settled herself in the wheelchair and was impatiently tapping her foot.

As they headed toward the elevator, Molly realized she hadn't said goodbye to Lucinda. "Just give me a minute," she said to Cheryl. "I'll meet you downstairs."

Lucinda seemed to be waiting for Molly as she approached the bed and smiled broadly. "I knew you would be in to say goodbye. You know, I really am going to miss your mother."

"It's not goodbye," said Molly. "I'll be gone for a couple of days, but when I'm back, I'll visit you every afternoon." She bent down and planted a kiss on the woman's forehead. She had come to really care for Lucinda and was surprised to find her eyes tearing up. "Gotta go now, but I'll see you soon. I promise," and she gave Lucinda's hand a squeeze before running to catch the elevator.

As she bundled her mother into the waiting car, Molly waved to Cheryl and mimed "call me." As they headed to the rectangular house she had grown up in, she realized with surprise that the usual stress that triggered was absent. Maybe her mother's near miss had softened something in her, maybe it was her decision to stand up to a threat and push back, or maybe it was simply time to let go. Whatever it was, she liked it. She liked it a lot.

"Looks like you have the whole place to yourself," said Cheryl brightly, as she brought Lucinda her medication. "There's a nasty rumor going around that if you keep getting better they might spring you from the joint," she added in a conspiratorial whisper.

Lucinda allowed herself to feel hope. The doctor had mentioned that her condition had radically improved and that, once again, they weren't exactly sure why. To be honest, they weren't sure what had caused her condition to begin with. One day she was fine, except for the aches and pains associated with a few too many birthdays, and the next she was suffering excruciating headaches, muscle spasms, and vomiting blood. She would go into the hospital for a few days, improve, only to have her symptoms recur a few weeks later. This had been the pattern for over a year, and she knew... everyone knew... that she couldn't go on much longer. This last time Helene had found her unconscious and called an ambulance. She had remained unconscious, comatose actually, for three days, and the doctor had hinted to Preston that the end might be near. When she fought her way back into consciousness, things were fuzzy and strange, and it took her a long time to feel like herself again.

Funny, she thought. Given the traumatic events of her life, she should probably have welcomed death, but she didn't. She wasn't ready to go. She had places to visit, mysteries to solve, and apologies to make. She was tired of being Lucinda and she wanted to let Lucy out for a while and see what happened.

As Cheryl was fussing around her bedside, Lucinda asked for a hairbrush and mirror. Cheryl looked surprised, but then laughed and said, "You bet… makeover time! But we need to get you doped up first." She handed her the medication and a glass of water, but as Lucinda raised the pills to her mouth, Cheryl stopped her and took the medication from her hand. She looked at the pills and then at the chart. Shaking her head, she said, "This doesn't look right, so let's hold off on the pills." She put them back in their paper cup and slipped them into her pocket. "Be back in a flash, but let's get to work on that makeover," and with that Cheryl dug out Lucinda's hairbrush and hand mirror from her overnight case in the closet.

Lucinda began carefully brushing the tangles out of her hair, enjoying the simple repetitive motion. She missed Shirley already. They had not really spoken much, but Lucinda found herself vicariously enjoying the budding romance between the Noble woman and the retired groundskeeper from the country club, Dick something… Holcombe maybe? They were like a couple of teenagers. *And why not… sure they were older, but what kind of idiot would say no to a second chance at love?*

Hit by the truth of that thought, Lucinda stopped brushing her hair and set the brush down. *What kind of idiot would say no to a second chance at love? Me… I'm an idiot… I'm such an idiot!*

When Cheryl bopped back into the room a few minutes later, she found Lucinda laughing softly to herself.

"Could you find me a phone book, dear? I think it's time for a second chance."

Chapter Eighteen

Getting her mother back into the house and her old routine was more of a job than Molly had anticipated. Rather than be pleased that her daughter had cleaned the house, Shirley was upset because now she wouldn't be able to find anything. At one time this would have upset Molly, but after all these years she recognized the old pattern and refused to play. She patiently listened and offered to find anything that she had inadvertently misplaced. Then Shirley carefully inspected the contents of the refrigerator and the pantry, and had Molly make a list of the things she had forgotten.

And finally, once she was settled into her favorite chair and tuned into an old TV murder mystery, Shirley suddenly made a show of sniffing the air, claiming to smell aftershave, and hinting very strongly that Molly had been entertaining strange men in the house.

"Entertaining? As in wowing them with my fast typing skills? As in seducing them with wild stories about sending my kids to college and paying the mortgage? As in dirty dancing in my moth-eaten sweatpants and 'I'm with Stupid' t-shirt?" Molly laughed in spite of the ridiculous nature of her mother's claim. "Honest, Mom, I didn't even stay here. All I did was clean your house and buy your groceries. And the only strange man I know is Dick."

For a moment, Shirley's expression darkened, but she couldn't keep it up and, in the end, giggled like a girl. "He really is strange, isn't he? That comb-over!" They laughed and laughed, until Shirley said it made her chest hurt. Molly made her mother a cup of tea and they sat in silence for a while, watching a roller-skating crime fighter solve the perfect murder. After explaining that she would be gone for a couple of days to take care of business at home, but would be back on Monday to get her mother to her respiratory therapy appointment, Molly got up and headed for the door.

"Wait a minute, honey," Shirley said and, surprisingly, turned off the TV. "I know it hasn't been easy for us. But I can see that you're different. I'm proud of you… really. You're a good person and a good mother. When it happened, I was just so upset about what everyone would think… and that people would blame me… I don't know why I couldn't have just… and all these years I couldn't just say… Oh, honey, I'm sorry." A single tear rolled down her cheek. "You're my daughter and I should have just loved you."

Molly knelt before her mother. "It's okay, Mom. It's okay." She held the woman for a long time, and shed her own tears. Those were words she had waited a lifetime to hear… words she had almost given up on. She had learned to live without them, but she couldn't pretend they didn't now mean something. As she gently kissed her mother's hair, Molly felt a sense of lightening. It was as if a fist deep inside her heart had finally let go, and she really did feel different.

She left her mother's house sometime later, smiling and humming David Bowie's 'Ch-Ch-Ch-Changes' under her breath. As she got into her car, she noticed a dark blue sedan with tinted windows, slowing down as it past her, and then abruptly speeding off. Molly was too busy singing the chorus to give it a second thought.

Nervously, Quinn went over his mental checklist again. Hair – somewhat tamed, although he thought it was getting too long; Shirt – long sleeved tee, casual enough, and without off-color slogan; Trousers – blue jeans, and not a front pleat in sight (he had, for some reason, really liked the whole front pleat trouser thing, even though it wasn't a good look on anyone and had been out of fashion for several years now). Shoes – the scuffed and well-worn work boots he wore while walking around drilling sites. He had briefly contemplated loafers, but that opened up the whole sock/no sock debate and he didn't feel up to the challenge.

"It's only a dinner... it's only a dinner..." he chanted to himself. As he squirmed around in his chair, hoping to strike just the right pose, he waited for her to walk through the door. He felt just like a teenager, he realized with a smile. Of course, his teenage dating experiences had mostly been the work of his ever ambitious father, trying to force some type of business or political alliance with one of Scotland's important families. Often times Quinn and his female counterparts from those families had gotten along well, both having a good laugh about playing the part of dangling carrot. He was kind to them and generally good-natured about the whole thing, and that resulted in him having a lot of friends who were girls, but he never really had a girlfriend until his college years when he had moved away from home.

Just as he realized that he had been shredding a paper napkin into tiny pieces, a pile of which littered the table in front of him, Molly entered the restaurant. Awkwardly, he swept the pile of paper bits into his hand and then looked around for a place to hide them. Finding nowhere, he emptied them onto his salad plate. He stood as she approached the table and gallantly pulled out her chair.

She settled herself into her seat and, noticing the paper evidence of his nervousness, said, "So, I see you started without me. I usually like to begin with the stuffed mushrooms, but I've heard the paper bits are excellent... not so filling."

He laughed, suddenly filled with relief. "I was feeling a bit peckish... I hope you don't mind. I took the liberty of ordering you some pencil shavings... a specialty of the house!"

They both laughed at that and then they made a big show of perusing their menus. After a couple of minutes, Quinn noticed that Molly had sheepishly donned a pair of reading glasses. Feeling less self-conscious, he did the same. He was surprised at how natural it felt and how comfortable to be himself in the company of this woman.

Momentarily disconcerted by the waitress, who was something of a contradiction with her short western skirt, cowboy boots, startling pink hair, and nose ring, Quinn quickly recovered and asked for stuffed mushrooms for an appetizer. Molly ordered salmon and Quinn went for the prime rib. When he asked her about wine, she said she preferred cranberry juice and soda so she could keep her wits about her.

"Love, are you worried that I might try to take advantage of you?" he asked, raising his eyebrow.

"Well, hope springs eternal," she answered sweetly, adding, "but if you do, I plan to enjoy every minute of it, unimpaired."

"Good point," he murmured, and ordered the same thing.

Quinn watched Molly as she chattered on about getting her mother out of the hospital. In spite of her traumatic experiences of the last day or so, she looked lighter and happier. It was as if a veil had been lifted and she seemed to glow.

After the drinks arrived, but before the appetizer, Molly excused herself to freshen up and Quinn occupied himself by looking around the room. There were a number of upscale restaurants in Hickok, ranging from the new Sushi bar to an exclusive Italian bistro that had just opened and actually screened its clientele. He chose this place, The Full Rack, because it was somewhere in the middle and the ambiance was true west, rather than "new west." And also, he had to admit, he liked the name. Maybe a bit dark, and even shabby, he enjoyed the worn plank floors, plain but sturdy furniture, and the decorating theme that included spurs, tack, old photos, and barbed wire. There was a massive old bar on one side of the room, and sitting there was an older gent, decked out in carefully ironed jeans, a western shirt, bandana, and slightly oversized white hat. The man had clearly dressed up to come to town and he was nursing what was probably his only beer of the night. *Now that's a real cowboy.*

It was early yet, but people were beginning to trickle in. The tourist season was over and these were mostly locals. Watching them greet the restaurant staff and each other, Quinn felt unaccountably jealous. They were rooted and connected and bound to each other in ways he had never experienced or understood. "But, it's not too late," he whispered to himself. "Not too late…"

He was roused from his reverie by Molly returning from the ladies room.

She planted a delicate kiss on his cheek and asked, "Miss me?"

"More than you know, lass, more than you know," he answered seriously, and Molly gave him a strange look.

Their food arrived and Quinn noted that Molly ate with great gusto, so different from other women he had dated. It had always annoyed him when they ordered something very expensive and then spent the evening picking at their food, sending most of it back uneaten. And dessert? Even suggesting dessert had been like asking them to drink drain cleaner. But Molly finished her meal and promptly announced that she was going to have a signature Full Rack dessert, which consisted of ice cream, rolled in semi-sweet chocolate chips and drizzled with fresh raspberry sauce. Laughing, Quinn ordered one of the same.

After dinner, they ignored the hovering waitress and sat for a long time with coffee and conversation. Not wanting the evening to end, Quinn reached across the table and placed his hand over Molly's. She leaned in and they both became very quiet.

At that moment, the door swung open and in walked Barbette, followed by a round-shouldered, balding fellow, whom Quinn assumed was the hapless Don. She stood for a moment, surveying the room and zeroed in on Quinn and Molly immediately. With a haughty look, she herded Don to a table near the bar, situating herself so that she could glare over at them without obstruction. Molly whispered, "Crap," under her breath, but Quinn just smiled and cheerfully waved to the couple. Don raised his arm to wave back, but Barbette knocked his hand aside and gave him the look.

But, since the romantic moment had passed and the ambiance had changed for the worse, Quinn and Molly got up to leave. As they walked past Barbette's table the woman hissed, just so they could hear her, "Moldy, Moldy, Moldy. When are you going to learn that you aren't welcome here?" Then she sat back, with a smug look on her face, and crossed her arms.

Molly took a step past the woman, then another. All at once, she stopped, spun around, and marched back to Barbette's table. Barbette looked surprised. "That's it... I've had it!" she said loudly but evenly, "I've put up with your crap for years. Years! But I'm done. The only thing I owe you is a good butt kicking. You open your mean mouth to me or about me one more time and I'll see that you get exactly what you deserve!"

Quinn was hugely impressed, but Miss Molly wasn't finished yet.

She turned to Don and said, "And you. You are such a loser... You could have had this (pointing to herself), and look what you ended up with!"

She whirled around and marched out the door. The room was absolutely silent. Quinn stood there for a moment, enjoying the stricken look on Barbette's face. He gave an apologetic shrug to Barbette's husband, and Don nodded ever so slightly. He waved to the rest of the room and headed for the door. As he left, he heard the room erupt into applause.

As he ran to catch up with Molly, he shook his head. What a puzzle this woman was! But he was, in fact, very good with puzzles.

Chapter Nineteen

Lucinda dozed and then woke with a jerk, remembering what she had done. After all these years she had contacted Eric Lentz. She still couldn't believe she had actually gone through with it. Over the years, she had picked up the phone again and again, but had never found the courage to follow through. How could she, after all her time with Cal? She shuddered to think how Eric must feel about her. But even during her miserable marriage, she had never stopped thinking about Eric and now, she thought, what did she have to lose?

He had not been home, and for that she was both relieved and disappointed, but his answering machine picked up and she managed to leave a somewhat tongue-tied message. She replayed it in her mind. *Eric, this is Lucinda... you know, Lucy. It's been so many years and my timing is, as always, terrible, but I was hoping to hear from you. Maybe we could be friends again. If not, I understand and it's okay. Like I said, my timing is terrible but it would mean something to me if... if... Well, anyway, I hope you're happy and I hope you can find it in your heart to maybe get in touch.* After giving him her telephone number she had paused for a moment, not knowing what else to say, and then quietly whispered, "Goodbye, Eric."

Okay, I've made the first move and now it's in his court." She felt better for actually having done something, but still experienced the same sense of embarrassment that had kept her silent that long-ago night in his pickup truck. With a sigh, she told herself to expect nothing so that she wouldn't be disappointed.

Disappointing would be a good word to describe her years with Cal. He had been handsome and powerful and very charming, at least in the beginning. Lucy had moped around for a long time after Eric left, and she had no heart for dating. When Cal made a habit of coming around her Daddy's store to see her, she felt flattered. He made her feel beautiful and desirable and he treated her like a queen. She wasn't interested in his money; although he made it known that he had plenty. Looking back, Lucinda realized that after three years of pining for Eric, Cal had made her feel alive again and she liked the feeling. As grateful as she was to Cal for "waking her up," she should have left it at that and looked elsewhere for affection. But when he wanted something, Cal was a force to be reckoned with and she allowed herself to be swept into a hurried marriage without love.

"Without love," she sighed to herself. She had always known that she didn't love Cal. She thought in the beginning that maybe she would grow to love him, but realized soon after the wedding that was not a possibility. And she also soon realized that he didn't love her. She was not sure he was capable of loving anyone, although she sensed he had been close to it with Cathy. If anything, Lucinda felt like more of a possession to Cal than anything else, but she managed to maintain her own identity and did not allow herself the luxury of regret.

Cal died suddenly one summer morning while on a horse pack trip with some East Coast financiers. He was impatient with his horse and had insisted upon "showing that no-good animal who was boss" with the help of a riding crop. The horse took off at full gallop, and then stopped suddenly at the edge of a rocky canyon. According to witnesses, Cal flew off the horse and over the edge, looking irritated to the end.

The funeral had been all business. Except for Lucinda, Preston and Helene, those in attendance were bankers, accountants, and Cal's numerous financial partners, none of whom looked very sad. His parents chose not to show, but sent an inappropriate and gaudy bouquet. Lucinda inherited the whole of his estate, and suddenly found herself to be very wealthy. Cal left nothing to Preston, his only living child, managing to humiliate the young man from even beyond the grave. Although Lucinda had later set things right for Preston, she understood that he was deeply hurt.

That had been over twenty years ago… twenty quiet and peaceful years. She couldn't honestly say those years were happy, but she had been content and that was good enough. Helene had been there for her and she maintained her relationship with Preston. She worked in her garden, she read her books, and she quietly and anonymously supported good causes, especially those involving children. She continued to travel and still secretly sang the blues, but mostly she kept to herself. It was safer that way, but it was so very lonely.

Well, nothing ventured, nothing gained. Feeling somewhat deflated, she reached over to the bedside stand for her book, but heard a sound from the doorway. Thinking it was the nurse, Cheryl, Lucinda turned with a smile.

"Eric," she said in surprise, her hand straying up to check her hair. She felt speechless and very vulnerable. "I guess you got my message."

He stood in the doorway in silence and Lucinda could hear the bedside clock ticking away the seconds. Suddenly, she was afraid that he would just turn away and leave her again. She didn't think she could bear that. "Eric, please…" she began, holding her hand out to him. "I'm so.."

Eric crossed the room and took her hand, then leaned over and gently kissed it. "Lucy, it was me. It was my fault. You were so beautiful and so perfect. You were everything I wanted, but I didn't think I was good enough. I should've told you that night in the truck but I was afraid. I was such a damned coward. And then I ran, thinking I would make something of myself and come back for you. But I was gone too long. Too long, Lucy… and I lost you." His voice was ragged with emotion. "It was my fault, and I'm so sorry."

Lucy felt a tear roll down her cheek. "Eric, oh Eric… I think about you every single day. I should have said something, but I didn't know you felt the same way. I should have called you sooner, I should have. ."

He put a finger on her lips, and said, "Lucy, we've wasted too much time already. Let's not waste any more on 'what ifs.' Let's start again right now, Lucy and Eric."

She smiled through her tears, "just for the record you never lost me."

"And you've always been my Little Runaway," he added, kissing her hand once more.

Chapter Twenty

Molly's black BMW flew along the highway between Hickok and the small town she had called her home for so many years. With her favorite music as a background, she took the back roads so she could catch the last of the beautiful fall colors before the Rocky Mountain winter arrived with a vengeance. Many things had changed during her brief time in Hickok, but the biggest change had been her own attitude. She felt so powerful and alive and happy… feelings she hadn't experienced in a very long time. Being around Quinn made her feel great, and the way she had dealt with Barbette the night before was uncharacteristic, unexpected, and, well… wonderful. She smiled, reliving the moment. *People shouldn't have to wait so long for a mid-life crisis.* She hummed happily.

After the breakup of her marriage, Molly had chosen the town of Monroe mainly because of its location… it was close enough to Hickok that her boys could see their grandparents, yet far enough away so that Molly could live her own life without the specter of her past. Monroe had become more of a bedroom community than a self-sufficient town in recent years, given its proximity to one of the larger cities in the region. Unfortunately, that proximity also meant that local stores could not compete with the bigger superstores down the road. The downtown businesses slowly died away, leaving a single grocery store, two auto part shops, a few churches, a handful of bars, and a restaurant or two. Gas was bought at the truck stop alongside the interstate and one rather shabby hotel adequately handled Monroe's infrequent visitors.

The town had two stop signs, no stoplights, and no soul. Although Molly had lived in Monroe for many years, she still felt like an outsider. When she worked for the construction company, she had her office friends and something of a social life. But when she got laid off they made excuses to stay away. She understood that they felt awkward around her and, to be honest, she felt the same way around them. They no longer had anything in common, and she suspected that deep down they might be afraid that unemployment was "catching." They were all so afraid of losing their jobs. Over the years, though, Molly had learned to "bloom where she was planted," and made the most of her situation in Monroe. She actively supported her kids, she worked for the community, and she maintained some really great business relationships. But even though she still had an occasional lunch with one or two of her old work friends, her social life was virtually non-existent.

As she eased into the driveway and parked, she sat for a moment and gave her home an appraising look. Charming older building, very well maintained, nice corner lot, mature trees, lots of flowers, wraparound covered deck... it all came together into a very nice package. When she first arrived, Molly had scraped enough money together to buy this "fixer upper" in the old part of town, and had never stopped working to improve it. Her "sweat equity," had paid off because now it was considered a real showplace. Molly realized with surprise that she could probably make a nice profit if she sold it in today's market. She knew that the boys considered it their family home, but she also understood that they would not settle back in Monroe after college. There was nothing here for them. And the house was way too big for her, too big and too empty...

Sell the house? Molly blinked in surprise at the direction her thoughts were heading. But once thought, the idea couldn't be "un-thought" and Molly realized that this might just be the next step in her new life. Shaking her head, she gathered up her things and went into the house.

After opening a couple of windows and doing some "compulsive dusting," Molly prepared some comfort food (grilled cheese sandwich and tomato soup), then settled herself in her sitting room to go through accumulated mail and catch up on some paperwork. Bills, credit card offers, catalogs featuring items they insisted she must have, a cheerful postcard from her dentist who wanted her to schedule an appointment, some organization she had never heard of asking for money, and more bills. Molly sighed and put the mail aside.

On top of the stack of paperwork she brought back from Hickok, was a manila envelope. Eric Lentz must have delivered it to her hotel when she was at dinner with Quinn because the suspicious night clerk handed it to her as she floated past him towards the stairs. The envelope contained copied crime scene photos of the Cathy Locke murder. In an attached note, he warned her that they were hard to look at and Molly thought that was a gross understatement.

There were copies of a few faded color Polaroids, but most of the photos were black and white. Molly couldn't help but think that this made it feel darker and more sinister. She glanced quickly over the pictures, taken from every angle, of Cathy lying on the kitchen floor. Her heart went out to Lucinda. Even though Molly was a stranger, she was also a mother and it caused her heart to ache. Lucinda had found her daughter like that. How could she ever get those images out of her head? How could she function at all? She gathered those pictures together and placed them face down on the table.

Molly made herself a cup of tea and then focused her attention on other photos of the house in general. She didn't really know what she was supposed to be looking for… never having been in the house, she had no point of reference. But she looked anyway. One photo showed Lucinda in the background, standing in a doorway and holding onto the doorframe so tightly that her knuckles were white. Another showed Calvin, his face a study of rage, rather than grief. She wondered about that but remembered what Eric Lentz had said about Calvin's behavior that night.

Finally, getting sleepy, Molly put the images back into the manila envelope, but set one photo aside. For some reason she kept going back to a picture of the kitchen counter near the back door. Something didn't look right. Something didn't seem to fit with the rest of the house. After a moment she realized that what bothered her was a small bouquet of flowers in a water glass. The flowers were somewhat worse for wear and looked like the impromptu bouquets Molly's boys used to bring her, sometimes when they were afraid they were in trouble and occasionally for no reason at all. She had treasured those childish expressions of love, but they stopped when the boys turned six or seven. Cathy was thirteen at the time, and Preston had been in high school. It just didn't feel right. *Well, that's curious. Very curious… maybe a neighbor kid… probably nothing, but I'll ask Lucinda about it.* Stifling a yawn, Molly put the picture away and wandered up to her big empty bed.

Well, well, well... the frightened rabbit ran away. Too bad she couldn't stay a bit longer... we could have had such fun together! But she managed to stir things up. Now there were too many others involved and great care must be taken to avoid discovery. But that's no problem, not really. People are, for the most part, sheep. Sometimes the killer longed for a worthy opponent. Not too worthy, mind you... just enough to add spice to the game. The killer liked to win.

One more major loose end to tie up... the old woman had to be silenced, and soon. Who knows what she figured out? The girl's involvement made things more difficult... difficult but not impossible. The killer welcomed the challenge.

A quick glance in the mirror -- *perfect* -- and out the door to once again play the part of wolf in sheep's clothing. The killer had the ability to blend perfectly, but underneath the innocent exterior was a genius that could get away with murder... already had, as a matter of fact, and planned to do so again. *Yes, indeed... and very soon.*

Chapter Twenty One

Quinn was a man with a plan. Last night, after he had dropped the ever surprising Miss Molly at her hotel, he had gone into action. Phone calls were made, favors were called in, and deals were struck. He was very good at making things happen and this particular "thing" was a vested interest for him. First, he contacted a close friend and business associate, who just happened to own one of North America's largest, and most discrete, private investigation firms. After Quinn explained what he wanted, his friend said, "No offense, old buddy, but this is out of character... even for you."

Quinn sheepishly admitted that it was about a woman, and his friend laughed. "Well, in that case I'll get right on it. Hope she's worth the outrageous fee I plan to charge you!"

"That and more," he whispered to himself as he disconnected. "Aye, that and more."

Next, he contacted a security firm he had used many times over the years. From experience, he knew their people were unobtrusive, thorough, and very well-trained. Twice these operatives had saved him from being abducted, and possibly even killed... once in Mexico City and another time in Malaysia. He asked for two security operatives to be sent out right away, but made a special request that they work covertly and be able to fit into the rural western scene. "Don't send me a couple of professional linebackers, and no suits," he said. "They'd stick out like a sore thumb. More like a couple of scruffy cowboys… or a rancher and a waitress… or a couple of lunch ladies…" Quinn realized he sounded like a moron, but if they thought so, they never let on and promised to have someone "on the ground" by Monday.

And finally, he placed a call to his secretary, the ever-intrepid Valerie. She let him know, in her proper British way, that she was still "reeling" from the additional work his absence had caused her and suggested firmly that he return to "civilization" in the near future. Forcing himself to remain calm, he explained that he would be staying in Hickok indefinitely, but had access to a computer and any telecommunications equipment he might need, in case of emergency. "In case of emergency," he repeated. Quinn could clearly visualize her tight-lipped expression of disapproval… it radiated from the phone. Realizing that Valerie was momentarily at a loss for words, he quickly said his goodbyes and hung up.

"Whew," he said, as he sauntered into Strange Brew. That last encounter deserved a nice cup of coffee and some moral support.

"Back of the line, Big Fella," said Lissy. "You're cute but you're not THAT cute," and she waved him behind a group of giggling high school kids.

"So much for moral support," he thought, but he sat at his usual table and waited patiently. Finally, as the door closed and the echoes of, "like totally, dude, uh, yeah, man, like totally" had faded, Lissy set a double mocha cappuccino on front of him.

"In honor of our AWOL friend," said Lissy, as she raised her cup in salute. "So," she added, cutting to the chase, "How we gonna solve this thing? I'm, so excited!"

Quinn laughed. No beating around the bush with Lissy. He told her he had made some calls and that he expected new information in the next couple of days. He chose not to mention his awkward call to Valerie. Lissy nodded approvingly and vowed to be "all ears," even more so than usual. They did a quick "high five" and Lissy trotted back to her station to deal with a new spate of customers.

His cell rang and caller ID indicated it was his private eye friend. He took a quick sip of coffee and answered. Yes, Quinn was a man with a plan.

Lucinda woke to the sound of her favorite nurse bustling around the room.

"Look at you," chirped Cheryl. "Just like the cat that got into the cream. I'd swear in a court of law you were purring! I heard about your gentleman visitor last night... managed to sweet-talk his way in to see you after hours. Wish I'd been here to check him out...the night nurse thought he was quite the stud."

Lucinda's face flushed with a rush of color. "Well, yes... I guess he could be called a, well a... stud. Actually it was Eric Lentz. He's an old friend of mine."

"Ironman Eric? You go, girl!" Cheryl whistled in appreciation. "He used to run that gym around the corner from the Calamity Jane... I think he was a cop before that. All of us high school girls used to walk by there after school trying to catch a glimpse of him lifting weights. He was an older guy, sure, but... wow! Even our mothers used to drive by real slow..." Cheryl caught the look on Lucinda's face.

"Oh... so sorry, didn't mean to embarrass you... got caught up in the past. We all wondered why he never married. I'm guessing you're the reason."

"Well, dear, I don't know why he never married. Maybe it was about me, but I would never wish that kind of loneliness on anyone... especially Eric. Anyway, he wants to spend some time together and we'll just see what happens." Lucinda smiled. She really did feel like the cat in the cream.

"Oh, you minx," laughed Cheryl. "I think there's more to it than that, but your secret's safe with me."

As she set out Lucinda's medications and poured her a glass of water, Cheryl said, "Since its pretty quiet around here right now, I'm thinking spa day. After breakfast I'll take you down to the whirlpool tub, and then later we can try something fancy with that great hair of yours. I get a couple of days off and they might just send you home if you keep getting better, so this might be our last chance for some girl time."

As Lucinda raised the last of her medications to her mouth, Cheryl once again stopped her hand. She took the pills, shaking her head. "Definitely not right," murmured the nurse. "I thought it was a one-off deal before so I didn't say anything, but these pills don't look like anything I'm familiar with. Wrong color, no stamp."

"Okay, let's just skip these for now, and I'll figure out what's going on. Our secret, okay?" Cheryl held out Lucinda's robe and slippers. "And now, without further ado, spa time."

Later, when Lucinda relaxed in her freshly made bed, she realized she felt happier now than she had in many years. While the hospital whirlpool room didn't exactly have the ambiance of an elite spa, the warm jetted water and the good-natured ministrations of Cheryl had lulled her into a wonderful state of relaxation. Her hair, which she wore fashionably short after the big "50," was beginning to regain some of its natural shine. Still dark brown, almost black, she had a sprinkling of gray, but a long way from salt and pepper. Her healthy skin tone was returning and her dark eyes were clear.

Not bad for an old woman. Not bad at all. She laughed softly to herself as she drifted off into thoughts of Ironman Eric.

Chapter Twenty Two

Molly realized with surprise that she was anxious to return to Hickok. After all these years it was such a strange sensation. She had gotten up at the crack of dawn and was on her way back to take her mother to her first respiratory therapy session, intending to stay until her mother was comfortable with her new schedule. Also, to be honest, Molly had felt something change between her and her mother, and she was curious to see where that went.

When she crossed the state line she felt a tingle of electricity and her heart rate picked up. Quinn, she thought. She had only known the man for a few days but she would be lying if she said she wasn't smitten. *Damn, damn, damn. Why do I have such rotten luck with men?*

Molly's ex-husband was an okay guy, but it was never a good match. He was smart and funny and very conservative. He knew about her past and didn't seem to care. He had been happy just to leave things low-key and uncomplicated, but Molly pushed it. Looking back, she suspected that he might never have married… he had his life just the way he liked it as a bachelor. And, to be honest, marriage hadn't changed anything for him; he still went off and did his guy things and made no effort to change priorities. Almost right away, Molly felt like a roommate rather than a wife and lover. It was very lonely.

Ironically, she thought she might have regained her mother's approval by marrying Dave, but even that hadn't worked out. Her mother approved of Dave, sure, but their marriage didn't seem to improve Molly's stock with her mother at all.

But Molly wasn't a quitter. Even though she was unable to utilize her educational skills in Hickok, she found a job that helped pay the bills, and worked full time. She took on the role of wife, cook, and housekeeper. And later, when the babies came along, she added full-time mother to her existing roles. Motherhood was her favorite job and she took it very seriously. Dave, on the other hand, hardly seemed to change at all. He still did everything he used to do before he was married, and more. As a couple, they had taken only one vacation together during their entire married life. Dave, however, continued to attend "guy" outings several times each year. But even though she wanted to, Molly couldn't blame Dave… not really. He was a "what you see is what you get" kind of guy. She had refused to believe that, though, and was sure that at some point he would change and become the type of man she needed in her life. It never happened. She knew that he loved the kids, and she supposed he even loved her in his own way, but for Molly it was a lose/lose situation. She probably could have spent the rest of her life in that marriage, many women had done just that, but she knew without a doubt that she would have lost herself and that was too high a price to pay.

When they divorced, Dave was hurt and bewildered, but eventually got over it. While they weren't exactly friends, they remained on good speaking terms. Molly's mother, however, was livid. She took their wedding photo off the wall and replaced it with a picture of Dave by himself. The photo was still there, in its place of honor, she had noticed during her last visit. Molly had been the recipient of her mother's famous "silent treatment" for years after that. She thought wryly about the fact that her mother only began returning her phone calls and letters after her other siblings had all moved out of the area.

Shaking those thoughts out of her head, she realized she was descending into Hickok. What was she going to do about Quinn? She felt like a teenager in the middle of a summer romance, but a teenager believed that love conquered all and that somehow they could make it last forever. Molly knew different. They would have this great time and then he would go away. That was it… bye, bye. Maybe he would call a few times and they would exchange emails, but eventually it would dry up and Molly would be left with a broken heart. *I'm too old and too smart for that kind of nonsense. I've done just fine on my own, thank you very much, and I don't need any more drama in my life. Yes, indeed.* She stiffened her spine and held her head up high as she parked in front of Strange Brew for a quick coffee fix and some female support before picking up her mother. *I am woman, hear me roar.*

But when she walked through the door, the sound she emitted was more like a squeak than a roar, and all of her sensible intentions disappeared into thin air. There was Quinn, at their usual table, with one of Lissy's "Lady Godiva" mochas and a big box of dark truffles waiting for her. Completely unable to control herself, she ran to him as he rose from the chair and threw herself into his arms, giving him a kiss he would remember for the rest of his life. He returned the favor and the candy was all but forgotten.

It had been forty-five minutes since the moment that Quinn's life changed forever. Forty-five minutes and there was no going back. After the life-changing kiss, they both tried to pretend that nothing had happened. Molly casually drank her mocha and talked about her trip home. Quinn politely listened and hoped that soon he would regain the ability to speak in coherent sentences. As she left to go pick up her mother, he managed to say, "Call me... more talk later." She looked at him oddly, then smiled and went out the door.

After a while Lissy came over and squirted him in the face with vinegar water from a spray bottle she kept behind the counter. "Wake up, lover boy," she said. "You got dragons to slay and damsels to save."

"Thanks, Lissy, I needed that," he said as he wiped his face with a napkin.

"So, were your guys here?" she asked, glancing around the room. Quinn had told her that two security people arrived early that morning. He'd also sheepishly come clean with her about who he was. Her response was, "Duh... I have the Internet and know how to use it, Mr. Oil and Gas. Tell me something I don't know." She did warn him, however, that he needed to spill the beans, and soon, with Molly. "Women don't like that kind of surprise, Mr. Big," she added, squirting him one more time, just because.

"Okay, I get the message," he laughed, wiping his face again. "They were here and, in my opinion, blended pretty well. One left before Molly and the other shortly after. I believe you would call it the "tag team" method here in the Wild West."

"Wild West, my ass," said Lissy. "Okay, let me guess. The first guy... tall, dark and ex-military... hair too short, shirt still had the off-the-shelf creases, and jeans so new they hadn't been washed yet. Didn't smile at all. Wearing Doc Martins… don't get me wrong… I love a man in Doc Martins, but they just didn't go with the outfit. Second guy was a lot harder to make. I'm thinking it was the short guy with the goofy smile, freckles, and huge biceps. Smiled too much. Great cover with tee shirt, jeans and runners. Fit right in until I heard the Boston accent. Am I right? I'm right, aren't I?"

Quinn was stunned. Shaking his head, he said, "Lissy, my dear, you never fail to amaze me. I just hope whoever tried to hurt Molly doesn't figure it out."

"Not a chance… Remember, I'm the professional Java Queen… You need information; I'm the go-to girl." Lissy headed back to her perch behind the counter.

At some point, Quinn wanted to ask the Java Queen about Molly's curious past, but now definitely wasn't the time. Feeling fully functional, he went over his to-do list. The lovely Miss Molly had briefly mentioned getting some crime scene photos from Eric Lentz, and agreed to bring them to Strange Brew when she stopped by around 6:00. Quinn intended to borrow them, scan them, and send them to his friend. Contacting Lentz was his next order of business, but Quinn found himself strangely intimidated by the man. The first thing he needed to do was tell the man everything about himself and what he was doing in Hickok. Lentz was not the type of man to tolerate deception on any level. Then he would explain what had happened with Molly. With her safety an issue, he was pretty sure that Lentz would rise to the occasion, as both advocate and information resource.

126

He had received some of the surface information regarding the old murder over the weekend, but his friend was beginning to dig deeper and was now sending information that was not exactly available to the public. He knew he was entering a gray area, where "don't ask, don't tell" was the rule of thumb. He intended to share this with Lentz, hoping it might lead to something new.

"No time like the present," he said to himself, and pulled out his phone.

Lentz picked up on the second ring. "Thought I might be hearing from you, Mr. Drummond," he said briskly. "I still have friends in the department and heard what happened to your pretty friend. So, what's your game here in Hickok?"

"Mr. Lentz," said Quinn, maintaining the formal tone. They were still circling the wagons. "I came out to look at some drilling prospects. I could have sent someone else. Hell, I could have sent a whole team, but I needed to get away. But then I met Molly and things changed for me." He paused for a moment to collect his thoughts. "When we were out there, I hadn't yet told Molly about who I was... still haven't for that matter, but hope to remedy that soon. Maybe you won't understand it, but I just wanted her to get to know me for myself, without the complication of wealth and power. I would never hurt her. I promise my intentions are good... the best... and for now I just want to keep her safe."

There was silence at the other end of the line. Finally Lentz spoke. "Okay, I can understand that. You care about someone, sometimes you get desperate. I understand better than you know. We both want to get to the bottom of things, and I think we can work together… be crazy not to. But if you ever withhold information or lie to me, I'll teach you the literal meaning of kick ass."

"Okay," said Quinn. Here was a man he could truly respect… and trust… a commodity that was scarce these days. "I'll agree to bring you the information I have and maybe we can dig deeper into what you know." They exchanged contact information and set up a meeting time.

"One more thing," said Lentz at the end of the conversation. "You hurt that nice girl, me and Jasper will hunt you down… and you'll be his new chew toy."

"Okay, then… chew toy." Quinn shuddered at the vivid image in his mind. "Good intentions, I promise."

As he left Strange Brew, Lissy, who was busy waiting on customers, gave him a conspiratorial wink. Here he was, shirking his business responsibilities, investigating a decades-old murder, trying to protect a woman who had run him down with a shopping cart, and being threatened by a tough guy with a crew cut and a big dog. The crazy part was that he hadn't had this much fun in years.

Chapter Twenty Three

Molly walked into her mother's house fully intending to share her new box of truffles. Really, she did. But there on the table next to her mother's chair was an enormous red cardboard heart-shaped box that was either six months too late for Valentine's Day or six months too early. Her mother had rearranged the objects on the table, giving it pride of place. *That Dick, what a romantic.* She had to suppress a smile as she dropped her own box of goodies back into her tote bag.

"Look what I got," her mother beamed. "Here, you can have one," she added, opening the lid and holding it out for her daughter to choose. Actually, it was the kind of cheap candy that made Molly's upper lip curl, but she was grateful for the offer. This was a long-standing ritual for them. They both knew that Shirley had poked a hole in the bottom of each candy with her little finger so she wouldn't have to guess what was inside. As Molly inspected each piece, she paid close attention to subtle changes in her mother's expression, warning her away from certain pieces that Shirley had earmarked for herself. Finally, after much deliberation, Molly chose what turned out to be nougat, not her favorite but not her mother's favorite either… a safe bet.

"Gee, Mom, I hope Dick doesn't think he can seduce you with candy and sweet talk," Molly said around a mouthful of sticky candy.

Shirley blushed a bit and said, "Honey, we're just friends." Flustered, she jumped up and gathered her coat and oversized brown purse. "He asked if he could take me to a movie, though. What do you think?"

Molly laughed, "Talk about role reversal. Let's see, you would have told me: Home before midnight and no hanky-panky in the theater. You also made me kiss you goodnight when I got home so that you could check for beer-breath. But honestly, Mom, I'm pretty sure you're a responsible adult… except for that brown purse thing… and I just want you to have a good time."

"What's wrong with my purse?" demanded Shirley, but she was smiling as they walked out to Molly's car.

The respiratory therapy session proved to be fairly painless, for Molly anyway, and she managed to get through some paperwork and study plans for a new database implementation being considered by one of her clients. Her mother, though, seemed tired afterwards and Molly took her home and fixed her a light lunch. She helped her mother adjust her oxygen, then made them both a cup of tea and stayed long enough to keep her mother company for one of her soaps. *Wow… These people make Jerry Springer look like Mister Rogers!* Soon, her mother was asleep in her chair and snoring gently. Molly covered her with an old afghan and slipped quietly out the door.

It was the perfect time to visit Lucinda. Molly grabbed a couple of bags from the back seat, after parking in front of the hospital. She had picked up a small CD player and a handful of CDs featuring various blues artists, both old and new. If Lucinda didn't want them, she would keep them for herself, but she had a hunch her gifts would be well-received… maybe because Lucinda hummed to herself, seemingly unaware of it, and maybe because she reminded Molly of an older Joan Baez. Molly's hunches were usually pretty good.

As she was waiting for the elevator, Cheryl ran by. "Just coming on shift, and I'm late" she huffed. "See ya later… "

"I'm feeling another chick flick coming on," Molly called after her, but she was probably out of range. As the elevator opened, she stepped in and almost bumped into Preston Locke.

"Oh, so sorry," she said, feeling awkward.

"Not at all… Miss Noble, isn't it? I've just been to see my mother and she mentioned that you might stop by. I really appreciate you making the effort to see her. I'm sure you have better things to do with your time."

Molly felt a flash of irritation. He made it sound like visiting Lucinda was an unpleasant duty. "Actually, I look forward to spending time with her. She's an amazing woman."

"She is that…" he said, almost to himself. "She is that." He made a point to look her up and down, then smiled, stepped around her, and casually strolled to the door. "I'll look forward to seeing you again," he added, just before leaving.

In an effort to calm herself, Molly hit the elevator button, and took a few deep cleansing breaths. She felt better, albeit somewhat dizzy, when she arrived on Lucinda's floor, but that didn't stop her from muttering "jerk" under her breath.

"Wow, you look great," she said to Lucinda, and it was true. Her skin was no longer pallid, but seemed to glow with healthy good color. Her eyes were bright and her hair was glossy. Molly ran over and gave her a big hug. "I've only been gone a couple of days, but it seems like forever. I really missed you!"

Lucinda smiled. "You look pretty good yourself... you look happy. Cheryl hinted around about someone tall, dark, and handsome in your life."

Molly blushed, "Well, yeah, and all I can say is 'It's about time!'"

"I know what you mean," said Lucinda softly. "I know what you mean." Suddenly, she frowned, and the color seemed to drain from her face.

"Lucinda, are you okay? What's wrong?" The woman drew her legs up into a fetal position and Molly could see she was in great pain.

Lucinda moaned, "No, not now... it's just not fair... not fair."

Molly leaned over to hit the call button and then ran into the hall looking for someone to help. Cheryl came running and Molly hurried to meet her. "I don't know what happened. One minute she was fine, great even, and then suddenly she was doubled over in pain... I didn't know what to do." She knew she was babbling, but she felt so helpless.

Cheryl went into nurse mode, calmly examining Lucinda, who was now gasping and shaking all over. "I don't like the look of this. She could go into seizure any minute..."

Suddenly, Cheryl noticed a crumpled paper pill cup in the trash beside Lucinda's bed. She bent to pick it up, looked at it a moment and then hit the emergency intercom. "Code Blue to room 407. Stat!"

Cheryl gently guided Molly out of the room, just as the on-call doctor arrived. "We need to work now," she said, as the room filled with emergency equipment and personnel. "Whatever happens, I'll let you know. I promise." Sick with worry, not knowing what else to do, she sat in a waiting room down the hall. There were two other people in the room,

132

and Molly thought she must look as terrified as they did. No one made eye contact. There was a small television bolted to the wall, and 'Walker, Texas Ranger' was making the world a better place. Molly quietly wept.

For Lucinda, the world began and ended with the pain in her gut, the pain behind her eyes. Everything else was a blur. There was noise around her and lots of activity. She tried to hold on to a thought, any thought, or a sound, maybe... but they disappeared behind the red wall of agony that consumed her. Then, for one bright lucid moment, she realized that the pain had vanished. She didn't know what that meant, but there was peace now, and silence. As her consciousness fled, she managed to find one thought and to hold on to it. She smiled just a bit, but everyone around her was too busy to notice.

Chapter Twenty Four

Quinn had been sitting in the squat waiting room for three hours now. The bad news was that they hadn't yet heard anything about Lucinda's condition. He reckoned that was also the good news. Molly had called him, barely holding it together, and he went to her right away. He quietly held her, and it was a while before she was able to tell him what had happened.

When he realized how serious it was, he called Eric Lentz. The man arrived shortly later and had been pacing ever since. Another woman, Helene Blanchard, had also arrived. She introduced herself as a close friend of the family and seemed very distraught, although she immediately went to Molly and offered grandmotherly comfort. Quinn noted that she kept glancing at the doorway, presumably waiting for Preston, who according to Miss Blanchard, had yet to be located. It soon became obvious to him that Miss Blanchard was an experienced care-taker, and he left Molly with the woman so he could talk to Lentz.

Lentz seemed so keyed up that Quinn was afraid to speak right away. Instead, he matched the man's pace and walked with him for a while. Finally, Lentz pointed to the exit sign and said, "I need some air, let's head outside."

Once out in the cool air, Lentz seemed to lose momentum and sat down on the front step. "I'm too close to this. I can't seem to get far enough away to focus," he said miserably.

"I know exactly what you mean," agreed Quinn, taking a seat next to him. "I don't know how else to say this, so I'll jump right in. Do you think this is a coincidence? Molly told me that Lucinda found something or remembered something about her daughter's murder. She thinks Lucinda didn't come right out and say what she's discovered because she doesn't know who to trust. She wants Molly to figure out what it means, but so far it's all riddles and rhymes. I think that's why somebody tried to run her down. I don't know about Lucinda's medical history but Molly told me they can't figure out what's wrong with her. Any ideas?"

"What are you saying? This might be about Cathy's murder? And you think somebody poisoned Lucinda?" asked Lentz, shaking his head. "If that's the case, why didn't they just kill her and be done with it? What kind of sick bastard would take a year to hurt her? What kind of..." He groaned, and put his head in his hands. "The same kind of sick bastard that would slit a young girl's throat."

"Listen, I don't want to be out here too long, but I think Molly is the key. She knows more than she realizes and it's now, literally, a matter of life and death to get it figured out." Quinn stood up and offered his hand to Lentz. The man seemed to struggle for a moment to get his emotions under control. Then he grabbed Quinn's hand a pulled himself up.

"So, you wanna be good cop or bad cop?" he asked Quinn, with a wry grin. Not waiting for an answer, he added, "Just kidding… you'd make a lousy bad cop."

As they approached the waiting room, a nurse came around the corner and headed straight for Molly and Helene Blanchard. Both women looked terrified of the news they might receive. The nurse – her name was Cheryl, Quinn remembered from Molly – addressed Helene.

"Ms. Blanchard, Lucinda has you and her son Preston listed as emergency contacts. We've been unable to reach Mr. Locke, but the doctor asked me to give you an update on her condition. Would you like to go somewhere private where we can talk?" asked Cheryl, gently.

Helene put a protective arm around Molly and said, "No dear, we're all family here. Please tell us what you know." She was all business, but Quinn noticed that her chin was quivering slightly.

Cheryl drew a deep breath. "Okay, first, I need to tell you that Lucinda is alive, but she has slipped into a coma. She was already in a weakened condition and this last episode was extremely violent. For a while there, it was touch and go. Now all we can do is wait. She's a strong woman, but, honestly, it could go either way."

Eric Lentz stepped forward. "Do you have any idea what brought this on?" His face was grim and his voice was carefully measured.

Cheryl paused and looked at Helene. "Lucinda has given authorization for you to receive health information on her behalf. Shall I continue?" Helene nodded. "It wasn't until we pumped her stomach that her condition began to improve. If we hadn't done that, she probably wouldn't have made it. This past year we have been at a loss as to what was causing these episodes, but it never occurred to anyone that it may have been something she ingested... maybe some type of environmental toxin or... ah, something else. We're having her stomach contents analyzed and then maybe we'll have a better idea of what's going on."

"Thank you, dear," said Helene and she gave Cheryl a hug. "I don't know what this all means, but at least we still have our Lucinda."

Cheryl, in turn, hugged Molly, and whispered in her ear, "It's gonna be okay." To the group she said, "Ms. Blanchard, the doctor will want to talk to you later, but in the meantime I think you all need to take a break and get some rest."

At that moment, Preston Locke charged into the room. He headed straight for Molly, his face livid with rage. "This is your fault. Things changed after she met you!" Quinn moved to stand between Preston and Molly.

"Preston, you know that's not true. Now come with me, because we have to talk," Helene's voice was full of authority and Quinn could tell she brooked no argument.

But Preston wasn't finished yet. He leaned past Quinn to continue his harangue at Molly. "You need to go away and stay away!" His voice was getting higher and louder.

"And you need to take it down a notch, son." Preston whirled around to see Eric Lentz standing right behind him.

Quinn couldn't help but notice the surprise, and maybe fear, in Preston's eyes as he recognized the former police detective from so long ago. His anger seemed to drain away and he stepped back.

Helene took control of the situation and gently guided Preston out of the waiting room and down the hall.

Shaking her head, Cheryl gave Molly one more quick hug and suggested to Quinn that he take her out for some air and something to eat. She promised she would let them know if anything changed. As they headed for the door, Quinn gestured for Lentz to join them.

"Thanks, but I think I'll just stick around for a while," he answered. Leaving, Quinn had the realization that the man intended to stick around for the rest of Lucinda's life, however long or short that might be.

Chapter Twenty Five

Molly smiled across the table at Quinn, mainly to reassure him that she was okay. She had been a basket case, and was embarrassed by her behavior, but had pulled herself together. Over the years, she had allowed herself the indulgence of falling apart now and then. But, since there was never anyone around to comfort her or help pick up the pieces, she would eventually give herself a good talking to and get right back on the horse. She had to admit that it was wonderful to have someone there to hold her and whisper reassurances. She could get used to that.

After their hospital ordeal, Quinn had insisted on coming with her to check on her mother. Molly smiled, remembering the shocked look on her mother's face when Quinn followed her through the front door. She introduced him, adding that he was only slightly strange. Quinn looked puzzled, but she whispered "in joke." Her mother gave him a careful once- over, before offering him a candy. Molly, standing behind her mother, mouthed "No!" but he chose one and popped it into his mouth, gallantly ignoring the hole in the bottom.

Over a cup of tea, Shirley Noble openly quizzed Quinn about his marital status, drinking habits, and career prospects. Molly's face burned red, but Quinn handled it with tact and humor. As they climbed back into her car, Molly said, "Okay, now that you've met my mother, I suspect you'll book the very next flight out of the Land of Amazon Busybodies.

Sorry about that… just please believe that in my case the apple falls very far from the tree."

Quinn laughed, "No worries. Now I won't be so nervous about taking you to meet my mum. She has interrogation down to a science. With her, it's more of an art form. And drama queen… well, she actually won an award for it!"

"So, since she's in Scotland, there's probably not much chance of that. I guess I'm off the hook," said Molly smugly, but she didn't fail to catch Quinn's raised eyebrow and "we'll just see about that" expression.

Now they were sitting at a quiet table in the Full Rack, where Quinn had brought her for an early dinner. The crying was over, but Molly was still upset and couldn't stop thinking about Lucinda. She felt like family and the thought of losing her was terrifying. For a while, they toyed with their meals and made small talk. Finally, she could stand it no longer, and blurted out, "Okay, this might sound crazy, but I think what is happening to Lucinda is on purpose and I think it has something to do with Cathy's murder. All of these weird things are connected and we need to figure it out."

Quinn surprised her by agreeing completely. "Something your nurse friend said, or actually what she chose not to say, tells me that Lucinda may have been poisoned. Eric Lentz wants in on it… don't think we could stop him if we tried."

"Excellent," said Molly, deciding she would have the dessert after all. "First we need to formulate a game plan, and then we need to…"

"Stop, Molly," said Quinn seriously, reaching to take her hand. "First I need to tell you something."

Molly looked stricken. "Crap," she moaned. "You're married, right? Or gay? Maybe married and gay? I knew it was too good to be true!" Her eyes widened. "Oh no, you're leaving... it was only a matter of time..."

"Hush," his grip on her hand tightened. "It's nothing like that... I should have told you this before, but I was... well, I was afraid. The truth is I don't actually work for the oil and gas company... I own it. I own a few other companies as well and controlling interests in some others. I just wanted you to know the real me, not the guy that gets plastered all over the newspapers and internet. I'm sorry I wasn't honest with you. I didn't expect to care, but I like you, Molly... I like you a lot." He paused for a moment to collect his thoughts. "And, just for the record, I'm not married, not gay, and not leaving."

Molly was silent for a moment; she smiled at him sadly and gently pulled her hand away. "Just for the record, I like you too, Quinn. I like you a lot, even though I tried hard not to because I thought you would leave. I'll probably forgive you for not being honest with me, but right now I just need some time alone." She stood, kissed him lightly on the forehead, and then walked to the door, leaving her dessert untouched.

Whoopsy Daisies... The mirror was an antique, elegantly framed in hand-carved walnut. It had cost a small fortune, but now it lay in glittering pieces on the floor. The killer liked mirrors because they reflected back the perfect mask, the non-assuming guise that allowed a genius to walk amongst the sheep. Hours were spent each day perfecting the disguise in order to blend perfectly and it worked. The checkout girl at the supermarket would never know that behind that beatific smile, the killer had calmly imagined her death in a hundred highly imaginative ways. The self-important bureaucrat had no idea that the killer had made it a point to casually stroll past the schoolyard during recess each day, patiently befriending the man's young daughter. *What a lovely child, and so trusting.*

But things weren't going quite so well right now... oh, dear. A lovely crystal vase joined the mirror in shards on the floor. The killer didn't like surprises, no sir, not one bit. *Now the nurse's aide will have to disappear, maybe permanently. Easy enough, though... just add an extra special ingredient to her "medicine."* The killer couldn't help but smile at the thought of that, and began to feel calmer and more in control.

Oh well, the old woman probably wouldn't make it anyway. At least that's what the local gossips were saying. The real problem now is the woman and her troupe of do-gooders, but no reason to worry, not really. All the killer had to do was play the part, and wait for just the right moment. *They were an inconvenience, but nothing more and they would all pay the price.*

An expensive porcelain figurine joined the ruined pretties on the floor, just for good measure, and the killer stepped out into the evening. *Showtime.*

Chapter Twenty Six

If it had been physically possible, Quinn would be kicking himself. He looked around for a brick wall to run headlong into. He felt like such a jerk, such an idiot. After all Molly had been through, he just had to hit her with one more thing. He breathed deeply, in an effort to calm himself down. *You had to give her the truth some time... the sooner the better. And she didn't exactly tell you where to shove it, so that's a good sign.* But, in a way, he wished she had. Then, she would have been angry, but she would have probably gotten over it. Right now she seemed hurt and sad and vulnerable. Quinn feared that getting past those emotions would be far more difficult. He took another deep breath, and then blew it out slowly. Women, with their mysterious emotions, were a minefield to him and he was beginning to think that brick wall looked pretty inviting.

But worrying about the future was a luxury he couldn't afford. There was too much going on right now, and the clock was ticking. Either Molly would come around, or she wouldn't, and he knew better than to try to force the issue. What he needed to do was figure out what had happened in the past in order to understand what was happing in the present. With Lucinda incapacitated, Molly was the key, but in the meantime Quinn intended to arm himself with all the information he could get.

Seeing Lentz walk through the door of Strange Brew, Quinn stood and waved him to the back of the room. After he explained what had happened to Lucinda and that Lentz was now part of the team, Lissy grudgingly agreed to stay open later, even though tonight was her weekly date with Ryan Seacrest. Lissy raised her eyebrow when Lentz asked for "a cup of real coffee, not that gawd-awful crap they try to sell ya these days." She handed him a steaming cup and they eyed each other suspiciously until he pronounced it "worth drinking." With a smug smile, she flipped over the closed sign, locked the door, and followed him back to where Quinn was waiting.

Introductions were made, though Lentz made it clear that he was uncomfortable having a woman on the team… too dangerous, he said.

Lissy barked out a laugh, leaning over to look Lentz right in the eye. "Get over yourself, Crew Cut. In one of my prior lives, I was a mail carrier in East LA. That makes this Podunk town look like Mayberry. Right now I'm the best spy you have. I hear all, know all, and the only thing I'm afraid of is boredom. So, either I'm in or you two are out," she added, pointing to the door.

Lentz was speechless for a moment, but then his face broke into a wide grin. "Yes, Ma'am," he said, giving her a jaunty salute. "And I just might need a refill of that brown water you call coffee."

"Brown water, my ass," muttered Lissy, but she was smiling as she refilled his cup. "Okay, then, down to business, cause I got a hot date."

Twenty-five minutes later, Lissy was shooing them out the door. Each had a task list and they agreed that they needed to share everything, however insignificant. "The devil's in the details," Lentz insisted, as he headed back to the hospital on foot, having set up something of a temporary camp there. Out on the quiet street, Quinn looked longingly at the Calamity Jane Hotel, which was just across the street and on the corner of the next block. More than anything he wanted to go to Molly and prove that he was for real, even though it had taken him too long to admit it. But, she had asked for some time and he was going to give her just that. He noted with approval that one of the security people he had brought in was sitting on the bench in front of the hotel, nonchalantly reading the local newspaper by streetlight. He finally located the other one, sitting by the window of a rather seedy establishment, on a side street across from the bar entrance of the hotel. He looked sullen enough to keep the locals away, and he was nursing a beer. He knew they would work as a team, guaranteeing that one of them was always on the job.

Not wanting to go back to his cabin yet, he wandered down to the Full Rack and sat at the old mahogany bar. There were only a few things he missed about Scotland, but McEwan's Ale was one of them. He ordered the closest thing he could find to that, and sat sipping the bitter dark beer. He noticed the old cowboy was at his usual seat, a couple stools down and Quinn nodded respectfully to him. The old gent nodded back.

As the fellow downed the last of his brew, Quinn offered to buy him another round.

The elderly cowboy gave him a smile and touched the brim of his hat. "Thank you kindly, Mister, but I made a promise to the Missus a long time ago and I ain't about to break it now." Noting the curious look on Quinn's face, the man continued. "I used to like my beer way too much and I made some bad choices, but when it came to deciding between too much beer and not enough good lovin', the decision was easy. I went with the good woman and there ain't a day goes by that I don't thank my lucky stars. So I have my one beer, and then I go home to the greatest woman in the world."

Quinn gave the man a sad smile and said, "Then you are a fortunate man indeed. I find that I have had too much beer and not enough love in my life."

The cowboy leaned over and said, "I seen that gal you was with the other night… right pretty she was, and I seen the way you was lookin' at her. I'm thinkin' you musta put your foot in your mouth and are tryin' to figure how to get it out."

Quinn raised his eyebrows in surprise at the man's astute guess.

"I'm just an old cowpoke, but I been married for fifty-some years and I guess I know a thing or two about the ladies. So, if you want to patch things up, just tell her she's right. Don't matter if she is… don't matter if she's dead wrong. Just tell her she's right and act all sorry like. Hard thing for a man to do, but I'm tellin' ya it works every time." With that, he stood up and ambled towards the door. "Be seein' ya," he said as he left, giving the two- fingered cowboy wave.

Quinn smiled to himself as he considered the sage advice he had just received. "A regular Rocky Mountain Deepak Chopra," he laughed to himself. Feeling better, he finished his beer, and went out into the cool night air, mentally going over his to-do list.

Chapter Twenty Seven

Molly put on a happy face when she went up to check on her mother, but she knew it probably wasn't necessary. The woman rarely noticed her daughter's moods and, on those occasions when she did, she would say, "Whatever it is, I don't want to hear about it. Now snap out of it because you're not good company." Molly sighed. She had been through some pretty traumatic events in her life, and they had made her a better person, but she sometimes longed for a shoulder to cry on.

Quinn was now the woman's topic of choice, and she peppered Molly with question after question until she called time-out. "Enough already, Mom... I've only known him for a short time. So, I'll answer as many questions as I can, and then we're done! Okay... Yes, I like him; yes, he likes me; yes, he's very tall; yes, he's from Scotland; no, he's not a terrorist; no, he's not a member of a cult; yes, he has a good job; no, he's not married (or gay, she added, although that was not one of her mother's questions); yes, he'll be here for a while; no, I don't know how long; and, yes, I'm pretty sure he liked your hair. That's it... end of topic!"

After that, they talked about Dick, her mother coyly confessing that the man liked her hair so much that he couldn't keep his hands off it.

"Okay, way too much information. Gotta go," said Molly as she checked the oxygen settings and planted a quick kiss on her mother's forehead. "Oh, and I forgot to tell you," she had hesitated to bring it up, not sure of how her mother would respond. "Lucinda Locke took a turn for the worse and is in a coma. Everyone is pretty worried."

Her mother made a kind of clucking noise and then returned to the topic of Dick's fascination with her hair.

"Mom, she was your roommate and she really liked you." Molly was disappointed with her mother's lack of empathy. She probably should have just let it go, but she was irritated. "It seems like you don't care at all."

"Well, I don't know what your problem is," her mother bristled. "She always acted like she was too good for us, driving around in her fancy cars and wearing her expensive clothes. Maybe I don't care and you shouldn't either!"

Shaking her head sadly, Molly said, "Okay Mom, whatever. I'll see you tomorrow."

She headed back to her hotel room, and did some computer work, though her heart wasn't really in it. She called the hospital, but Cheryl was busy and the night nurse told her there had been no change in Lucinda's condition. Finally, longing for a friendly voice, she called her younger son. As luck would have it, he was not involved in a video game and they had a nice visit about this and that. He seemed to sense something wrong though, because he said, "You okay, Mom? Did something happen with Grandma?" Molly reassured him and told him she was just tired. After she hung up, she realized it was true and brewed herself a cup of chamomile tea to take to bed with her. But it was a long time before she managed to sleep, and she couldn't get Lucinda or Quinn out of her thoughts.

In her dream, Lucinda was driving around in a version of the old rodeo car. In real life, it was an old pink Cadillac convertible that had been customized with a set of longhorns attached to the hood. It drove around all day during tourist season, advertising the Hickok Rodeo and blaring old time country songs at full volume. In the dream it was bigger and pinker and louder. Molly was walking down Main Street, with the uneasy feeling that she was being watched or followed, or both. Lucinda, in the rodeo car, came up alongside of her and slowed down almost to a crawl. She was shouting into the bullhorn, "Hickok Rodeo tonight... come and experience Cowboy Daring-Do!" but as she passed Molly she leaned over and whispered, "Remember the words, little girl. You know what to do... just be careful!" Then Lucinda stiffened and drove off before Molly could respond.

Uneasily glancing behind her, she realized that she was being followed by a rodeo clown. This made her heart pound, because she didn't like clowns to begin with and this one seemed more sinister than most. In fact, it reminded her of the old clown wall hanging that had terrorized her as a child. The clown was getting closer, and Molly took off in one of those frustrating dream runs where you can never go fast enough. Beginning to feel real panic, she ran to Strange Brew and tried the door. It was either locked or stuck and she was terrified. She kept pulling at the latch and pounding on the door, knowing that this was her only chance. All of a sudden the door swung open and she literally fell through the doorway and into Quinn's arms. But, looking over her shoulder, she realized that her pursuer was standing on the other side of the glass, just inches from her. The clown pointed to her and smiled. It was the most terrible thing she had ever seen. Then it was gone. Quinn held her and stroked her hair as she sobbed. He told her everything would be okay, but she wasn't so sure. When she woke up she was holding a wet pillow, and there was a knot in the pit of her stomach.

"Well, look what the cat dragged in," said Lissy, but not unkindly. She handed Molly a Mexican Mocha and a cranberry muffin. "Honey, any word about Lucinda?"

"No," answered Molly miserably. "Cheryl says that a coma is a way for the body to concentrate on healing, but that it could go either way." She sat near the counter so they could chat while Lissy served the other customers that were beginning to trickle in. She lowered her voice, and added, "And then there's this thing with Quinn..."

Lissy rolled her eyes, "I wish you'd just hurry up and DO the thing with Quinn. The sexual tension around here is so thick you could cut it with a knife!"

"Lissy!" gasped, Molly, her face turning red. "Not THAT. It's just that I found out he wasn't honest with me. I don't know if I can have a relationship that starts off that way."

"Listen, honey, I tell my online pen pal that I'm a twenty-two year old fashion model who can yodel and twirl baton. He tells me he's an Olympic speed skater who happens to look a lot like Orlando Bloom. Truth is, he knows I'm a middle aged woman who sits on her butt all day and makes coffee. I know that he's an overweight computer programmer named Chester, who still lives with his mother." Lissy leaned closer to Molly to make her point. "The way I see it, no harm, no foul, as long as nobody gets hurt."

"But, but," stammered Molly. "He should have been upfront with me about everything."

"Poor baby, I see what you mean." Lissy pursed her lips in mock sympathy, "Here's this tall, dark, handsome... and rich... guy who just happens to be crazy about you. Did I mention rich? But he didn't tell you about the rich part right away because he wanted you to like the tall, dark and handsome part first. Wow, and how tough is that?" She shook her head. "Now your dream man fesses up to the fact that he is filthy, stinking rich. What a bummer!"

"If it's all too much for you, you could settle for a regular guy. In fact, you could make a play for him," Lissy said, pointing out the window. "I hear he's a real catch!"

Molly glanced up to see Curt Golden passing the shop with his odd bouncy stride. He smiled blandly and waved to the women. They waved back without much enthusiasm. "Eew," said Molly after he passed.

"My point exactly," said Lissy. "You might want to get down off your high horse and take what's offered. Oh, and about being completely honest, that street goes both ways, Miss Secret Past." She arched her brows and nodded knowingly.

Molly choked on her muffin. "Oh, well, about that..."

"Later," said Lissy. "Right now we have a mystery to solve and the other team members should be here any minute."

Feeling chastened, Molly quietly finished her breakfast and thought about her feelings for Quinn.

Chapter Twenty Eight

As Quinn walked through the door of Strange Brew, he saw everyone already gathered around a large table in the corner. He felt like the stereotypical late guy at the business meeting. Molly was there, looking tired, but beautiful nonetheless. Lissy was standing in the corner, keeping one eye on the door. She gave him a curt nod as he entered. Lentz was giving her a hard time about frou-frou coffee, and she was giving him an equally hard time about crew cuts. He noted with surprise that Cheryl, from the hospital was also there. She wasn't in uniform, but she kept glancing nervously at her pager.

"Sorry I'm late... just got off the phone with one of my contacts and he'll be sending updates later today," he said as he grabbed the nearest chair. Addressing Cheryl, he asked, "Any change in Lucinda's condition?"

"Well, since you're all family, according to Ms. Blanchard, I can tell you that she's still comatose, but her vital signs have improved and she is breathing on her own. It's just a matter of time."

Lentz asked, "So, you folks any farther along in knowing what caused this?"

Cheryl hesitated for a moment, then answered, "Well, our lab found traces of an unidentified alkaloid substance in the stomach contents, but we had to send it off for further analysis." She hesitated again, and then blurted, "Okay, I'm just gonna say this. Nothing in any of her medications could have caused this. I noticed, twice actually, that some of her pills looked unfamiliar. The first time, I just tossed them and fetched the right ones. The second time, I took them to the hospital pharmacy and asked them what the heck was going on. They were completely surprised. As far as their records showed, the correct medication had been sent up to the fourth floor on both occasions. They couldn't identify the pills, either... said they almost looked homemade. We all agreed it was strange but then it got busy, and I put them in my pocket and forgot all about the whole thing." She paused, and when she spoke again, her voice was thick with emotion. "I should have done something... I should have reported it right away, but this is Hickok! I really like Lucinda and I can't help but feel it's my fault." A fat tear rolled down her cheek.

"Listen here, young lady... " Lentz surprised Quinn by gently putting his arm around Cheryl's shoulder. "It's not your fault. You didn't do this thing. We got a predator out there that got away with murder once and thinks he can do it again, but we're gonna make damn sure that doesn't happen. Now, if you still have those pills, we can get 'em to a lab and find out just exactly what we're lookin' at."

Cheryl wiped her tears away and smiled gratefully at Lentz. "I was hoping you'd ask," she said as she dug through her oversized purse. She handed him a small plastic bag containing a crumpled paper pill cup. "I'm pretty sure the hospital plans to call in the police as soon as they figure out what the substance is, but there's the liability issue and, well... it might take a while. Right now I'm afraid for Lucinda... and for you, too, Molly.

They all jumped when Cheryl's pager went off, and she stood up. "Gotta go… on call," she said. "But I'll let you know if anything new or interesting turns up. Thanks, Mr. Lentz, for asking me to be a part of this." He nodded his acknowledgement. She looked like she wanted to say more, but instead pantomimed "call me" to Molly and trotted to the door.

After she left, Lissy went to the counter to wait on a couple of customers who had wandered in and Lentz followed her, empty cup in hand, leaving Quinn and Molly alone at the table. Finally, when the silence became too awkward, Quinn said, "I am so sorry I didn't tell you everything right away. I was economical with the truth and you had every right to be upset. It was my fault."

Molly looked flustered as she reached over and touched his hand. "So, you're rich and important. Big deal. That's good news, right? I mean, now I won't have to feel guilty about ordering dessert when you take me out to dinner. Not like feeling guilty ever stopped me from ordering dessert… But the truth is, I can't quite figure out why you'd be interested in me. I mean, I grew up in a rectangular house… and you've met my mother!"

Quinn gave a sigh of relief. He brought her hand up to his mouth and gently kissed her fingers. "Hush, Molly dear. The heart wants what the heart wants, and right now my heart wants to know everything about you."

Molly stiffened slightly and broke eye contact. "Uh, about that… about knowing everything, there are some things I should probably tell you. But… I'll wait for a better time," she quickly added as Lissy and Lentz returned to the table.

154

Lissy gave him "the look," and Quinn released Molly's hand, willing himself not to blush. It wasn't working. "Hope we're not intruding," she said.

Lentz was smiling to himself as he settled into his chair. "Let's finish this meeting and then you two can go somewhere and pump each other for information all you want," he added, trying to keep a straight face. Lissy hooted and punched Lentz in the shoulder.

"Good one... Much as I hate to admit it, I like this guy... except for the crew-cut, that is!"

Quinn and Molly couldn't help being drawn in. When the laughter died down, Molly glanced at her watch and said, "Oops, I only have about fifteen minutes before I need to pick up my Mother." She pulled the manila envelope containing crime scene photos out of her tote and pushed them across the table to Quinn. "You said you wanted to see these?"

As he leafed through the disturbing images, Quinn frowned. "What kind of monster would do such a thing?"

"I know," said Molly. "I can't get the pictures out of my head. I did find one thing I thought was strange, though. Probably nothing. I was going to ask Lucinda about it but... uh... I didn't get the chance."

Alert with interest, Lentz leaned forward and said, "I'd be mighty interested to hear what caught your attention. I've looked at those pictures a thousand times over the years, but it's always good to have a new set of eyes."

Molly went through the stack until she found the one she was looking for. "Like I said, probably nothing, but I just don't think that these flowers belong in that kitchen. Maybe they came from a neighbor child, I don't know. Anyway, it's just a feeling..."

"In my business, Ma'am, that was called a hunch and a smart cop never ignores a hunch." Lentz studied the photo carefully. "I see what you mean. I can't believe I never noticed it before…"

"I think it's a girl thing," Molly volunteered. "I've been giving it a lot of thought. If it wasn't a neighborhood child, then maybe, just maybe, it could have been a gift to Cathy from a hopeful suitor. If that's the case, then someone else was at the house… if not the murderer, maybe somebody who might have seen something that could help."

"Damn," said Lentz, and he whistled appreciatively. "It never occurred to me. Course, we need to know if the flowers were there before Lucinda and her ass of a husband left that night, but it gives us a whole new direction."

As Molly got up to leave, Lentz gave her an affectionate hug. The man seemed energized with a new sense of purpose. Molly shyly returned the hug and then headed to the door, stopping in front of Quinn to plant a very sweet kiss on his cheek that left him feeling warm and fuzzy.

When she had gone, Quinn suddenly found himself also energized with a new sense of purpose. After surprising Lissy with an exuberant hug, he overpaid her and happily followed Lentz out of the shop, ready to slay any dragon that had the bad sense to get in his way.

Chapter Twenty Nine

Molly was afraid that her mother might still be upset over their "Lucinda Locke" conversation the night before, and she mentally prepared herself for the silent treatment that usually accompanied a slight, either real or imagined. But, thankfully, the older woman seemed to have forgotten all about it. Molly was surprised to see that she had painstakingly tamed her fluffy hair, dressed in one of her better pantsuits, and even doused herself with Eau de Toilette, a nice perfume with an unfortunate name.

"Mom, you didn't tell me you were having lunch with the Queen today! I'd better run out and buy some crumpets!" Molly shook her head and laughed. "You are one hot mama!"

"Oh, pshaw," the older woman waved away the compliment, but she couldn't quite hide the prim smile that showed she was pleased. "I've had this old thing for years, and I just wanted to try something different with my hair... that's all."

"Well, you look fantastic, d-a-h-ling," Molly said, as she helped her mother into a light jacket and handed her the infamous brown purse. "This way to the limo, Madam... your adoring fans await."

Molly managed to get a lot of work done during her mother's respiratory therapy session. She did her usual maintenance work for existing clients, and then focused on the never-ending paperwork and documentation necessary for billing. When she checked her email, she was excited to learn that she had been chosen for a second phone interview to further discuss what she could bring to a huge database conversion project. If she was actually chosen for the contract, it would keep her busy for months, maybe even years, and greatly enhance her rapidly dwindling college fund. It wasn't exactly a done deal, but she still indulged in some mental happy dancing.

After the session, the young therapist with spiky blue hair walked out to visit with Molly. In a serious tone, that belied the hair color, he informed her that even though they were just beginning the therapy, Mrs. Noble's stubborn attitude was making their work somewhat difficult.

"Nonsense, I've always had faith in my mother's ability to blow hot air," said Molly with a straight face.

He answered, with an equally straight face, "To be honest, she blows at sucking and sucks at blowing."

They looked at each other in stunned surprise for a moment and then both cracked up. Her mother, who was standing just out of earshot, looked bewildered. Realizing she was pushing her luck, Molly eventually got herself under control and assured the still-laughing therapist that she would work on the attitude. Before her mother could demand an explanation, she hurried the sputtering woman out into the corridor.

The respiratory therapy department was located at the back of the clinic wing of the hospital and it took Molly all the way to the front door to convince her mother that it had just been a corny respiratory therapy joke, and one not worthy of her attention. Finally placated, the woman took a detour to the ladies room before they left the building.

While waiting for her mother, Molly was alarmed to see Preston Locke come out of the elevator and head towards the door. Uneasily, she stepped back, hoping he wouldn't notice her, but no such luck. He stood for a moment and then walked purposefully in her direction. With nowhere to go, she stiffened her spine and prepared for an onslaught.

But it never came. Instead, he gently put his hand on her shoulder and said, "Ms. Noble, Helene… ah Miss Blanchard… says I need to apologize and she's absolutely right. I was just so upset and worried about my mother that I wasn't thinking straight. There's no way this was your fault. I mean, how could it be? Being a jerk runs in the family, I guess, but that's no excuse for my behavior. I hope you can forgive me."

Molly blinked in surprise. "Well, of course… Forgiven and forgotten." His apology felt just a bit too slick, but she wanted to give him the benefit of the doubt. "Any news about Lucinda?"

"Sadly, no. The old gal has had a rough ride, but she's strong. I'll give her that." He sounded concerned, but his eyes didn't quite match his tone. "Please don't be afraid to visit her. I know she… uh… cares for you," he added, as he walked away.

Molly watched him leave, shaking her head. *I can understand Lucinda not knowing who to trust… how very sad.*

"Another young man buzzing around, Molly? Really!" Shirley Noble had obviously witnessed some part of the exchange between her daughter and Preston Locke and was the epitome of matronly disapproval.

"Not buzzing around, Mom. That was Preston Locke and we were just talking about his mother. I met him a couple of times at the hospital."

"Preston Locke… the Preston Locke? Why, he's quite a good looking man and a local to boot. You know, honey, if you play your cards right you won't have to settle for that foreigner. Preston Locke would be a good catch for you… and the Lockes have money!" The woman looked absolutely pink with excitement.

Molly rolled her eyes, "Yeah, Mom, great catch." But muttered under her breath… "Wouldn't be caught dead…"

Chapter Thirty

Disappointingly, the report that Quinn had expected yielded no new information. His investigator friend explained to him that the lengthy elapsed time proved to be a stumbling block. Some of the players had passed away, while others were no longer in the area and difficult to track down, especially those who were not interested in being found. He commented that, to him and other investigators on the team, it felt like considerable political clout had been used to keep important details out of the public eye, and possibly even out of the investigation. He noted it was obvious that the girl's father had the connections to make this happen, but found it rather curious since it had also severely impeded the case. The man added that the Hickok police had really gotten the short end of the stick with what appeared almost to be an intentional smear campaign. "The regional news was fairly unbiased, but the local newspaper was unusually vicious," he said. "We are looking into who else in town might have that kind of power, other than the father, of course."

Before signing off, the man mentioned that the name "Eric Lentz" had come up a few times and they had been trying to contact him the last couple of days, thinking he would be a good source. Quinn quickly told them that he was already working with Lentz, and that he would gladly share any new information with them.

"Don't usually put clients to work on their own cases, Old Buddy," the man laughed. "We'll have to start you out at entry level, so don't expect anything above minimum wage."

Next, Quinn reviewed the surveillance reports he received by email from the security company. In order to protect their covers, it was understood that the two agents and Quinn would have no physical contact. Daily reports were sent to headquarters, quickly reviewed, and forwarded on to Quinn, along with comments and potential threat assessments. Nothing earth-shattering, although each agent had noted seeing a dark blue sedan circle the block around the Calamity Jane... both times at night, but neither agent had managed to see the plates.

He sighed. Frustrated, he padded into the roomy kitchen, flipped on the electric teakettle, and then perused the refrigerator for anything interesting.

"Nice digs."

Surprised, Quinn whirled around to see Eric Lentz standing in the doorway.

"Sorry. Guess I didn't knock very hard and the front door was open, so..."

"No problem," Quinn answered. "Just preoccupied, I suppose. I was just about to make myself beans on toast. Care for some?"

Lentz looked unsure for a moment, but answered, "Sure, I'll try me soma that exotic Brit food."

"Trust me," Quinn said, wryly. "There is absolutely nothing exotic about British food, except for the names. I mean, you haven't lived until you've tried Bubble and Squeak, or Neeps and Tatties, or Toad in the Hole... and don't forget Spotted Dick... "

162

Catching the thunderous look on Lentz's face, Quinn held out his hand, laughing. "That's what I mean. I'm talking about fried leftovers, turnips and potatoes, pigs in a blanket, and Spotted Dick is a steamed suet pudding with raisins. Really."

Lentz didn't look convinced but he said, "Well, I'm game for the beans and toast, but I'll have to get to know you better before I try the rest… specially that suet pudding thing."

A short time later they were sitting at the kitchen counter, polishing off a big batch of beans on toast and eyeing half an apple pie that Quinn's housekeeper had left for him.

"So, like I said, nice digs," repeated Lentz, casting his eye around a kitchen that was larger than his entire cabin.

"Yeah," agreed Quinn. "Ironic. The more money you have, the less you have to spend. There's always someone who wants to trade favors. This cabin, for instance, belongs to an old friend from college who wants me to sponsor him for a board position at an international bank. I like the guy and I trust him, or I wouldn't be here. But he wouldn't take no for answer." He shrugged.

"Well, I guess it's better than the Tomahawk Motel just up the road, where a good scalping comes with every room," said Lentz, as he finished his pie and pushed himself away from the counter.

They wandered out to the dining room, where the huge wooden table was covered with file folders, loose papers, and photographs. Lentz smiled sadly. "Brings back my old police days. Never really gets out of the blood, ya know. But I been stuck on this case for most of my life and it's time to put it to rest."

They both sat down, and Quinn gave Lentz an update on the reports he had received. He also expressed his frustration at the lack of progress. "I think I can help pin down some of the people your investigator mentioned," Lentz said. "I always took this case real personal and kept tabs on the comings and goings of anyone involved with it… even kept track of their families. But you might wanna tell your big city friend to take care not to spook anybody. I had two messages on my answering machine and they don't know me from Adam. Might force the killer to either bolt or do something, uh… unpredictable. Not a good plan."

Quinn shuddered as images of what "something unpredictable" might be passed through his mind. "Right, I'm on it," he said, and hurriedly called his investigator friend. After that was done, he looked miserably at the piles of paperwork, wondering where to begin.

Lentz reached into an old leather satchel he had brought with him and pulled out a thick stack of paperwork. "Before I left, I made copies of anything having to do with the case. Probably shouldn't a done it, but after it all came down no one in the Police Department had the energy to care much." Keeping the top half of the stack, he pushed the rest over to Quinn. "So get a move on, partner! Grab yourself a stack, put on your cheaters, and keep the coffee coming!"

Chapter Thirty One

Molly felt like her face was going into rigor as she left her mother's house. She had to massage her cheeks to make the frozen smile go away. Once the woman had fixated on the idea that Preston Locke would be a good suitor for her daughter, there was no stopping her. It had been relentless… the loaded questions, the thinly veiled hints, and the overabundance of motherly advice. Molly knew, from previous experience, that the only thing to do was put on the game face, smile and nod occasionally, saying as little as possible. The time between lunch and her mother's mid-afternoon soap had been an eternity.

When she was finally able to escape, she drove around the block, stopped in a convenience store parking lot, dug into her tote, and indulged in two Godiva truffles. No guilt, though… she had earned every cocoa-laden calorie.

Her next stop was to see Lucinda at the hospital. She really hoped that since Preston had already been there today, she wouldn't run into him again. *Not enough truffles in the world for that!* Fortunately, he was nowhere in sight and she took the stairs up to the fourth floor. Cheryl was on the phone as she walked by the nurse's station, but gave Molly a wave and mouthed, "We need to talk." Nodding an acknowledgement she continued on to Lucinda's room.

"Hi, Lucinda." Molly had no way of knowing whether or not the woman could hear her, but it didn't matter. She believed that Lucinda would be aware of her presence on some level and that was enough. "You didn't get a chance to listen to the music I gave you the other day, so I brought a CD player so we could hear it together." She chose a CD at random and cued the first track at low volume, pulling her chair close to the bed. Molly smiled as Bessie Smith belted out a gutsy tune. *Nice choice*, she thought. *I can almost hear Lucinda humming along.*

She stayed through the whole album, sometimes having a one-sided conversation about her kids or her mother or Quinn. At other times she just sat and quietly listened to an entire song. It felt almost as if Lucinda was doing the same thing, and Molly felt a comforting sense of camaraderie with the silent woman.

Toward the end of the CD, Molly took Lucinda's hand and was surprised at how warm it was, and soft to the touch. As she stood to leave, she leaned close to the woman and whispered, "I know you're in there. Take your time and save up your strength, because when you come back, we've got some butts to kick!" Kissing her cool brow, Molly said goodbye and went looking for Cheryl.

"Cafeteria, ten minutes," called the cheerful nurse as she ran past down the hallway. "I missed lunch!"

Knowing that spare time wasn't a big commodity in Cheryl's world, Molly bought her a chicken salad sandwich, side of coleslaw, and strawberry shortcake for dessert. "You're my hero!" Cheryl gave her a big hug and then wasted no time in digging in. After a few minutes, she slowed down and said. "Whoa, that's better. I get spacey when I don't eat. I wanted to tell you that one of the nurse's aides, a new girl who moved here from… I think Denver, maybe… hasn't shown up for work since Lucinda's episode. We've been calling the number on file, but no answer. Anyway, her name is Rochelle Martin and I think she lives in one of those trailers down below the baseball field. May be nothing, but the timing just feels weird, if you know what I mean. Haven't heard back yet from the lab, but it always takes a long time. Mr. Lentz and your guy might hear back sooner on the pills."

But the sound of Cheryl's beeper cut the visit short and before she raced off, Molly assured her she would pass along the information and let her know if anything new developed. As she watched her friend head for the stairs, she stifled a yawn. Still tired from her restless night, a nap sounded wonderful, but she knew that her mind was too busy to let that happen. Finding herself alone in the cafeteria, she sighed.

Musing as she headed back to the hotel, she remembered that Cheryl had called Quinn "your guy," and she found herself hoping that was true. Following that train of thought, she envisioned her mother's reaction to being told that her daughter had no intention of marrying into the Locke fortune. Silent treatment, most assuredly, but after today that sounded almost inviting. She wondered what her mother's reaction would be to the fact that Quinn could buy and sell the Locke family several times over. "Oh, now that would be interesting," she laughed to herself. "But I think I'll just keep that tidbit of information to myself for the time being." She swung out into late afternoon traffic singing, "Piece of My Heart" with Janis Joplin.

Chapter Thirty Two

"Mama? Mommy?"

With a great sense of reluctance, Lucinda came back to herself. She had been floating, fragmented into uncountable moments, the glittering pieces of her life. All around her was a cool darkness. Not long ago, although time was a slippery concept for her, she had sensed music. It had been such a revelation for her. She had forgotten there was such a thing. Moving through the darkness... surrounding her, almost touching her, like an elusive spirit. It was wonderful. Then, as the music faded away, there was a blue light that warmed her. That was love, she thought, another revelation.

"Mommy?"

With an effort that seemed impossibly difficult, she cast her mind in the direction of the voice. She first sensed, and then saw a vague shape there. As she gained focus the shape slowly resolved into a young girl in a pink satin dress and diaphanous gauze wings. She wore a tiara and was holding a raggedy stuffed rabbit.

"Mommy!" cried the girl, as she skipped over and plopped down in front of Lucinda, who was inexplicably sitting cross-legged on an old saddle blanket.

Lucinda looked at the child with wonder and fear. "Cathy? Can it be you, baby girl? Am I dead? Are you an angel?"

"No Mommy, I'm the princess," the girl laughed, shaking the poor rabbit by its ears. Lucinda suddenly remembered the outfit her daughter insisted on wearing during every waking moment for weeks. She had to sneak it out of her room and wash it when the girl was asleep. It had been a gift for her fourth birthday.

"Baby girl, I missed you so much." Then she paused, "What happens next?" She was afraid of the answer.

The child looked at her oddly, and then slowly transformed into an older Cathy. She had pink barrettes holding back her unruly dark hair, a pink mohair sweater, and the hint of strawberry lip gloss. Around her neck was the extravagant pearl necklace that her father had given her when she turned thirteen. She smiled sadly, and the expression in her eyes was both old and wise.

"Oh, Mommy, it's up to you. I'll always be here, but you need to be ready. Are you ready? Can you let go?" The girl reached up gently and touched Lucinda's face. It was a soft, sweet touch but Lucinda felt herself falling back into the world of darkness. As the light faded, "are you ready?" echoed in her mind, "are you ready?"

Quinn pulled out the chair for Molly, ignoring the obvious eye-rolling from the Lissy/Lentz contingent. She smiled sweetly at him, and his heart skipped a beat or two. Intruding on his "moment," Lissy unceremoniously plunked a drink in front of him and he eyed it suspiciously. It was wildly fancy, with pinkish whipped cream and generously topped with either sugar sprinkles or glitter. Quinn hoped it wasn't glitter.

"What can I say," Lissy shrugged. "I can't help it if I'm a creative genius. I call it the Dark Choco Disco Delight."

He looked to Lentz for sympathy, but the man just shook his head and said, "Man up, Drummond... she made me drink some crazy thing called a Berry Cherry Mocha. Didn't kill me... yet... "

Lissy elbowed Lentz in the ribs, and then turned her gaze to Quinn.

Buckling under the force of "the look," Quinn reluctantly sipped the fluffy drink. He was surprised to realize that it wasn't half bad... drinkable, even. He raised his cup to Lissy in mock salute.

After they were all settled in, Molly told them about what she had learned from Cheryl. And just moments ago, when she had called the hospital to check on Lucinda, Cheryl had added that the missing nurse's aide, Rochelle Martin, was still unaccounted for and another nurse's aide had gone to her house to check on her.

Quinn quickly went over what he had learned from his investigator friend, and Lentz just sat back and listened, adding a detail here and there. It was obvious that they didn't have a lot to go on.

Quinn leaned towards Molly. "So far, all you have are riddles and rhymes... at least that's what you told me, but it seems that Lucinda thought you could figure it out. So let's hear it all, and don't leave anything out."

"No pressure there," laughed Molly, nervously. But she took a deep breath and jumped right in. Beginning with the first day her mother was in the hospital, she described her initial encounter with Lucinda and how their relationship had developed over time. She talked about Lucinda's lullaby, and recited the poem that she had been given. "I was supposed to burn this," she said sheepishly. "I kept promising her that I would, but… oops, here it is, still in my jacket pocket." She pulled it out and set it on the table. Lentz picked it up gently, read it, and then set it down. He seemed lost in thought for a moment, but quickly recovered and prompted Molly to continue.

She went on, but at the mention of the toy chest, Quinn interrupted her in surprise. "She had a toy chest delivered to you at the hotel? That seems like an odd thing to give you, especially since it must have had great sentimental value for Lucinda."

"I know, I know. I tried to talk her out of it, but she insisted I have it. She had Helene Blanchard pack it up and send it over. In some way it might tie in with the poem and also the lullaby. In fact, I think everything is connected, but I just don't know how."

"Okay," said Lentz. "Since then you came pretty near to becoming road kill, and somebody tried to poison Lucinda." He was silent for a moment and a vein in his temple throbbed. Everyone at the table had the good sense to patiently wait for him to continue. "That tells me that somebody thinks we're on the right track and somebody wants to shut us up. The good news is that the more we shake the tree the more reckless that somebody might become. The bad news is that more reckless means more dangerous. We don't know who we're dealing with, here, so we're all on red alert. Got it?"

Everyone around the table nodded vigorously. Lissy was the only one who seemed completely unfazed. She casually strolled over to serve a couple of late customers, and returned with some gingerbread cookies decorated to look like members of a famous punk rock group. "What? I get bored, okay?" she said, in response to the odd looks she was getting. But, hey, food was food, and no one hesitated to bite the frosting spiked hair and nibble on the tiny army boots.

"All right," said Quinn, licking frosting off his fingers. "I think we need to see this toy chest. There must be something special about it."

As Quinn, Molly, and Lentz headed for the door, Lissy bowed out with a nod-nod-wink-wink-say-no-more. Really getting into the cloak and dagger thing, she said she didn't want to blow her "cover." Quinn had to smile.

They walked over to the Calamity Jane. Quinn noticed that the dapper gent behind the desk gave both him and Lentz the once over as they followed Molly to the stairs. The man shook his head, and Quinn felt, inexplicably, like a sneaky adolescent who had just been busted.

Quinn thought Molly's room was charming, in an old fashioned way. He was a bit disappointed that he hadn't been invited up under different circumstances, but he forced himself back to the task at hand. Kneeling in front of the toy chest, both men admired the workmanship, and closely inspected the whimsical paintings. "I see what you mean about this being connected with the lullaby." Quinn traced the rainbow on the inside of the lid, while Lentz checked to see if anything had been hidden in the lining of the box.

"Nothing," pronounced Lentz. "I guess this means it's all in the words. What do you think she meant about the words that don't belong?"

Molly opened her mouth to answer, but at that moment her cell rang. "Cheryl," she said. "I had better take this." To her friend she said, "Hey girl..." but that was as far as she got. She listened for a minute and then hung up, with a stunned look on her face.

"Lucinda? Did something happen with Lucinda?" Lentz grabbed Molly's arm, his face rigid.

"No, no. Not Lucinda." Molly sat down on the edge of the bed. "You know that missing nurse's aide? A co-worker went over to check on her, found the door unlocked, went in, thinking the girl might be sick or something. She found her in the bathroom, dead. The police are there now and the girl's pretty upset, so Cheryl's going over there to get her calmed down and take her home. The girl told her that there wasn't any blood, but there was white foam around her mouth. Cheryl said it sounded like a drug overdose and thought we should know."

"Damn," said Lentz. "You two stay together for now. I'm headin' over to the department and see what I can find out. I don't know about you," he said, addressing Quinn. "But I'm pretty sure this ain't a coincidence."

As Lentz ran pounding down the stairs, followed by Quinn and Molly, the night clerk looked up in surprise. They had only been upstairs for five minutes. "That's gotta be some kinda record," Quinn heard him mutter. As he looked back, the man shook his head slightly with an expression that said, "I really have seen it all."

Chapter Thirty Three

Twenty minutes later Molly found herself sitting in a quiet corner of the Full Rack. She and Quinn were toying with an order of nachos, but her mind was elsewhere and she might as well have been eating paper bits. The place was relatively empty, but people were beginning to wander in. She was trying hard to ignore an old cowboy sitting at the bar who kept winking at her and giving Quinn the thumbs-up. *A few too many brewskies.* But she was surprised to see Quinn wave to the man and nod an acknowledgement. "Uh, what's up with your new best friend over there?" asked Molly, not sure she wanted to know the answer.

"Not exactly my new best friend, but he's a nice old character, and very wise in the mysterious ways of women."

"Who knew?" said Molly, wanting Quinn to elaborate, but trying to remain cool. "Actually, it's a big mistake to judge people by their appearance around here. For instance, the man that just wandered in… the one who looks like a cross between Albert Einstein and the homeless guy who rides his bike up and down Main Street… he's the head of the hospital board. And the guy in the black suit and white tie, who looks like he should be the head of the hospital board, is the local barber. They call him, fondly I hope, Butcher Bob."

The door opened and Barbette strode in, followed by Don. Suddenly the restaurant became very quiet, in anticipation of fireworks, and

Barbette glared in her direction. Molly leaned back, crossed her arms, stuck out her chin, and raised an eyebrow at the woman. After a tense moment, Barbette whirled around and stormed out, dragging Don with her. With a collective sigh of disappointment, restaurant patrons returned to their own conversations.

"Damn, that's better than chocolate... maybe even better than sex, although it's been so long I can't remember." Realizing what she had just said, she felt herself blushing. "Didn't really want to advertise that, but it felt so good!"

Quinn laughed. "Well anytime you want to polish up on those old skills, I'm the man for the job. I hear it's just like riding a bike..."

"Just like riding a bike... not much of a recommendation," replied Molly. It was Quinn's turn to blush. "No openings right now, so to speak, but send me a resume and I'll keep it on file."

They both laughed and then, with the tension gone, they reviewed what they knew about the long-ago murder and the recent incidents.

"I can't help but think that the toy chest is pivotal," said Molly. "I think the words that don't belong are words from Lucinda's lullaby, nonsense words like stinky skunks and elephant trunks. There are skunks and elephants painted on the toy chest so there must be a tie-in. There has to be something we're missing."

"I agree," said Quinn. "And as for suspects, my sources tell me that everything points back to young Preston, but he was at a party and had a pretty good alibi. There were a lot of other kids coming and going, but all of the ones interviewed didn't remember him leaving. One of the witnesses even said he was passed out by the pool for most of the party. A couple of the kids mentioned that early on, there had been some kind of fight… two guys came to blows, but it was never clear who exactly was involved or what it was about. They agreed, though, that it must have gotten resolved, because the rest of the party was pretty "happening."

"That was over at the Golden house, right? I guess that used to be party central until Jeff got killed. He was in a car accident, by himself, going way too fast, and hit the side of a bridge abutment. The papers said there wasn't any sign of him trying to stop or even slow down. No sign of braking at all, but there was the rumor of alcohol involved. That was just a couple of months after Cathy's murder. I always thought his accident sounded more like suicide, but he just didn't seem the type."

Molly sighed. "I didn't know him at all. He was older than me and ran in different circles. His dad was a doctor and his mother came from money. To be honest, what I do remember about him was scary. He was a bully and would hurt other kids who got in his way or somehow annoyed him, and you never knew what would set him off. He was one of those guys you tried to avoid. It felt like he was above the law and knew it. I guess that's true, in a way. He used to get into these huge fights. I remember he attacked this boy I knew for no good reason and almost killed him... stabbed him with a butter knife. But nothing happened. It got covered up and just went away."

At that moment, Eric Lentz came through the door and walked to their table with purpose.

"Man, what a night," he said, pulling out a chair and gesturing to the barmaid for a beer. The old cowboy gave him a wave and he nodded back.

"It looks like our candy striper was into some bad stuff. It was a drug overdose, but I won't guarantee it was accidental. I'm guessing she was the one who swapped Lucinda's pills… saw some at her place that looked just like the ones we got from the nurse… and somebody wanted to make sure she didn't talk. Probably gave her a "bonus" and it was more than she bargained for. She and her low-life boyfriend have been living in an old trailer down by the river for about six months. Neighbors say they haven't seen the boyfriend for a while and that the girl has been acting strange lately, nervous and maybe even scared." He stopped to take a long pull from the beer he had ordered.

"The guy that lived next door said she had recently put a padlock on an old garage at the back of the lot, more like a shed. Said the boyfriend used to spend a lot of time out there. The police cut the lock and found the remnants of a meth lab. They also found an old blue Chrysler that matches the description of the one that tried to run you down." He looked at Molly. "They even matched the paint from the car he sideswiped when he drove off. Course, they need to prove it, but I'd bet good money it was the same car. Nobody knows where the guy is." Lentz paused for a moment. "My guess is that he's as dead as his girlfriend."

Molly shivered. This was so out of control. So beyond anything she was prepared to deal with. Seeming to sense her fear, Quinn put his hand over hers and gave it a squeeze. Surprisingly, Lentz took her other hand. "We're in this thing together and there's no going back, even if we wanted to. We're gonna find the monster responsible for what happened then and what's happening now, and we're gonna make him pay. You have my word, little lady."

There was no doubt that he meant it, and she hoped he was right. She really did. But Molly suddenly remembered how she had felt in her nightmare about the back room of Save-Mart. She had the same sense of foreboding, the same knot in the pit of her stomach, and *"Goodbye, Yellow Brick Road,"* echoed in her mind.

Feeling in a very good mood and humming tunelessly along with the Bee Gees… 'I Started a Joke', the killer slowed the car to a crawl and took in the scene with relish. *Busy bees… see our tax dollars at work. Hickok's finest scurrying around the trailer and that wreck of a garage, clueless, just like the other time so long ago.*

One or two of the policemen glanced over at the car, but no worries. The curious had been driving by all night and there was nothing alarming about this particular car… nothing out of the ordinary. In fact the car was almost too ordinary, but it had once belonged to the old woman and the irony of it was….well, priceless.

It had been so easy; like giving candy to a baby or, rather, nose candy to a baby-faced nobody. The girl had been surprised in the beginning, surprised that someone like the killer could supply her with the drugs she needed. But she got over that soon enough. Everybody had their price and she was happy to do whatever she was asked, as long as she got her fix. But the girl was getting antsy, wondering where her boyfriend had gone, and realizing that her little switcheroo at the hospital might actually have killed a nice old lady. Meeting her behind the Save-Mart, giving her lots of sympathy, two hundred bucks, and the promise of a lot more, the killer slipped her a special "job well done" bonus. "It's really going to blow your mind, my dear, but you deserve it." It did and she did. The boyfriend had fallen for the same thing and ended up in the deep end of the reservoir.

Another couple of loose ends tied up and it was almost effortless. Feeling energized and just a bit daring, the killer circled the block and drove slowly past the busy trailer again. The next Bee Gees song came on. *Stayin' Alive? I intend to do just that, but as for the other loose ends... Well, we can't always get what we want..."* The killer's laugh was hollow and humorless.

Chapter Thirty Four

From a great distance, Quinn heard a sound he couldn't quite place. Bagpipes, maybe... but he had always liked the sound of bagpipes, even found them comforting. This was more shrill and annoying. Almost like a banshee, shrieking just outside his field of vision. Though he had never actually heard a banshee, he had listened to the stories his pals whispered when they were caught out in the chill Scottish evenings; heard the tales that the old folks told when they had indulged in a wee bit too much whiskey-laced coffee after a holiday dinner. *This must be what they sound like.*

So, it was a banshee he decided but, again, that didn't seem quite right... He felt himself stir and suddenly realized it was the jarring ringtone he had chosen for his secretary. He reluctantly opened his eyes and saw the cell phone vibrating a few inches from his head. The shrill British ambulance ringtone made his teeth hurt. Knowing he was not prepared to deal with the ever-efficient Valerie, he waited until the phone stopped ringing. Almost immediately it rang again. She was nothing, if not persistent. When it finally stopped, Quinn took stock of his situation. He had apparently fallen asleep at the big table in his cabin. Toppled over like a tree. His head lay dangerously close to the remains of a peanut butter and jelly sandwich and a cup of cold tea. Papers were scattered around him and the light above the table was still on, although it was full daylight. He swore under his breath and sat up, blinking in the morning sun. As he went to run his hand through his unruly hair, he found a large Post-It note mysteriously stuck to his forehead. He pulled it off and read it with a groan:

Stopped by to work on our game plan, but figured you needed your beauty rest. Give me a call and I'll meet you for coffee. And lock your door, you dumb-ass! Lentz

Feeling sheepish and ever-so-busted, Quinn had to laugh. He was really beginning to like the crusty old guy.

Last night had been difficult for everyone... the poor nurse's aide most of all. Because of Molly's near death experience in front of the theater and the discovery of the vehicle at the dead girl's house, the police were now involved. Even if they concluded the girl's death was a suicide, they would want to find out how Molly might be involved. A valid question, but Quinn and Lentz agreed that this might complicate their own investigation.

And then there was Molly... Quinn had noticed a change in her over the last few days. Rather than making her more careful and circumspect, recent events seem to have made her stronger and more focused. She appeared more grounded and had acquired the habit of holding her head high and sticking her chin out ever so slightly. It was her "bring it on" look and Quinn loved it. She was afraid, that she admitted freely, but was she going to back down? Not a chance.

When he walked her to her hotel last night, he had offered to stay with her... Sleep on the sofa or even rent an adjoining room, but she read him the riot act.

"What, you think I'm some delicate wallflower or fragile shrinking violet? You think I'm going upstairs to cower in the corner and cry my eyes out?" She took a step forward and raised one eyebrow. "Well, you're dead wrong, mister. I have a lot of work to do for my neglected clients and I have a whopper of a mystery to solve, so if you'll excuse me...." The chin appeared. "This isn't getting it done!"

He was speechless at first, but then gently touched her arm and admitted -- realizing as he did so how true it was -- that his wanting to stay was actually more for him.

"Oh, so that's how it is. You men are all alike!" she said, punching him in the arm, but Quinn was relieved to see that she was smiling.

"I kind of like the idea of caring enough to want to protect someone, even if she is the Bionic Woman. So you see it's more about me than about you. The truth is, lassie, I do want to be there to save your life, but I think maybe you've already saved mine."

She looked at him for a moment, and then stood on tiptoe to plant a chaste kiss on his lips. "Good night, Mighty Quinn, and get some sleep… there'll be plenty of time to save the world tomorrow." She gave him a sweet smile, strode through the hotel lobby, and disappeared up the grand old staircase.

Quinn had stood there for a moment, breathing in the chilly night air. With relief, he noted his security people were in place, one in his customary seat at the bar window across the street and the other, who had managed to rent a room across from Molly's, was sitting in the lobby nonchalantly reading a travel magazine. He knew he should probably tell her about the "security detail" but thought that, after her outburst, it could wait. He toyed with the idea of sharing a beer with the old cowboy, but decided his time would be better spent looking for some clue to this big mess they were all in. With a sigh, he wandered back to his car and drove out to the cabin. Lentz's car was parked right in front as he passed the hospital. There had been no change in Lucinda's condition.

As he took a quick shower and helped himself to a big serving of the housekeeper's homemade peach cobbler, he remembered last night's feeling of frustration. Quinn had gone over every single piece of paper, revisited each witness interview, and peered at all of the disturbing photos more than once. His investigator had continued to add bits of information but, so far, nothing helpful. He had also sent off the strange pills to a highly reputable lab, recommended by his friend, but the results were still pending. Honestly, the only headway they had made came through the cryptic clues Molly had received and her surprising insights. But he didn't want to miss anything, so with great reluctance, he went through the stack one more time. The next thing he remembered was waking up to the sound of a London ambulance, but thinking of his secretary he guiltily believed that a banshee might not be too far off the mark.

As if on cue, the phone began to ring again. There was no mistaking the ringtone, so he swallowed the last of his cobbler and mentally prepared himself for a conversation with Valerie.

"Mr. Drummond," even the tone of her voice told Quinn that his secretary was mightily peeved. "I have had some difficulty in reaching you, but decided to persevere since the matter was of some importance." There was a slight pause. "I do hope this is a convenient time."

"Of course, Valerie... how can I help?" Quinn was surprised at how easily he had resumed his business persona.

"Well, Sir, Mr. Steinmetz and Mr. Lowell are adamant that your absence be explained. They are of the impression that you are undertaking a business venture that may impact the home company and feel that they have the right to know what is going on."

Quinn wasn't quite sure what he had just heard. Steinmetz and Lowell were high level corporate officers and trusted business associates. But he had communicated with both of them shortly after he had decided to extend his stay in Hickok, explaining that his reasons were of a personal nature, though he could be reached in case of emergency. They had been very understanding, supportive even, and he had taken calls from both of them, relating to various business decisions, since then.

"Valerie, could you hold for a moment?" Quinn set down the phone in order to collect his thoughts. In all the years he had known the woman, she had never been anything but honest…sometimes bluntly so. But this was a fabrication and he couldn't understand why, unless… Unless this was Valerie's way of demanding that SHE know what was going on.

"Oh, no," he whispered. "There is none so blind as a man that will not see." In a rush, he remembered all the presents she had brought him from her infrequent vacations. She made a big show of arranging them artistically in his office. She insisted upon running personal errands for him, ordered his lunches, and had even taken over his personal calendar so that she had a better idea of family birthdays than he did. Recently she had gone so far as to accept and reject personal engagements for him, something that annoyed him greatly. He had taken it for granted, thinking her the apex of efficiency. He had never been attracted to her, but he could see now that she had felt differently.

Taking a deep breath, he picked up the phone. "Valerie, you were right to call. Misters Steinmetz and Lowell certainly do deserve an explanation. Please tell them that I chose to remain here for personal reasons. Tell them that I have met a woman and want to stay until I see how things work out. Tell them that I'm happy, happier than I've ever been, and that I trust them to continue to do their best. Tell them that I appreciate their great work. And, Valerie, please know that I appreciate you and everything you have done."

There was a long silence on the other end. "I see. Well, then, Mr. Drummond. I will certainly convey that information." There was another long pause. "And, sir, I am glad you are happy." Her voice cracked just a bit and the line went dead.

"Oh, Valerie," whispered Quinn, sadly. He had never led her on... never, as far as he knew, encouraged her in any way. But again, the heart wants what the heart wants. His heart wanted Molly.

Chapter Thirty Five

It would have been so easy for Lucinda to just drift way, for her to follow her daughter into the cool darkness. She wanted more than anything to do just that. No more pain. No more sadness. No more unanswered questions. "Just let me go. I'm so ready… I want to let go," she whispered. But Lucy was pestering her, reminding her that there was something she had yet to do, some detail she had to remember, someone she had to help. It all hovered there, just out of reach.

"Go away," she said crossly to Lucy. Lucinda was curled up into a tight ball, but Lucy kept nudging her shoulder, whispering in her ear.

"Get up old woman, you're not done yet. Get up! Move it… shake a leg!"

"Go away," Lucinda repeated, but she could feel her resolve weakening. Lucy had kept her going all these sad and lonely years and Lucy always got her way. "Leave me alone, I just want to sleep." Even Lucinda could detect the pathetic whine in her voice and she knew that Lucy wouldn't tolerate it for a moment.

"All right, old woman, you asked for it," and Lucinda's body was hit with a sudden painful jolt.

"Stop it, leave me alone!" Lucinda wailed, but Lucy answered, "No such luck, you pansy, now get your butt in gear… in gear… gear…"

"CLEAR." Another sudden jolt and the darkness began to retreat "CLEAR" and she again felt herself go rigid. Lucinda's eyes fluttered open to white lights and worried faces.

"She's back," someone said and Lucinda was confused. She had not completely returned to her body and everything was too bright and too loud.

"Lucinda, stay with us… Lucinda…" it was a voice she recognized, and when the nurse took her hand and told her everything was going to be okay, she believed it.

"Cheryl," she whispered. Her throat was dry and sore from disuse. "Not done yet." She smiled and then let herself drift back to sleep. Not a coma this time, just deep healing sleep.

Chapter Thirty Six

Molly's night had been rough, very rough. She had managed to put on a brave front for Quinn, and when she left him in front of the hotel, she made sure her head was held high and her stride was purposeful. But by the time she got to her room, she was a quivering bowl of Jell-O… yellow Jell-O, to be exact. She was trembling so badly, it took her a couple of tries to get the old fashioned key into the lock, and once she was in the room she quickly engaged the deadbolt and added the flimsy chain for good measure. After a thorough room search – under the bed, closet, bathtub, behind the drapes – she felt safer and plopped down on the bed. "Not a delicate wallflower, not a shrinking violet," she murmured to herself, almost like a mantra. She gazed longingly at the corner of her room, wanting desperately to curl up there and cry her eyes out. But instead, she sat still, tried to clear the mental chatter from her mind, and took several deep breaths.

When she felt better, she sighed and fired up her laptop. Her work wasn't exactly mindless, quite the contrary, but she knew she could lose herself in it and right now that was exactly what she needed. So she popped in a compilation CD her oldest son had made for her, put on headphones and softly sang along, as she began to map out a complicated table conversion. Three CDs later, she finally shut down the computer and wandered over to the pink toy chest. It was late, but she was way too keyed up to sleep. She sat on the floor in front of it and pulled Lucinda's poem from her pocket. She thought about Lucinda's nonsense lullaby, and suddenly realized that all of the animals in her song were painted on the toy chest. On some level, at least in Molly's mind, that meant that those words did belong. "So what about the words that don't belong?" she wondered. She reread the poem, returning to a couple of lines that seemed out of place.

Momma says look where bluebirds fly,
Momma says the mirror doesn't lie.

"Where do bluebirds fly," she asked herself and, out of nowhere, a young Judy Garland answered her tunefully. "Beyond the rainbow, why, oh why can't I?"

"Well, duh," Molly shook her head. How had she missed that? She had grown up with a generation of kids who could recite the movie almost word for word. Hers was a generation of kids who longed for their own Land of Oz and had a healthy respect for tornados. Okay, so it had to do with the rainbow and the mirror.

Molly opened the lid of the toy chest and traced the sweet rainbow above the mirror. "The mirror doesn't lie," the poem read. She had to sadly agree as she gazed at her tired, pale reflection in the mirror mounted beneath the rainbow. The dark circles under her eyes were becoming ghoulish. "Just in time for Halloween... maybe I could be the Zombie Princess," she thought wryly. It had to have a deeper meaning, didn't it?

But what could it be? Eventually she closed the lid and rested her head on the toy chest, trying to chase down a clue. She got nothing.

It was dusk, and Molly found herself sitting alone in Lucinda's empty hospital room. Strangely, as often happens in dreams, it seemed much larger than it should have been, and she couldn't see beyond the shadows at the edges of the room. She didn't know where her friend had gone and was afraid that something bad had happened. Hearing a laugh, she turned, expecting to see Lucinda, but instead it was a young girl, wearing pink, standing in the doorway. The girl skipped over to Molly and gave her the once over. "Are you me?" she asked, as if it was a perfectly normal question.

"No, I'm Molly."

"Molly," the girl echoed. She thought for a moment and then said, "I don't know you, but you love my mother so it's okay."

"Yes, I guess I do love your mother," Molly answered, knowing that she meant Lucinda. She realized that the girl was Cathy.

"Here, you can wear this," the girl said. She undid the clasp of a pearl necklace that was around her neck and handed it to Molly. "Ask Mama about it when you see her again," she said as she skipped back to the door.

Molly ran the pearls through her fingers, marveling at their coolness and perfection, and then slipped the necklace into the pocket of the suede jacket she was wearing. When the girl reached the dark doorway, she stopped and turned.

"But stay away from the clown," the girl said, her eyes wide and serious. "The clown wants to hurt you. The clown wants to hurt everybody." She looked nervously down the corridor and then disappeared.

Molly could now hear the faint strains of music... "Goodbye Yellow Brick Road..." and she knew that she couldn't stay there any longer. She darted into the dark hallway, trying to remember the way to the exit. She ran for what seemed like forever, but soon realized she was hopelessly lost. Knowing she could no longer find her way back to Lucinda's room, let alone the exit, she felt panic wash over her.

From the dark end of the hallway, the shadows began to resolve into a shape. First the clown wall hanging that she had always feared and then it came to life as the rodeo clown that had chased her before. Smiling a terrible smile, it walked toward her slowly, nonchalantly, even adding comical dance steps to the Elton John song. But it wasn't funny. Molly turned to run again, but the long hallway had disappeared. In fact, she was faced with the proverbial brick wall. She had two choices. She could either wait, terrified and passive, for the clown to reach her, or she could run, though still terrified, right at it and take her chances. Her heart was pounding, but she steeled herself and took off at a dead run straight at the smiling entity. Right before she hit, she thought she saw a flicker of something in its eyes. Fear maybe? She hoped so. There was a collision and...

Molly awoke on the floor of her hotel room, in front of the toy chest. The last thing she remembered was resting her head on the box and she must have slid off. Feeling self-conscious, even though she was alone, she glanced around the room. The bedside lamp was still on and her travel alarm told her it was 4:00 a.m. She groaned and stood up stiffly, then washed her face, and collapsed into the bed, hoping she could get some sleep before her alarm sounded. After two hours of listening to the clock ticking, she got out of bed and began preparing herself for another crazy day.

Lissy took one look at her and said, "Oh, honey, you look like the prom queen's morning after."

"Thanks a bunch," answered Molly, but she gratefully accepted a large steaming mocha. "Mmm, this is the solution to every problem. You know, I haven't been up all night, but it feels like it… and apparently looks like it. Did you hear what happened to the nurse's aide?"

"Sure did," said Lissy, but gestured for Molly to wait. When a lingering customer finally wandered out, she leaned over and said, "Had most of the police force here first thing. It was all they could talk about. Seem to be evenly split as to whether it was suicide or accidental overdose. A couple of the younger ones were skeptical, though. Said they had experience with junkies and weren't buying the suicide thing, and they also had some questions about it being an accidental overdose. They said that usually happened when extra pure stuff, or maybe stuff that wasn't properly cut, made it to the street. When that happens there are usually a number of deaths, not just one. They'd really like to find the missing boyfriend."

As a couple of new customers walked in, Lissy handed her a freshly baked cranberry muffin, and quickly added, "Anyway, they talked about the car they found in the garage and how it looked like the same one that almost hit you, so expect a call."

Molly nodded and wandered over to her usual table. She had almost finished her muffin and was valiantly trying to talk herself out of another one, when Quinn came rushing in.

"Molly, I just got a call from Lentz. He's at the hospital."

"Lucinda," she said, suddenly remembering her dream. "Oh, no, something has happened!" She jumped up and headed for the door.

"No, no... calm down, it was good news." Quinn gently placed his hands on her shoulders. "She's awake. Well, actually, she's asleep, but she came out of her coma and spoke to Cheryl. They almost lost her early this morning. Her heart stopped and they kept trying to bring her back. They were almost ready to give up when she opened her eyes. She opened her eyes and told Cheryl that she wasn't done yet. The hospital staff was amazed. They were reluctant to use the word "miracle," but Cheryl told Lentz that's exactly what it was."

Molly seemed to collapse into his arms and then leaned in to embrace him. "Thank you, oh, thank you," she whispered. Then she dropped back in her chair and wept openly, in both relief and joy.

When she had composed herself, Quinn told her that Lucinda was still dozing off and on, but that Lentz was at her bedside nonstop, so she decided to let them have their time together. Later, after her mother's respiratory therapy session, she would stop by. She and Lucinda had a lot to talk about... and they had a major butt-kicking to plan.

So, the old gal pulled through after all. Gossip traveled faster than the speed of light in this burg. Feeling strangely ambivalent about the news, the killer piled bags of Halloween candy into a shopping cart, and then moved on to the frozen food aisle. *No worries... she doesn't really know anything.* The killer amused other shoppers by performing a bossa-nova to "The Girl from Ipanema" Muzak that was drifting through the store.

Next step... do nothing; just patiently wait and see what happens. The nurse's aide was deceased, her charming boyfriend was "missing," and the hit and run vehicle was tied to them. The killer smiled winningly at the check-out girl. *What a perfect dead end.*

Chapter Thirty Seven

Quinn had some spare time, since Molly was tending to her mother and Lentz was tending to Lucinda, and he used it wisely. Back at the cabin, after his brief visit to Strange Brew, he read a preliminary report that had come back on the mysterious tablets they had gotten from Cheryl. It seemed that the base ingredient was an alkaloid found in a plant commonly called water hemlock. The plant was found throughout the United States and was easily identifiable. Although not as deadly as one of its cousins, poison hemlock, water hemlock was still considered very dangerous. Ingestion of even small amounts of the plant had been known to cause seizures, as well as nausea, vomiting, abdominal pain, tremors, confusion, and oftentimes death. For those who survived, recovery was usually complete. But, depending upon how much was ingested, death was a real possibility. The lab reported that two of those tablets represented a lethal dose for a healthy adult. One would have done it for a child, elderly person, or someone in poor health. Quinn's investigator friend had added that almost anyone with backwoods training could have located the plants, but that processing the poison was another matter entirely. Even making the tablets was a skill usually limited to either pharmaceutical professionals or drug dealers.

Truly, the fact that she was still alive attested to Lucinda's strength. Quinn remembered that the onset of her symptoms began about a year ago and made a mental note to suggest to Lentz that all foodstuffs and medicines in her house be removed and, if not tested, then destroyed. In fact, if they could find out how she had originally been exposed to the poison, they may have a clue as to who delivered it. He shook his head. It was a faint hope, but a hope nonetheless. He also made a mental note to find out who Lucinda had confided in about her suspicions a year ago. She had said or done something that made someone nervous enough to up their game. That "someone" was very clever and very cruel... and very, very dangerous.

The analysis from the security company had yielded nothing new and had, in fact, determined that the threat assessment to Molly was quite low. Given all that had happened recently, Quinn felt deep down that the opposite was true and extended his surveillance and protection agreement indefinitely. He also requested, since Hickok was such a small town, that new operatives be rotated in so that no one became unduly suspicious. With what he was paying them, they were more than happy to oblige.

Finally, having decided that he needed a break, Quinn threw on a jacket and headed outside, intending to take a quick walk around the small lake that bordered the cabin. As he stepped off the porch, he glanced up the driveway and then stopped. There was a dark blue car with tinted windows idling on the road in front of the driveway. Just such a car had been mentioned in a couple of the security reports, and Quinn thought it was too much of a coincidence to be ignored. Rather than going off down the path to the lake, he jogged over to his car, got in and quickly took off down the long driveway to the main road. The sedan moved forward and then flipped a U in front of the driveway and headed back in the direction of town. Quinn turned onto the highway and followed, but the driver of the blue sedan increased speed and kept far enough ahead that the license plate remained unreadable. Quinn hit the gas but the other driver seemed to anticipate pursuit and did the same thing. Just as they hit the city limits, the sedan veered off recklessly into a residential neighborhood. Seeing a police car in the oncoming lane, Quinn barely managed to slow down to the speed limit, and when he was finally able to make a left turn the other vehicle had disappeared.

Feeling frustrated, he decided to go back to Strange Brew. Even though he hoped for sympathy and moral support, he was surprised to realize that he actually looked forward to the ridicule and abuse he was likely to receive from Lissy.

Quinn walked through the door of the coffee shop, but before he could even say a word, Lissy handed him a mop and a bucket.

"What on earth?" Pretty much everything within a five-foot radius of the counter was covered with a foamy glop, featuring chunks of what he hoped was fruit. There was what looked like chunks of pineapple sliding down the side of the counter in the ooze.

Lissy aimed a fierce look in his direction. "Don't say a word... I mean it, Mister. Let's just say my experiment with a coco-loco tropical smoothie was not a success and leave it at that."

Quinn stifled a laugh. "Okay, then," he said, looking at the lumpy ooze. "But that had better be banana or no deal." He dutifully dipped the mop in the bucket and began to clean up.

Later, when every surface had been wiped down and the floor was no longer a sticky mess, Lissy handed him a tall coconut latte. "That's as close to tropical as it's gonna get today," she said, as she plopped back onto her stool. "I think I'll let my creative genius have the rest of the day off."

Quinn sat at the counter, on a freshly cleaned stool. The odd thought occurred to him that before today, he had never before used a mop. How strange his life had suddenly become. Sipping his latte, he asked Lissy if she knew anyone who drove a dark blue sedan with tinted windows.

She frowned thoughtfully for a moment. "Ya know, I might know the one you mean. Seen it around lately… just in the past few weeks. But with those tinted windows I could never see the driver. Never did like tinted windows… it makes me wonder what they're doin in there, if you know what I mean."

Quinn laughed, "Yeah, I know exactly what you mean. Too bad I'm not an expert on American cars. Looked like an older model to me, and it was pretty good-sized, compared to British cars."

Lissy looked at him like he was from outer space. "Well, honey, if we're talkin' about the same car, let me give you a lesson. It was a Lincoln Town Car, mint condition, 1993-1995."

Quinn's jaw dropped. "Oh, great and powerful Java Queen, is there anything you don't know?"

"Well, duh," she answered. "I don't know who's drivin' the thing."

At that moment Lentz walked through the door. He looked both tired and happy.

"Hey, Crewcut," Lissy called. "You know who drives a 1994-ish dark blue Lincoln Town Car with tinted windows?"

Lentz stopped in front of the counter. He had an odd look on his face. "Well, I know who used to drive one." He looked from Lissy to Quinn.

"Well, spill it, tough guy," Lissy urged.

"Lucinda... It was Lucinda's."

"Hey, woman," Molly said, planting a light kiss on Lucinda's brow. Her eyes fluttered open; she smiled slightly, and whispered, "Back atcha." Then she drifted off again.

Humming happily, Molly arranged a new stack of CD's on the bedside table, an eclectic assortment of music she thought her friend might appreciate as she recovered. Cheryl had caught up with her in the hallway and told her that Lucinda was still very tired and more than a little confused about what had happened to her. It would probably be a while before she was able to sustain even a short conversation. Between the seizures and the other toxic effects of the poison she had ingested, she was lucky to be alive, but Cheryl warned that it may be awhile before her mind was completely clear. It was likely, even probable, that she would never remember the time right around this last episode. It looked like their "chat" would have to wait, but that was okay. Right now, Molly was just grateful that her friend was still among the living.

Cheryl had added in a whisper that the hospital administration was hemming and hawing about the results of their drug analysis, calling it inconclusive, but that everyone knew there had been an attempt on Lucinda's life and they were all watching her like a hawk. "As long as she's here," Cheryl said, with fire in her eyes, "She'll be protected." Molly believed it. Then Cheryl's ever-present beeper went off, and she gave Molly a quick hug before trotting off to the next emergency.

As she headed back to her car, she saw Preston Locke, and his friend Curt Golden, going into the hospital. They waved to her and she waved back. It was all very civil, but still left her feeling just a bit uncomfortable.

After the wonderful news about Lucinda, the rest of Molly's morning had been fairly uneventful. When she picked her mother up, she found the woman ready to go and waiting at the door. She was sporting a new purse; in Molly's opinion, the ugliest purse she had ever seen. "Wow Mom," that's some dandy handbag you've got."

The woman stroked it lovingly and beamed. "Well, I confided in Dick that you were always mocking my brown purse, so he went to Save-Mart and bought this for me." She struck a funny fashion-model pose. "I told him my favorite colors were orange and green... and look! He found a purse with both colors in it."

"Orange and green paisley..." Molly whistled appreciatively. "It just doesn't get any better than that."

"Exactly," agreed the older woman happily.

Her mother was in such a great mood, that Molly risked having a chat about her attitude during respiratory therapy, taking care to phrase it in such a way that her mother did not feel criticized. Apparently, it paid off because the young technician gave Molly a thumbs up after the session. He also asked the older woman where she got the great "retro" purse, and she proudly told him her "boyfriend" had given it to her. Molly had to smile at the idea of her mother having a boyfriend. She wondered if she should break it to her siblings or... maybe more fun to let them find out for themselves.

She took her back up to the house, fixed them both a quick lunch, and then sat through a couple of soap operas. Her mother held the purse firmly on her lap the whole time.

"You know, Mom," said Molly. "Your next therapy session isn't until next week, and I'm going to be gone a few days. I have some business to take care of back in Monroe, and I really need to be home for

Halloween. An empty house is just asking for a good egging. You gonna be okay?"

"Well, of course," the woman replied primly. "Dick will be around if I need anything. Oh, I forgot to tell you he was going to take me to the Rotary Club's Annual Haunted House and then to the Sundae Best for ice cream." She fanned herself coyly. "Honestly, I feel like a young girl again." She had to admit that her mother did look more animated and happy than she had seemed in a long, long time… maybe ever. And her budding romance took her mind off such things as fixing her daughter up with Preston Locke. Molly sent Dick a big mental "thank you," then gave her mother a hug and told her to stay out of trouble.

Strange Brew was a hive of activity, when Molly walked through the door. The local quilting group had taken up residence at the large table in the center of the room, and they were busy doing anything but quilting. An officious older woman was trying to make eye contact with Lissy and was loudly chortling demands for a new round of coffee drinks for her "girls." Sensing imminent violence from the expression on Lissy's face, Molly quickly jumped in, offering to take the orders and bring the drinks to the table.

As she stood at the counter, waiting for the complicated and, at least to Molly, confusing order, she glanced back to where Quinn and Lentz were seated. Actually, only Quinn was seated. Lentz was on his phone and was pacing back and forth. Quinn smiled at her, but she thought they both looked a bit tense.

"Sugar-free nonfat mocha with extra whipped cream… my ass," grumbled Lissy. "I'd like to give her a secret ingredient, the pompous old

202

hag." As she said this, Molly noticed she was looking at a mop bucket in the corner that contained the remains of something unpleasant.

"Just say no to the bucket," whispered Molly. "Think happy thoughts."

"Okay," Lissy answered, reluctantly. "But my happy thought involves watching that old biddy slurping away at the contents of the mop bucket, with extra whipped cream, of course." She got a far-away look in her eyes and smiled. "Okay, better now."

Molly delivered the drinks, without receiving so much as a thank you, picked up her own steaming drink, and then hurried over to see what was going on with Quinn and Lentz.

Quinn stood as she approached and gave her a warm hug. "Lovely as ever," he said, brushing a stray curl back so he could kiss her forehead.

"Nice," smiled Molly, as she slid into her usual chair. "So, what's going on?"

"Well, this morning I had a close encounter of the weird kind with a dark blue sedan with tinted windows, an older model Lincoln Town Car, according to the Java Queen."

"Oh, now that you mention it, I've seen that car, too… driving past my mother's house and a few times on Main Street. I didn't think anything of it, except that those tinted windows kind of creep me out."

"That seems to be the general consensus," Quinn agreed. "Apparently it looks just like one that Lucinda used to own and we don't think it's a coincidence. Lentz is working his magic with the police department to track down ownership and registration."

"Before he gets off the phone, I need to tell you I'm going up to Monroe for a few days. My mother doesn't have therapy again until next week, and I need to take care of some business at home. And, to be honest, I want to be there for Halloween. I have this great old house and I usually get trick-or-treaters from all over town." Molly noted that Quinn looked absolutely crestfallen.

At that moment, Lentz pulled out a chair and plopped down. "Another dead lead," he said, tossing his phone on the table. "Looks like the car was purchased from a retired couple in Fremont just a couple of months ago. They bought it, way back when, from a dealer here in Hickok, who had taken it in as a trade from Lucinda. I talked to the woman and she said it was all kinda funny. They hadn't even thought about selling it, but one day some fella knocked on the door and asked if he could buy it... offered them way more than it was worth. They thought he was kidding, but he had the cash with him, so they signed the title and got it notarized. He drove off with it that very same day. Said he was a young fella. She had a funny feeling about the guy, because he had an earring and a ponytail, but his money was good."

Lentz continued. "I got pretty excited, thinking maybe we finally caught a break. But it turns out that the car is registered to Leonard Pantoni, our dead girl's missing boyfriend." He pounded the table in frustration, causing the leader of the quilting gang to send a disapproving look his way. He gave it right back to her until she made an odd harrumphing noise and turned away.

Molly stifled a grin, but when she turned back to the table everyone looked so tired and so serious. She took a deep breath and said, "Look, I have to be gone for a few days, so I suggest we take a step back and let things percolate. Lucinda will be safe as long as she's in the hospital and I think the rest of us might need a break... I know I do. Whatever we're missing is probably right in front of us, but we're too deeply involved to see it. So... I vote we meet back here on Tuesday and compare notes."

Lentz was silent for a moment, then slowly nodded. "Maybe you're right, young lady. Jasper's getting so lonely, he's threatening to take off with some frisky she-wolf, and I gotta top up my winter woodpile." It went without saying that he would be spending the rest of the time with Lucinda.

Quinn didn't look too happy, but he agreed that he should probably get some actual work done while he was here.

As she said her goodbyes to Lissy, the quilting woman began demanding a refill, and she saw her friend's eyes stray once more to the mop bucket. Molly laughed out loud, but walked through the door and didn't look back.

Chapter Thirty Nine

The thought occurred to Lucinda that she was back, but "from where," she wondered. Her mind seemed a jumble of chaotic images and whenever she tried to focus on one, it drifted away... and remained just out of her reach.

She opened her eyes, and there was Eric, dozing in the chair next to her bed. He was holding her hand firmly, though, even in sleep. Lucinda smiled. The afternoon light filtered through the windows, and she watched as golden leaves fell from the big cottonwood tree outside. It was late autumn, and she realized with surprise that she loved this time of year. Another revelation.

She didn't know what day it was, couldn't remember her address, or even her age. But she wasn't worried. Things were beginning to come back, and she knew her mind would clear in time. Right now, though, as she began to drift off, she felt a wash of contentment. It was autumn, she was alive, and Eric was holding her hand. Everything else could wait.

Quinn was at a loss. He was restless and agitated, feelings he had managed to avoid quite nicely for most of his adult life. Calm was a state of being that he had worked hard to cultivate and it had served him well in his business dealings. In recent years, though, he had felt himself moving from calm to cold, and he had seen himself described in the press as the "Stone Man," about as feeling as a block of Scottish granite on the shores of the North Sea. At the time, he had been proud of the description, but not now.

He was driving around aimlessly, looking for the mysterious sedan. even though he knew it was probably a lost cause. After Molly left the coffee shop, he and Lentz agreed that given his "chase scene," unless the killer was an idiot, the car would probably either disappear or be found abandoned. Neither one of them thought the killer was an idiot. He also filled Lentz in on what he had learned about the water hemlock poison used first to sicken, and then in an attempt to kill Lucinda.

"Stuff grows all over around here," Lentz said with a sigh. "Anyone with half a brain knows to stay away from it. Some of the Indians even used to dip their arrows with the poison, so that if the arrow didn't kill a fella, he'd a wished it had."

"So, we might be looking for a drug dealer or someone with a medical background, or both." Quinn said, wryly. "Drug dealers probably won't be advertising their professions, but we might think about looking into anyone with a medical background."

"Way ahead of ya, partner. Went over all over the players from Cathy's murder and, with the exception of one kid who became a medic in the Army, nothing else came up. The kid died fifteen years ago in a hit and run. Drug dealers, more likely, but like you said… they don't exactly offer up that information."

Quinn headed down another path of investigation, when Lentz interrupted him.

"You know, old buddy, that pretty gal of yours is right. We're beatin' this thing to death and we need to give it a rest, at least for a few days." He stood up and stretched. "So, I'm gonna go buy some flowers for a pretty gal of my own, and then I'm gonna get some sleep. You can't get very far when you're runnin' on empty."

Tiring of his fruitless search, Quinn pulled into the Save-Mart parking lot to pick up a few things for the weekend. The front of the store was crowded with Halloween merchandise, and it made him wonder if he should pick up candy it case anyone knocked on his door. He didn't know the etiquette, since Halloween was not quite the same on his side of the Atlantic. Lissy had tried to talk him into dressing up and handing out goodies to the trick-or-treaters that would mob Main Street before it was even dark. He told her he would think about it.

Actually, he was thinking about Molly in her big house, answering the door to all manner of whimsically costumed children. He could see how she would love it. He wondered what her costume might be and pictured her opening the door as Glinda the Good Witch, smiling at all of the little Munchkins gathered on her doorstep. He really wished he could be on the receiving end of that smile.

Suddenly, he made a decision, and headed off down the costume aisle. Of what was left… a cheesy Jack Sparrow pirate outfit, a cow suit complete with plastic udders, and a colorful Sponge Bob ensemble made of Styrofoam… nothing fit him, and for that he was eternally grateful. He wasn't sure what to do, but he thought he knew just the person to call. He flipped open his phone and called Strange Brew.

Lissy laughed, when he explained what he planned. "Oh, honey, I love a challenge. Pick up a funnel, grey wig, several feet of dryer venting, work gloves, a jumpsuit, two cans of silver spray paint, canvas shoes, and some chain. We'll improvise the rest. Meet me here before I close tonight and we'll get you costumed up."

"But, but... what am I supposed to be?"

"You're a work in progress, Big Guy. We won't know till we're done." She paused for a moment. "And by the way... this is gonna cost ya big time," she added and then hung up.

Quinn stood blinking for a moment and then hurried to jot down Lissy's shopping list before he forgot anything. Whatever Lissy did to him, he was pretty sure it would be worth it when he knocked on Molly's door and said, Trick or Treat." He was really hoping it would be "treat".

Chapter Forty

Molly woke up feeling refreshed and happy. After arriving in Monroe the night before, she had gone to bed early and didn't remember a thing after laying her head on the pillow. She hadn't realized just how weary she was, both mentally and physically. She let herself stay in bed after waking, an indulgence she seldom allowed, and reveled in the warm morning light that washed over her. Finally, stretching like a cat, she got up, threw on an old sloppy bathrobe and padded through her big empty house. On mornings like this, she really loved her home... the tidy, colorful rooms, the smell of freshly ground coffee, and the muffled sounds of the neighborhood... all adding up to a sense of security and belonging.

But other times, especially at night, she realized it was too big and too empty. Her boys would continue to visit during holidays, and sometimes for no reason at all, but the dynamic had changed and they all knew there was no going home. Sighing, she added "call realtor" to her to-do list. Then, afraid that if too much time passed she might talk herself out of it; she went ahead and called the realtor, who sounded very excited and promised to stop by later in the afternoon. "Change is good... change is good..." she chanted and, although it was scary, she knew she was ready for it.

After giving the house a once over, she took a quick shower, then called a couple of neighborhood kids to come over and tackle the ever-increasing leaf pile that was her yard. She and her boys used to take care of it, making it into a game, but it was a huge job and right now, time was of the essence. She had once made the mistake of waiting until after an early snow, and raking the ordinarily fluffy dry leaves had become more like shoveling wet cement. As soon as they arrived, she hopped in the car to make a candy run and check the mail.

Monroe was actually a nice enough small town, although small was the keyword, and while it had been a relatively safe place to raise kids, there wasn't much for Molly there. She knew most everybody in town, but after all these years was still considered an outsider. She had many acquaintances and a few friends, for the most part outsiders like her, but had never been allowed into what she thought of as the inner circle. That was reserved for those whose great-grandparents were buried in the cemetery on the outskirts, whose grandparents had owned and operated the big ranches that surrounded the town, and whose parents were immortalized in old sports photos on the wall of the newly expanded high school.

It was hard to compete with history but, deep down, Molly was glad not to be trapped in a system that honored the past, yet refused to learn from its mistakes. She smiled sadly when she realized that saying goodbye to Monroe wouldn't be that difficult.

It being Halloween day, the candy selection was pretty picked over, but she managed to load her cart up with what she thought she might need. Her house was close to the edge of the older part of town. Only a block away, began a neighborhood featuring smaller, mid-century ranch style homes, and a few blocks past that, towards the city limits, were the bigger more modern homes. Her location guaranteed that she got children from all three neighborhoods… that plus the fact that she liked to dress up in her own crazy costumes, and was known for being overly generous with candy. Molly loved Halloween… it was actually right up there with Christmas as her favorite holiday.

Piling candy into the huge bowl that she kept on the table by the front door, she headed down to the basement to put together an impromptu costume. She had a thing about dressing up… the high school drama coaches had loved her, calling her basement their one-stop costume shop. She was the go-to girl for such things as old fashioned sequined gowns, zoot-suits, wigs of all types, and a variety of masks and make-up. After giving it some thought, she decided upon a "Cinderella in Rags meets Zombie Queen" theme, and was pleased that all of the odd bits and pieces came together for a very interesting look. The raggedy clothing was a bit whimsical but worked well with the white makeup and dark circles under her eyes. She teased her hair into a study of unkempt corkscrews, and finished it off with a child's plastic tiara and a dash of bright red lipstick. "Lovely, Dahling," she said, blowing a kiss to her reflection in the full-length mirror.

The doorbell rang, surprising her. "A bit early for the greedy goblins," she murmured, as she hurried up the stairs. She grabbed the candy bowl and swung open the door, expecting to see the first of the trick-or-treaters but, instead, came face to face with Peggy Gamble, the town's realtor extraordinaire and most prolific gossip. She was surprised, but not as surprised as Peggy.

There was a moment of shocked silence, and then, "Oh, aah… Molly, dear. You look, aah… good. Is this a bad time?"

"No, it's a great time, Peggy… I'm just getting ready for Halloween. Come on in." She set the candy back on the table and urged the woman inside.

"Oh, right, Halloween," Peggy visibly relaxed and stepped through the door. "I forgot that you always get somewhat, aah… enthusiastic about this time of year."

Before Molly could say anything else, the woman pushed past her and wandered from room to room making notes and commenting on her eclectic taste in decorating. The woman said "eclectic" like it left a bad taste in her mouth, and Molly had to work hard to keep from saying something she might regret.

Eventually, after completing her self-guided tour, Peggy sat primly on the edge of an overstuffed sofa in the front room. "Being something of a design expert myself, I would normally recommend that you get rid of all of this, aah… stuff, before you even think about showing the house," she said waving vaguely around the room. Molly felt her jaw jut out, ever so slightly. "But, lucky for you, it just so happens that I have a waiting list of people who have contacted me over the last few years, asking that they be informed immediately if your house ever goes on the market."

Molly blinked in surprise.

Peggy brought out her calculator, ran some numbers, and then gave Molly a selling price that surprised her even more. "If you agree to that starting price, I'll put together the paperwork and be in touch. If we play our cards right, dear, we may even end up with a bidding war." The woman's eyes gleamed at the thought.

"Wow," thought Molly, after Peggy left. "This is really happening…"

But the doorbell rang again, and this time she was greeted by the first trick-or-treater of the day, a shy toddler wearing a lady-bug costume over a puffy coat, firmly holding on to her daddy's leg. "Tweat," she whispered, holding out an orange plastic pumpkin.

Molly smiled, "You are just too cute! Take two pieces, baby bug." The first wave usually consisted of the tiny ones, maybe even first-timers, with their parents. The next wave, when it was beginning to get dark, was groups of older children, with a parent or two waiting vigilantly at the sidewalk or, if the weather was bad, driving slowly down the street and idling in front of each house.

When it began to get late, it was down to the older kids, middle school and even some high schoolers. Molly liked these best because their costumes were usually self-made, oftentimes funny, and occasionally even brilliant. She also liked to give them a hard time and engage in good-natured banter. Secretly, she had to admit that they reminded her of her boys. One particularly persistent group had been to her door three times now, swapping costumes between them and concocting wild stories each time. They were a lot of fun, but the game was getting old, so when the bell rang again she swung the door open, ready to call a timeout.

But what stood on her doorstep defied imagination. It was an enormous… what, robot? Space creature? No, it was more like the Tin Man from the Wizard of Oz. And as she stared, open mouthed, it held out a large silver-gloved hand and said, "Trick or Treat?"

It was Quinn, wearing metallic spray painted clothing, silver theatrical makeup, a gray wig, and a funnel on his head. He looked about as uncomfortable as a man could possibly look.

Molly let him squirm for a few moments more, and then hoping his paint was dry, gave him a big hug and pulled him into the house. "Well, if you're looking for a heart, I'm not exactly the great and powerful Wizard of Oz," she said, with a dazzling smile.

"Actually, I did have a heart but lost it to a beautiful fairytale zombie princess. I was hoping you could help me find her."

"Fairytale zombie princess... Hmmm... I'll have to ask around. But in the meantime, you can stick around and help me answer the door and chase away the hooligans." Molly looked at him seriously, and added softly, "Quinn, I'm so glad you're here. This is the best treat ever!"

Quinn grinned so hugely, it made his makeup crack. Molly thought she had never seen anything so sweet.

Halloween was nearly over, the doorbell had long since stopped ringing, and the killer happily basked in the success of the evening. So many adorable rug rats; the girls dressed as fairies, and mermaids, and princesses... the boys as hobos, and pirates and superheroes, with their parents beaming proudly a few feet away. Each child was asked to explain his or her costume, and no treats were given without a please and thank you, but if the kiddies wanted candy they learned to play by the rules. And, of course, no worries about late-night pranks... even the most mischievous of adolescents had somehow intuited that it would be a very bad idea to toilet-paper or egg this particular house.

Finally, after turning off the porch light, blowing out the sputtering jack-o-lanterns, and locking the front door, the killer paused at the full-length mirror in the hall to indulge in a well-earned moment of self-admiration. *What a marvelous costume... it was custom designed, exquisitely detailed, and painstakingly sewn by hand. And so worth the outrageous expense... worth every penny, yes indeed.*

Remembering the way that the children's eyes had widened in alarm when the door opened, brought a smile. Some had backed away, and a few had even refused to come any closer. Their loss, the poor poppets. This year, however, a few of the parents had also flinched.

But despite whatever went on in their safe, sheltered minds, they would eventually shake their heads and dismiss their apprehensions in favor of common sense. The killer laughed, knowing that none of them would be able to articulate their sense of unease. *After all, what could possibly be more innocent than a clown?*

Chapter Forty One

Quinn found himself singing along with a country CD he had picked up in a convenience store in Monroe, where he filled his car with gas for the return trip to Hickok. *What in the world brought that on?* He had never been an impulse shopper, nor had he ever had the slightest interest in country music, but there it was, twanging away on his car stereo. And he liked it!

Thinking about music in general, Quinn realized that was one area in which his education was sorely lacking. Raised in an atmosphere of stuffy upper class silence, time-tested church hymns were obediently mouthed each Sunday, and sedate string quartets were tolerated for those functions that might require such a thing. Other than that, the general rule of his childhood home was quiet. When he was small, Quinn could remember his mother singing nonsense ditties and sometimes even crooning away to a current love song on the cook's radio in the kitchen, but eventually that stopped, leaving nothing but the creaking of the old building and the ticking of the ancient grandfather clock in the hallway.

It made him suddenly feel sad, as if he had missed something important. In truth, he had missed many important things. He had never had a best buddy, an overnight, or a camping trip. He had never had a pet or even an imaginary friend. The one time he had worked up enough courage to complain to his stern father, the man was dismissive and quick to point out that Quinn had everything a young man could need. And he supposed it was true in a way, but needing and wanting are two different things. He sighed, pulling his thoughts back to the present.

Molly... now that was a thought worth dwelling upon. He would forever treasure the look on her face when she opened the door, looking like a rag-tag queen of the night, and realized that Quinn had made an enormous fool of himself just for her. It was an honest expression of joy, with just the right amount of humor mixed in, and he was almost positive that her eyes had misted up just a bit.

He had arrived there later than anticipated, since Lissy had indeed charged a fee for costume design. He thought she was kidding, but no... Quinn was put to work handing out candy to the horde of Main Street trick-or-treaters that surged through Strange Brew until Lissy flipped the signed to "closed," and turned off the lights. The kids seemed to love him, as did the parents, and he actually had a good time, but he would never admit it to Lissy.

After she closed, Lissy handed him a double Macchiato in a to-go cup, gave him directions to Molly's house, and then told him to hang a left onto the interstate and drive for two hours. She also told him he had better get a move on if he wanted to get there before Molly turned off her porch light. "No porch light, no treat," she said raising one eyebrow meaningfully.

And he did just that. Without bothering to change clothes, he drove straight to Monroe, eliciting many interested looks as he drove through the small towns and passed other vehicles. Once, he even forgot he was costumed, until an activity bus filled with middle-schoolers overtook his vehicle, children hanging out the windows shouting, "Hey,

Tin Man, you're not in Kansas anymore!" He was enjoying himself immensely.

He helped Molly take care of the last of the Halloween stragglers, and then she turned off the porch light, made a pot of herbal tea, put on soft music, and they talked for hours. Molly's home was warm, comfortable, and inviting, and he loved the colors and the successful mix of styles. Quinn realized he had never before felt so utterly at ease.

Finally, not wanting to fuel the gossip machine in Molly's town, Quinn kissed her goodnight and then checked into the local motel, causing quite a stir with the elderly couple who ran the establishment. They grudgingly took his money, but asked that he not get silver spray paint on the furniture. Again having forgotten he was in costume, he sheepishly promised them he would shower and put the painted clothes in the trunk of his car. Luckily, he always traveled with a set of site inspection clothes, or he would have been in a bind.

Breakfast had been an absolute riot. Again, for the sake of propriety, they met at a small, but very busy restaurant, called The Chitchat. The woman who brought their menus, Fern, was short, wide, and had the voice of a long haul trucker. Her husband, who waved to Molly from the kitchen, was named Spud, and had the thin, wiry build of a circus acrobat.

Quinn admitted he was hungry, and Molly suggested he get the chicken fried steak breakfast. When it arrived it actually hung over the plate and even Quinn was not sure he could do it justice. But he did and he enjoyed every bite, although he thought he might never have to eat again.

As they were finishing up their coffee, a woman who had been staring in their direction since they arrived, finally came over to the table, introducing herself as Peggy Gamble, Molly's realtor.

"Realtor?" Quinn asked Molly. "You're selling some property?"

"Oh, well… The boys are in college and the house is so big… I'm thinking about downsizing," she glanced at Quinn.

"Molly, dear," said the realtor. "Now I understand the reason for your sudden change of heart." She was looking straight at Quinn, with a smug smile on her face. "I'll get the paperwork to you right way. You two kids be good," she added with a smirk as she hurried back to the table to pass on her newly acquired information.

Molly sighed. "So much for my spotless reputation. I get the feeling that she's been waiting for this moment for years. I guess if I'm going to give them something to talk about, I might as well have fun in the process." With no warning, she leaned over the table and gave him a huge, noisy kiss.

Quinn glanced over to see the shocked expression on Peggy Gamble's face, then threw some money on the table, said goodbye to Fern and Spud, and dragged Molly, laughing, out the door. They said goodbye and kissed again in the parking lot, clearly visible through the plate glass windows. Then Quinn got in his car and headed back to Hickok to actually get some work done. In the rearview mirror, he saw Molly, still standing in front of the building, blowing kisses until he turned the corner. He marveled at her courage, thinking that she might be the one person he knew that could have stood up to his father. He smiled at the thought, and then laughed aloud.

Now, still an hour from Hickock, he played the CD again, cranked up the volume, and sang along loudly with "Ah dreamed ah was there in Hillbilly Heaven…"

Chapter Forty Two

Within half an hour of leaving the Chitchat, Molly was pretty sure that news of her exciting new romance was all over town. The phone was ringing as she walked through the door and she noticed that there were four messages on the machine. *Wow,* she thought, *Wallflower to Belle of the Ball in minutes flat.* She let the machine pick up the call, but listened as one of her former work associates, a brassy woman with a fondness for partying, but who had never once invited Molly to join her, called to "touch base" and see what was new in Molly's life. *Yeah, I'll get right on that,* she thought wryly, shaking her head. The phone continued to ring about every fifteen minutes.

Finally, having reached the upper limit of her patience, she re-recorded her voicemail message, saying, "Hi this is Molly. Yes, I have a boyfriend. No, I don't want to talk about it. If you want to discuss something other than my social life, call me on my cell, otherwise have a nice day." She turned off the ringer, fired up her laptop, and began preparing for a telephone interview she had scheduled for the first thing Monday morning. She was nervous about this particular project, not because she doubted her skills, but because it was a very large company and it functioned (or not) from a level of bureaucracy she found intimidating. She was used to a certain amount of hoop-jumping, feather-smoothing, and hand-holding, but for this project she would need to up her game to a place that was well outside the comfort zone. It occurred to her that she could talk to Quinn about it, but decided to do that only as a last resort. She wanted her accomplishments to be her own and she thought that her intrepid Scot could probably afford to buy the company, maybe even owned it already, and she was having trouble getting her head around that kind of wealth. Squaring her shoulders, she took a deep breath and jumped into her work.

A couple of hours later, when she came up for air and a nice cup of tea, her cell phone rang. "Uh, Mom?" It was Alex, and his voice sounded strange. "I, uh, just called the home phone and got this crazy message. What's the deal?"

"Oh, son, why did you call the home phone... you always call the cell!"

"Well, my friend Derek got a call from his mom in Monroe, who wanted him to get all the details from me about your new boyfriend. She told him there was a message on the answering machine at the house." There was a long pause... "So...?"

Molly swallowed. "Oh Alex, I meant to tell you and your brother before the whole town knew, but... well, you know how fast news spreads in Monroe." She paused to gather her thoughts. "I met this man while I was down taking care of your grandmother... actually, I ran into him with a shopping cart, but I like him. I like him a lot. His name is Quinn and he's from Scotland. We've only had coffee together a few times and a couple of dinners, but we get along so well. And, in spite of the shopping cart thing, I think he really likes me, too. He dressed up as the Tin Man and surprised me on Halloween, and then we went to breakfast in town... Uh, I mean we met for breakfast... you know, in separate cars, but, anyway, that's what all the fuss is about."

There was a momentary silence on the other end of the line, and then, "Well, Mom, all I can say is… it's about time!" He laughed, "You don't have to explain yourself to me or anybody else. I just have two questions… is he good enough for you, and when do we meet him?"

Molly blew out the breath she had been holding and smiled. "Thanks, son… I needed that. I think he just might be the one, and I'll try to get him up here for Thanksgiving so he can meet the other men in my life. Then, you can decide for yourselves whether or not he passes inspection."

"Oh, and I'll invent some crazy story for Derek to tell his mother… maybe something involving alien abduction or spontaneous combustion, and we'll see how long it takes to get back to you." They both laughed at the thought. "Love you, Mom."

"Love you, too, son." She ended the call, thinking about how lucky she was. The cell rang again, and this time it was her younger son, Jack. She took a sip of tea, then answered the call and proceeded to tell him the happy news. He was just as supportive as his brother had been, and when the call ended Molly marveled at what great people her sons had become.

She spent the rest of the day preparing for her interview, ducking out long enough to get herself a coffee and pick up a few groceries, and then settled in for a long, quiet evening. She left the telephone ringer off, knowing that if it was anything important, she could be reached through her cell, but chuckled when she saw that she had seventeen messages waiting. "Let 'em stew."

Monday morning came early. Nervous about the scheduled interview, she was up before sunrise, researching innovations and rehearsing answers to questions she might be asked. When the call finally came, twenty minutes late, she sat up straight, smiled into the phone and endured the forty-five minute interrogation as gracefully as possible. After the call ended, she sighed in relief. She felt it had gone very well, but knew better than to count on a certain outcome, when six different managers had to agree with each other in order for that to happen. Mentally crossing her fingers and toes, she finished packing up and readying the house for her return to Hickok.

Thinking about Quinn, she threw in a couple of her nicer sweaters, two long skirts, and a pair of boots she hadn't worn in several years. She might have to relearn how to walk around in the modest heels, but they just might come in handy. *You never know...* she thought, humming *'These Boots Are Made for Walking'*.

Finally, convinced she had not forgotten anything, she loaded up the car and made a last-minute house inspection to make sure toilets were flushed and windows were closed. As she finished up, the doorbell rang and she found Peggy Gamble on her front step, with a sheaf of papers and a hungry expression.

"Hi, Peggy... I'm just heading out... is this something that can wait?" "Well, Molly, dear, this really is very urgent. I have the paperwork for your listing and I need you to go over it right now, and sign it so we can get the house on the market as soon as possible." She shoved a manila folder towards Molly but kept looking past her into the house, presumably hoping to spot Quinn.

Suddenly realizing that she had forgotten to mention to her sons that she was thinking about selling the house, Molly thought for a moment.

Oh, and by the way, boys, I'm selling your childhood home... just didn't seem to play well, and she knew she needed to think things out better.

"Tell you what, Peggy, I'll take the paperwork, look it over, and get back to you when I return to Monroe." The woman's eyebrows shot straight up and her mouth formed a shocked "O". It was obvious that Peggy Gamble was not used to being put off. "Not sure when that will be, though," she added, taking the folder.

"Well, gotta go, but I'll be in touch just as soon as possible." Shouldering her bag and picking up her computer case, she stepped through the door, locking it behind her.

"But, but I, but..." sputtered the woman as she followed her down the steps, but Molly waved to her gaily, climbed into her car, and headed for Hickok, a place she was once more beginning to think of as home.

Chapter Forty Three

She was sitting in Eric's truck, eyes closed, swaying to '*Little Runaway*,' on the radio. What a nice dream... no, not a dream. Lucinda opened her eyes and was disoriented for a moment, but soon remembered that she was in the hospital, after having had a very close call with death. '*Little Runaway*,' ended, and '*Teen Angel*' began playing softly... one of the CDs that Molly had left on the bedside table. She glanced around the room, noting the mid-afternoon slant of sunlight coming in through the windows. Eric was sitting in the chair next to her bed, going through a stack of papers. He had his cheaters on and was scowling, intent upon whatever it was he was reading. She thought he had never looked better. She gently placed her hand on his shoulder, and he looked up at her with a start.

"Well, hello pretty lady," he said with a grin. "You gonna ever drag your lazy ass out of bed?"

"Put a sock in it, cowboy," she laughed. "I do what I please."

He stood up and gallantly kissed her hand. "My lady, your wish is my command. Whose sock did you have in mind?"

"I'll give the matter serious consideration," she answered haughtily. She had never seen him so playful and she found it endearing. "You know, things are coming back a bit at a time, but I still have big blanks. You said you had some questions for me; I may not have the answers yet, but at least thinking about them would give me something to do while my "lazy ass" is stuck in bed."

"Okay," he said hesitantly. "We'll begin with one and see how it goes." He rifled through his stack until he came to a photocopy of one of the old crime scene photos, and then held it out to her.

Lucinda flinched, afraid for a moment that it was one of those nightmare images of her daughter, but when she realized it was a picture of her kitchen counter, she was bewildered.

"Molly had a question about the flowers in the water glass. She didn't think they belonged. We wondered if you remembered them being there that day before you left for the charity dinner."

"Oh, my," said Lucinda, casting her thoughts back to that horrible night. "You know, I don't remember seeing them before we left. If I had, I'm sure I would have asked Cathy where they came from and I probably would have put them in a vase." She looked at Lentz quizzically.

"Molly was thinkin' that maybe some friend of Cathy's... maybe even a wanna-be boyfriend... brought them over after you left. If that's true, then knowing who that friend was might give us some answers."

Lucinda frowned. "I was such an idiot to play silly rhyming games with Molly about what I knew. I was still out of it from being sick before, and I didn't know who to trust, but I should have just come right out and told her... about... something... it was something important... Damn! I just can't remember!"

"Hey, hey," Eric shushed her and stroked her hand. "It'll come, and in the meantime we have plenty to keep us busy."

"Oh, Eric, I'm so lucky to have you."

"Luck had nothing to do with it, pretty lady… it was always a sure thing."

Chapter Forty Four

When Molly dropped in she found her mother elbow deep in sticky dough, flour everywhere. "Thought I'd get a jump on my holiday baking," the woman chirped.

"Mom, the closest you get to baking is eating cookie dough ice cream straight out of the tub. You haven't made anything from scratch in twenty years."

Now that she thought about it, Molly couldn't actually remember her mother doing much cooking at all. The woman was a child of the depression, when meals were hard work and took a lot of preparation and imagination. She had decided, somewhere along the way, that new was better than old and she delighted in all things quick and easy; rarely serving anything that didn't come out of a can, box, or the frozen food section of the grocery store. Molly remembered meals of boxed macaroni and cheese so orange that it seemed to glow, with potato chips on the side, followed by bright red gelatin and canned fruit cocktail for dessert. And then there was her mother's famous "Hawaiian Delight," which consisted of fried Spam and canned pineapple chunks, served with margarine slathered white bread, and instant banana pudding for a big finish.

"There," her mother would say, happily. "Every food group and so colorful…"

As a child, Molly remembered pining for such things as apples, carrots, and meat that wasn't cooked to the approximate consistency of shoe leather. But, considering her current healthy eating habits, maybe that hadn't been such a bad thing.

"Here, let me help," said Molly, quickly washing her hands, then checking the recipe in the hopes of figuring out why her mother's cookie dough looked more like wallpaper paste. She made a few adjustments, used educated guesswork, a big dose of common sense, and soon had the sticky mess looking more recognizable. "Not holding my breath, though," she murmured to herself. She set her mother to the task of rolling the dough into balls, flattening them with a sugared glass, and then adding a candied pecan to the middle of each one.

As she got the first batch out of the oven... drum roll, please... she was relieved to see that they looked edible. She carefully lifted a hot cookie from the pan and nibbled the edge. "Divine," she pronounced, popping the rest of it into her mouth.

It took them most of the afternoon to bake the remaining cookies... it was a triple batch, but Molly found herself enjoying the day. The kitchen was warm and cozy, and she and her mother worked with a sense of contentment and quiet rhythm that reminded her of a Norman Rockwell painting.

After the dishes were washed, the cookie jar was filled, and the rest of the surprisingly good cookies were tucked away in the freezer for future use, Molly's mother drifted into the living room to watch an old black and white movie. It had been a nice afternoon, but she had other things to do, so she gave her mother a kiss and reminded her that respiratory therapy was scheduled for Tuesday, bright and early.

As she turned to leave, her mother said, "Oh, honey, I forgot to tell you that I had a nice time at the Haunted House. Dick bought me a caramel apple, but I couldn't figure out a way to take a bite without making a mess of my face. So he started it for me and then finished what was left when I was done. We're kind of a good team," she added, looking at Molly shyly. "I might ask him if he wants to drive me to therapy."

"Well, you go, girl," said Molly with a smile. "Much as I love it, I can't be your unpaid servant forever. It was always the plan that after you got used to the therapy, you would have the Senior Bus take you. But going with Dick is even better. So, I'm all for it. Just let me know when you want to make the switch."

"Well, I'm not quite ready… but soon," the woman said with a coy smile. "I wouldn't want to be too forward and give him the wrong impression."

Molly suppressed a grin, as she stepped through the door. "Yeah, Mom, you wouldn't want him to get the wrong idea." The older woman agreed with a serious nod.

As she drove to the Calamity Jane, she envisioned her mother trying to daintily eat a caramel apple and had to laugh out loud.

Having left her suitcase at the hotel, taking only an overnight bag to Monroe with her, she was bringing back more than she realized and, through careful balancing and sheer luck she managed to get through the lobby without dropping anything. The desk clerk made no effort to help her, but did give her a slight head nod and what could have been a smile. *A definite improvement*, she thought as she staggered up the stairs. *I think he likes me.*

Molly fumbled with the key and swung the door open with her hip to find... chaos. She stood in the doorway for a shocked moment, and then set what she was carrying on the floor and turned around to look at the wreckage of her room. The bedclothes were in a pile on the floor and the mattress was leaned against the wall. The drawers and closet had all been emptied and her clothing lay strewn about the room. Her suitcase was empty, but it had been slashed several times. And, in the corner, Cathy's pink toy chest lay in pieces. "Oh, no," she moaned, thinking of how much it must have meant to Lucinda.

Later, after she had alerted the desk clerk and sat waiting for the police, Molly perched on the edge of the naked box spring and took a mental inventory of her room. Some, but not all, of her clothing was damaged, and her suitcase was a total loss. Many of her cosmetics had been opened and then thrown carelessly on the floor, and someone had gone to the trouble of emptying her shampoo bottle into the bathtub. The heavy lid of the toilet tank was ajar, and the trash can was lying on its side. Thank goodness she had kept her computer with her, as well as the files relating to Cathy's death. It was obvious to Molly, that someone had been looking for something, and she hoped against hope that they hadn't found it.

But saddest of all, was the colorful pile of wood that had once been a whimsical toy chest. Molly wandered over to it and knelt down. The mirror was a spider web of cracks, but the lid was still in one piece. And, despite the fact that the pink satin lining had been ripped out, the box had been broken along the seams so she felt a glimmer of hope that it might be repaired. Gently she lifted the lid up and leaned it against the wall. As she did this, a piece of the mirror broke away and fell to the floor. She went to pick up the jagged piece of glass, but her attention was drawn to something that had been behind the glass; it looked like paper. Old and slightly yellowed, but it was definitely paper.

Molly rummaged around in her computer bag until she found the small pouch of tools she always carried with her, and then carefully pulled the pieces of broken glass out of the way. Finally, she took the tweezers and gently extracted a folded note from behind what was left of the mirror. "The mirror doesn't lie." Repeating the line from Lucinda's poem, she suddenly felt foolish for not having figured it out sooner.

But, before she could read it, there was a ruckus outside the open door, and Molly turned around. The police had arrived, bringing with them the distraught desk clerk, one of the hotel maids, and a number of curious hotel guests hovering just outside the door.

Suddenly, Molly could understand why Lucinda didn't know who to trust. She discretely slipped the note into her pocket and stood up to greet Hickok's finest.

Chapter Forty Five

Lissy's message consisted of two words. "Come now." There was no mistaking the sense of urgency, and Quinn wasted no time in getting to Strange Brew. As he walked through the door he saw that Molly was back in town and he grinned, but he knew right away that something was wrong. She and Eric Lentz were seated at their usual table, but there was a seriousness about them that alarmed him. Molly glanced up as he approached the table and smiled; Lentz glanced up and didn't.

Lentz pushed a chair out from the table with his foot, and Quinn sat down. A moment later, Lissy handed him an unidentified coffee drink and perched herself on the arm of an old wingback chair. Lentz waited until he was settled and then said, "Bad news is it looks like we've made our killer mighty nervous. Took advantage of Miss Molly being out of town and tore her room up. Good news is, because he tore her room up, she found something… probably what he was lookin' for. But we haven't seen it yet… she wanted to wait for you." Lentz gave Quinn a sharp glance and then looked expectantly at Molly.

She reached into her pocket, pulled a folded piece of paper and pushed it to the middle of the table. "I read it when I first got here, but you all need to take a look. It definitely explains the flowers."

Lentz gently opened the yellowed piece of paper, smoothed it, and then sat back so they could all see. It was a note to Cathy, pencil-scrawled in an oddly childish hand. There was a crudely-drawn heart with an arrow through it at the bottom and, at the top, was written a date... a few days before the girl's murder. The note read:

Cathy, you are the most beutifal girl in the world. You are the best thing that ever hapened to me. I know we have to be secret, but I want the world to know about our love. If it's OK for me to come over Saterday, leave the back gate unlocked. I will dream about you until then. Love forever, your Romeo.

Quinn blew out a breath, "Well that explains a lot... just not who it was." "Maybe not, old buddy," Lentz said, "but it sure gives us a lot more to go on. She found it under the mirror in the lid of the toy chest, after it got broken up." He glanced over at Molly and added, "And not to worry, young lady, I'll fix the thing as good as new."

Molly nodded gratefully. Quinn noticed that she did not seem terribly upset about the invasion of her space. She calmly sipped her drink and nibbled on an oatmeal cookie. When she saw that he was looking at her, she gave him a wry crooked smile and raised one eyebrow in a way that made him blush and look away. *Oh, that woman!*

"So," offered Lissy, as she watched the door. "She obviously had an admirer, and I'm guessin' she felt the same way or she wouldn't have hidden the note away from her folks." Lentz looked skeptical, but Molly was quick to agree. "It's a girl thing," added Lissy.

236

"So, our first priority is to find this fella. I'm thinking that he either killed Cathy or would have a pretty good idea who did." Lentz looked around the circle. "Probably lookin' for a kid around the same age, maybe even younger, judging from the spelling."

"You know, having had two teenage sons, one who struggled through high school, I can honestly say that a percentage of every graduating class is functionally illiterate... a significant percentage, sadly." Molly looked at the surprised expressions around the table. "I'm just saying that this could be a high school kid or even an adult."

Lentz shook his head. "Okay, that still narrows our search parameter some. We know it's a male, we know it's someone Cathy knew, probably someone her parents even knew, and we know the kid wasn't exactly an over-achiever. The timeline fits. Maybe she changed her mind and told him to get lost. He got mad and killed her with whatever weapon happened to be on hand. Sounds like something a love-crazed teenager might do."

He gingerly picked up the note and handed it to Lissy. "Got a photocopier? I'd like some insurance that this doesn't mysteriously disappear. Everybody gets their own copy, I'll give one to the police and we'll put the note itself in a safe place." Lissy gave him some lip, but took it with her to the back room. When she returned with a stack he distributed the copies, tucking away the original into his leather satchel.

Before anything more could be said, the door opened and in walked Preston Locke and Curt Golden. Quinn noticed that Molly cringed a bit, but they casually waved to the table and then paid them no more attention. Lissy quickly got up and returned to her stool to take their orders. Lentz gave the two a good long look, and then said he was heading over to the police department and made his goodbyes.

That left Quinn and Molly alone together and there was an awkward silence. He reached across the table, took her hand, brought it to his lips, and kissed it gently. "So, lass, I want to hear every detail. Leave nothing out."

She sighed, disengaging her hand and sinking back into her chair, and told him what she remembered; beginning with cookie-baking and ending with her hotel room in chaos, discovering the note and her subsequent experience with the police. The police had found no evidence of tampering with the door lock, and the maid insisted that she had cleaned the room the day before and it had been intact. The desk clerk was offended when asked if he had allowed anyone into the room, and said he had not seen anyone who was not a registered hotel guest go up the stairs or even loiter in the lobby. He couldn't vouch for the other clerks, though. He also said there was a back staircase which, though not exactly common knowledge, was often used by hotel employees and sometimes by guests. He also grudgingly admitted that since they still used metal keys, it was possible that somewhere along the line duplicates had been made. He was adamant, however, that nothing like this had ever happened before, and had looked accusingly at Molly, implying that it was her fault.

She declined Quinn's offer of a place stay, insisting that she had been given a new room and that it had a proper lock. In fact, she had already gathered her things and moved them in. He wanted to insist, but wisely backed off.

Quinn sat quietly for a moment, trying to decide how much he wanted to disclose. "Well, Molly my dear, you seem to be taking this very well, but I have some real concerns about your safety." She began to sputter a response, but he held up his hand. "I've hired some professional security people to make sure nothing happens to you."

He watched the play of emotions on her face range from surprise to embarrassment to anger. Anger won out because her chin jutted out and she sat straight up on the chair. "What, you think I'm some kind of... you think I can't take care of myself... now look here, mister..." Her hands were drumming the table and she was working herself into a respectable fit of pique.

Quinn leaned forward, covering her hands with his own, and looked her straight in the eye. "Be angry, that's your perfect right and, to be honest, you're lovely when you're mad, but I won't take no for an answer. People are getting hurt here, and I intend to make damn sure you're not one of them." Molly wanted to say something, but he put a finger to her lips. "I am not doing this because I want to control you; I'm doing this because I... ah... like you." She smiled. "No, wait a minute...that's not true."

"What? Oh, you are such a..." She looked absolutely crestfallen and he noticed her lip quiver a tiny bit.

"Hush, Molly, dear. The truth is I think I love you."

Chapter Forty Six

She sat there a long time after Quinn left, thinking. When she stammered a reply to his declaration of love, he shushed her, kissed her hand, and then, after she again assured him that she had been given a new room with a proper lock, took off to take care of some business. At one point, Preston Locke and Curt Golden came over to say hello. She said "hello" back but didn't invite them to sit down and, after an awkward silence, they returned to their own table, leaving soon after. They seemed to be arguing about something, though, and Curt Golden slammed the door on his way out, eliciting a stormy look from Lissy.

During a lull, Lissy came over and plopped down, putting her feet up on a chair. "So, honey, you look like Santa left a turd in your stocking."

Molly almost choked on the coffee she was sipping and laughed in spite of herself. When she was able to stop laughing, she sighed deeply and said, "I need to tell him, Lissy. He thinks he loves me, but he doesn't know who I am... what I've done." She was absolutely miserable.

"So, tell me about it. Let's hear all about this big, bad mystery."

Molly blew out her breath, looked to the ceiling, and then said, "Okay, here goes... When I was in high school, I was this super-smart geek and I really didn't fit in very well... that's actually a huge understatement. Kids would call me to help them with their homework, but that was about it. Most of my spare time was spent working at the market down the street or babysitting. Parents loved me because I was never busy and I was so… so… well, normal. Maybe dependable would be a better word… if you knew my home life, normal probably wouldn't apply. Well, anyway, the summer between my junior and senior year, I drove a couple of my babysitting kids down to swimming lessons and waited for them in the park next to the pool. This guy would be there and we talked… you know, just chit-chat. He was an older guy, but he was really nice. We talked about poetry and songs and movies… stuff like that. I thought we had a lot in common and I used to look forward to seeing him there. When swimming lessons ended, I managed to meet him a couple more times, but then he stopped coming and I thought that was it."

"Hold that thought," Lissy said as she hurried up front to help a small group of older women. When she returned, she brought coffee and spice cookies with her. "This is better than a chick flick," she said as she settled back into her chair.

"Okay, so when school started, I walked into my creative writing class and there he was… he was my teacher. I blushed and didn't know what to do, it felt so awkward, but he just smiled and nodded. Well, pretty soon, he was giving me these extra research assignments and then asking me to stop in after school so we could discuss them."

She took a nervous slurp of coffee, burning her tongue, and crumbled a piece of cookie into bits. "You have to understand, Lissy, I was so lonely and so inexperienced. And here was this smart, good-looking guy who couldn't take his eyes off me. At the time, I don't think I had much of a chance. One night, when I was supposed to be at the library, he asked me to go to his place… he rented a garage apartment close to the park where we first met. And we… well, let's just say that after that, he couldn't take his hands off me, either. That was my first time." Molly stared off into space, with a sad smile.

"And then, just before Christmas break, we went to see a special production of The Nutcracker in the city. The students all rode in the activity bus, but he brought his own vehicle… an old Volkswagen van. After intermission, instead of going back into the theater, we went out to his van. He gave me a gold ring with a tiny sapphire and told me I was his Christmas star. I thought I was in love, Lissy… I really did. We were kissing and then, all of a sudden, the door swung open and there were a whole bunch of kids from my class. Apparently this one girl, a really awful girl, saw us leave and rounded up some other kids to follow us out. She said she had been suspicious for a long time, but just wanted everyone else to know what a slut I was."

Molly had to stop for a few minutes to compose herself and stop her hands from trembling. "After that, things were terrible… so terrible. The girl's mother called my mother and, apparently, everyone else in town because the news was all over. It became intolerable for me, and for him, too, because he didn't return after Christmas break. I don't know if it was his decision or theirs, but the school administrators announced that he had left 'to pursue other interests.' My mother was publicly shamed and I don't think ever forgave me for it. I lost my job at the store and was never again called to babysit. In fact, the only calls I got after that were anonymous prank calls asking for "Moldy the Whore". That was the year from hell, and the only thing that kept me going was the knowledge that I could leave as soon as I graduated."

242

"I remember my mother took to her bed for a week and most of her friends stopped coming around. My brother was dropped from the basketball team and they were cruel to my sister and called her all kinds of awful names. The town was very religious back then, and I heard there were whole sermons about my "wickedness." No forgiving and forgetting around here, that's for sure. My grandmother never spoke to me again. My sweet Grandma... and she died a couple of years later. Oh Lissy, it's like I destroyed my whole family. There's so much guilt; it never seems to go away and just being here..." A tear rolled down her cheek.

She was quiet for a while. "His name was Marcus. I heard from other people that he moved back east, but he never even tried to contact me. I want to believe he was a nice guy and I want to believe he cared for me. We had this chemistry... but, that's all water under the bridge." She shook her head. "Anyway, how can I tell Quinn what I've done and expect him to still love me? How can you still want to be my friend?"

Molly waited, eyes downcast, for a response from Lissy, but it wasn't the one she expected.

Lissy laughed, not a chuckle, but a huge guffaw. She laughed and laughed and laughed. Finally, after she had regained her breath, she wheezed, "Is that it? That's your big mystery?" She wiped a tear from her eye. "Honey, I knew all that before I ever met you. When I first came to town, there was this skinny rat-faced woman who brought her posse in here a couple times a week. It wasn't long before I heard every piece of gossip there was in this town. And trust me; your story was Sunday school, compared to some of the steamy stuff I learned. It also wasn't long before I realized that my regular customers stayed away when she was around. So I told her to piss off."

It was Molly's turn to laugh. "No way! I know exactly who you're talking about… she's as awful now as she was back then, and I want to hear every detail."

"Oh, honey, if looks could kill, I'd be double dead. I said she wasn't good for business and told her not to let the door hit her in the butt on the way out. Some of her "girls" snickered behind her back, but she put her pointy nose in the air and walked out in a big huff; they ran along behind her. I think some of her "girls" broke ranks, though, because they come in on their own and are very well-behaved. Anyway, she circulated some rumors about me and tried to bring me down, but, hey… folks do like their coffee." She reached over and patted Molly's arm. "I think you overestimate your secret past and underestimate your guy. He really is smitten."

As Lissy ran to take care of some new arrivals, Molly gathered up her things and headed for the door. She felt like a weight had been lifted and for the first time she allowed herself to picture her and Quinn as an item. *I'm smitten, too… smitten like a kitten.*

Chapter Forty Seven

Lucinda looked out the window, into the gathering dusk of early evening, letting her mind wander. They had not yet brought her another roommate and she surprised herself by being glad of the fact. She had her own life to think about and her own future. In the past, she had enjoyed the comings and goings of those who shared her hospital room, as well as their friends and families. Although undoubtedly vicarious, it had made her feel somehow connected to this community and its people. Since her marriage to Cal, she felt like an outsider in her own world, but also had herself to blame for the years of self-imposed isolation after Cathy's death. Now she wanted back in… Lucy wanted back… and Eric was holding the door wide open for her. She smiled to herself.

The note… she remembered it now. Eric had stopped by and told her what had happened to Molly's room, and as soon as he mentioned the toy chest it all came flooding back. About a year ago, she had been cleaning out Cathy's old room and was moving the chest into the closet. She opened it to make sure it was empty and noticed that the screws holding the mirror in place seemed loose, so she got a screwdriver to fix it. But she noticed something peeking out behind the glass so, curious, she removed the mirror and there it was. A note… something her sweet daughter had hidden from her. Her hands had been shaking as she opened it, afraid that it would be something she didn't want to see;

something that might hurt what was left of her family even more. But it was just a childish love note, similar to ones she had received back in her youth.

She remembered the sense of relief she felt at not recognizing the handwriting, and it allowed her to put to rest the nagging suspicion that her stepson Preston had somehow been involved. She loved the boy, always had, but back then he was an angry teenager, rebellious and determined to punish his father for the way he was treated. His behavior had changed after Cathy's death; changed radically. He became overly polite and helpful, taking Calvin's abuse without complaint. Lucinda knew it was an act, and that Preston remained deeply wounded, but the sudden turnaround unnerved her.

After returning the note to its hiding place, she had casually asked Preston if he knew if Cathy had a secret boyfriend, or if there were any boys he knew that liked her enough to send a love letter. His negative response was innocent enough, but Lucinda saw him tense up and could tell he was hiding something. She had a similar conversation with Helene, and got pretty much the same response. Her intellect told her that it was because no one wanted to revisit that horrible time, but her gut insisted they were being evasive and knew more than they told her.

And, shortly after that, her attacks had begun. She chased away the dark thoughts and suspicions that fought for attention in her mind. She loved them both and was pretty sure they both loved her. So one or both of them had told someone else and that was the path their investigation should follow.

She looked at the photocopy of the note one more time and then set it on the bedside table. She was able to stay awake for longer periods, but her body was still weak and weary. Cheryl bustled in with her dinner and chattered away as she arranged the tray and uncovered the plates with a theatrical 'voila.'

"Your dessert tonight was tapioca pudding... again, but I think you've earned yourself some strawberry cheesecake, so I smuggled you a piece from the cafeteria."

"Well, life is short so... dessert first," said Lucinda as she picked up her fork and dug in. She closed her eyes to savor the first bite. When she opened them again, Cheryl was standing at the side of her bed staring at the photocopied note with an odd expression on her face.

"That's weird," said Cheryl softly. "I haven't even thought of it in years." She picked up the piece of paper and held it closer to her face.

"What is it, dear? Do you recognize the handwriting?" Lucinda felt her heart begin to pound.

"Well, yeah... sort of. I saw this handwriting in a message spray-painted on my brother's truck after he was chosen for All-State in basketball during his senior year. The message read something like 'you think you're a jock but you're a jerk. If you go to the tournament, you'll be sorry...' but it was spelled all wrong and the handwriting was just like this." Cheryl continued. "Jimmy did go to the tournament and scored big... we were so proud of him, but when he got back all four tires were slashed and his windshield was smashed."

"So, do you think it was someone on the same team as your brother... a rival, maybe? Any idea who? Can you give it some thought?" There was a hint of desperation in Lucinda's voice.

Cheryl snorted. "Oh, I don't have to think about it... we all knew who it was, everybody knew but we were afraid to do anything... it was Jeff Golden."

Chapter Forty Eight

Lentz was nursing a beer, looking none too happy, and Quinn pushed away a cup of tea that had long since grown cold. The crowd at the Full Rack had thinned out and a tired-looking barmaid was wiping down tables and stacking chairs. The old cowboy, sitting a few stools down, was the only other patron, and he stood up, tipped his hat in their direction, and sauntered out on bowed legs. When the barmaid glanced at them, Quinn shrugged his shoulders and asked if they should leave, but she assured them they could stay as long as they liked.

To be honest, Quinn was tired. It had been a long and exhausting day for them all and he marveled at Lentz's endurance. Molly had laughingly told him that the man's nickname was "Ironman Eric," and now he understood why.

"Okay, old buddy. So it looks like the Golden kid wrote the note to Cathy. Your handwriting experts need to confirm it, but I don't have much of a doubt. She hid the note away, like it was special to her, so I'm guessing she must have had some kinda feelings for the guy."

"Sounds about right," agreed Quinn.

"What I'm having trouble wrapping my head around is the fact that this kid was as bad as they come. And I'm not talking 'troubled teen' here.. Jeff Golden was the business end of mean. He was a bully, and a loose cannon, and he hurt a lot of people. Hell, when he was killed, about half the town breathed a big sigh of relief. So what did this sweet girl, pretty like her Mama, see in a guy like that?" Lentz shook his head and took a long pull of beer.

"Maybe she was the music that soothed his savage soul... maybe she was the only one that made him feel normal."

Lentz looked at him strangely, "Now don't go waxing poetic on me... but I know what you mean. The kid was mean, but he probably had good reason to be. His old man was all about the power and the image... never had a good thing to say about anybody or anything. He was a big city doctor who moved here for what he called the simple life... just wanted to be a big fish in a small pond, if you ask me. I heard rumors he was forced out of his big city job, but never did hear why. He used to push the boy real hard in sports... told everybody he was headed for the Pros."

The kid's mother married for status and couldn't have cared less about her boys. They were allowed to do anything they wanted, as long as it didn't embarrass her. She also had a fondness for the bottle, and back when I was on the force we were called to their fancy neighborhood several times. Once we found her sitting on the neighbor's porch swing in her underwear, belting out show tunes. Another time we found her passed out in the bushes beside the old Lutheran church. It was on a Sunday morning and people just walked right by, pretending they didn't see her there. Anybody else we woulda tossed in the drunk tank, but Mrs. High-and-Mighty got an apology, a free ride home, and we were told to forget it had ever happened. Same thing with the kids... well, just the one kid, actually. The other one, Curt, was almost normal, compared to the rest of the family."

Lentz set his empty bottle down on the counter with a thud, and the barmaid looked up hopefully. Quinn signaled that they were done and paid the tab, rewarding her generously for her patience.

"You know, old man," said Quinn as they stepped into the chilly night. "I don't think someone like Jeff Golden could have kept his feelings a secret. He wasn't that smart. Somebody had to know about it, or at least suspect and I think a good place to begin would be with Preston Locke."

The image of an enraged Locke, looming over Molly at the hospital, and loudly blaming her for his step-mother's illness replayed in his head. Had Lentz not intervened, Quinn suspected it could have become physical. He found the man's apology and sudden show of remorse to be equally disturbing and recently, his cheerful waves and overly friendly manner seemed so disingenuous and manipulative that it made Quinn's teeth hurt. Over the years he had relied heavily on his gut feeling, and if such a man had approached him with a business proposition, he would have shown him the door without giving it a second thought. He smiled, imagining that very thing.

"Yup, gotta have a chat with Mr. Locke," Lentz agreed. "He's the spittin' image of his Daddy so I'd love to knock that smirk off his face, but Lucinda thinks of him as a son, so I'm gonna have to take it nice and easy." He unlocked his Jeep. "I gotta get home... Jasper's probably howling at the moon. So, get some rest, partner, and tomorrow we knock on doors."

Quinn climbed into his own vehicle and as he drove past the Calamity Jane, the radio came on with 'Knock, Knock, Knockin' on Heaven's Door.' *Just a coincidence... not gonna happen.* But he couldn't stifle a shudder as he made sure his doors were locked, and drove towards his very big, very dark cabin.

And so it begins. The next few days would be challenging, but the killer welcomed the excitement. It was obvious that they knew something… had found something. And even though it would lead them to another dead end, it was one step closer to the truth.

The truth… now that's funny. Some people wouldn't recognize the truth if it looked them right in the eye. They insisted that it was a fluid thing that existed in many shades of gray, shifting this way or that with religious perspective or political correctness. Their version of the truth gave people excuses for their mistakes and their shortcomings… it gave them permission to be stupid, and that was truly laughable.

But truth was a simple thing, really; it was white or black, good or bad, right or wrong… that's all there was to it. No shades of gray, no maybes, no exceptions. Outsiders threatened a reputation that had taken a lifetime to build… that was wrong. Meddlers wanted to uncover a secret that could send a person to prison… that was bad. And the whole affair was forcing a normally sunny disposition into the blackest of moods.

They all had to go… and that was the truth.

Chapter Forty Nine

When Molly left her new hotel room, she checked twice that it was locked and told the maid not to worry about cleaning. Intellectually, she was pretty sure that nothing would happen, given the fact that the police were now involved, the hotel staff was on heightened watch, and Quinn's security people were renting rooms on either side of her. But emotionally, she still felt violated and vulnerable. Someone with malicious intent had broken into her private space, damaged her property and handled items of apparel that had never seen the light of day. She salvaged most of her clothing, but her winter coat was a total loss, with the lining ripped out, and her long fuzzy bathrobe had also been torn apart. Her big suitcase was in shreds. "Okay, shopping opportunity," she murmured with false cheer. The hotel had reimbursed all of her rent up to that point, so she could go crazy, but much as she loved shopping, that wasn't really her priority right now.

Her mother was running late when Molly arrived to take her to her therapy session. She helped the woman tame her fluffy hair, locate a missing glove, and take her morning pills. But they were unable to find a tube of lipstick Shirley insisted was her favorite. "I know it's here, someplace," she said, rummaging through bathroom drawers. "When was the last time you wore it, Mom?" Molly asked, helpfully. To be honest, she couldn't remember her mother ever wearing lipstick.

"Well, I know I wore it when your father was made an officer at his Lodge..."

Molly was shocked, that had to have been at least fifteen years ago. A tube of lipstick that old would most likely have degenerated into something fairly unpleasant. "Okay... I'll tell you what. It's probably not a good idea to wear lipstick at the therapy session, so maybe we can stop at Save-Mart afterwards and I'll treat you to a brand new one... they have some really great colors now. In fact, I have to pick up a few things, myself, so we can have some long overdue girl time!"

Her mother looked skeptical, but allowed her daughter to herd her to the car. "Well, I hope they have Midnight Orchid, because I don't think anything else will do... It matches my coloring, you know."

Molly smiled to herself but reassured the older woman that they would certainly have something to match her coloring.

The therapy session went well and the subsequent shopping time was actually fun, much to Molly's surprise. Her mother was like a kid in a candy shop, and bought several lipsticks and nail polishes in bright candy colors. But when the woman fixated on bright blue eye shadow, however, Molly had to draw the line and hinted that blue eye shadow might be over-the-top. Her mother looked at it longingly, but, to her credit, walked away.

After a light lunch, the obligatory afternoon shows, and a mini-makeover, Molly kissed the woman on the forehead and headed out the door. Dick was pulling up just as she left and she waved to him. She still didn't know him well, but she could tell he was devoted to her mother and Molly credited him as the bringer of positive change.

When she arrived at Strange Brew, she sat at the counter so she could visit with Lissy until the others arrived.

"So, did ya spill the beans?" Lissy handed her a double mocha and a raspberry tart.

"Not yet, but I plan to do it today. You know, just talking to you made me feel better. All these years I thought that I, personally, was the black mark on Hickok's reputation, but I realize now that I wasn't even a blip on the radar. How arrogant was that? I really did put my family through a lot, but they put me through a lot, too… so, I'm thinking it all sort of evens out." Molly sipped on her drink. "You know it's crazy, but I think of you guys as family… but better because you accept me for who I am."

"I know, honey… you're like the bratty, annoying kid sister I never had, Crew Cut is the cranky weird uncle with the heart of gold, and Quinn is the good-looking first cousin I have the secret crush on… "

Molly choked on her drink… "Lissy, you are incorrigible!"

"Thank you… I do my part. But be forewarned, once a mail carrier, always a mail carrier… just don't make me go postal!" They both laughed. When Lentz and Quinn arrived, they looked oddly serious so Molly grabbed what was left of her drink and pastry and followed them to the back table. Lissy brought drinks and cookies a few minutes later.

"We had ourselves a visit with Preston Locke." Lentz wasted no time in getting to the point. "We asked him if he knew that Cathy's secret boyfriend was Jeff Golden and he about swallowed his tongue." Molly noticed that he smiled at that, as if he enjoyed the memory. "The guy hemmed and hawed, trying to think up a good story, but I cut to the chase and told him we knew he was hiding something."

Quinn cut in, "Right at that point, Lucinda's friend, Miss Blanchard showed up. Locke took her into the kitchen and they had quite a conversation. Voices were raised, but they must have settled something, because when they came back, Miss Blanchard did all of the talking and she said they had something to say... something that should have been said a long time ago."

"Well, what was it?" breathed Molly.

"Don't know, yet. The old woman was adamant that the story be told in front of Lucinda, so we're gonna meet them there in about..." he looked at his watch, "fifteen minutes."

Chapter Fifty

Lucinda propped herself up in the hospital bed. With each passing day she felt better and stronger, but right now she was shaking all over and found it increasingly difficult to breathe. Eric reached over and took her hand.

"It's gonna be okay, Lucy. It's gonna be okay."

She looked up at him and nodded, but was desperately afraid that whatever had to be said would reopen a wound that had nearly killed her. She swallowed, forcing herself to breathe deeply and still the trembling that betrayed her emotions. She sensed the beginning of resolution, and in spite of her fear, she needed to understand what had happened so long ago.

Eric was at her side, as he had been since she woke from her coma, and Molly was sitting a few feet away. Behind her stood a very tall, nice-looking man, who approached her shyly and introduced himself as Quinn. She had heard so much about him, she felt she knew him already, and she smiled at the way he hovered protectively near Molly, even though he was clearly out of his element. Cheryl stood quietly near the door, not wanting to intrude upon the family, but Lucinda insisted she be a part of this.

Helene Blanchard walked through the door, followed a moment later by Preston. She stopped a few feet from Lucinda's bed, and it was obvious that whatever was about to be said had taken a toll on the woman. Her face was pale, her eyes were swollen from weeping, and her cheeks burned red, as if they had been rouged. Lucinda had the sudden realization that she looked like one of the antique porcelain dolls her friend was so fond of collecting.

Preston was dry-eyed, but nervous and had the deer-caught-in-the-headlights look. He stood behind Helene almost as if he thought she could shield him. Maybe not such an odd thought, Lucinda realized, since Helene had indeed protected him for most of his life.

Helene's mouth worked, but no sound came out.

"My oldest friend… my son," said Lucinda gently. "You're my family and I love you both, so say what you need to say and let's all get through this."

"Oh Lucinda, if I thought this would have helped I would never have waited. But things were just so ugly then, so awful, and this would have made it so much worse… so much worse for everyone."

"What is it, Helene… just tell me," Lucinda whispered.

"That night… that terrible night… I was at the church; it was a fundraiser and I can't even remember what for. Anyway, the pastor's wife was on her high horse about something… she was always going on about this or that, not very Christian if you ask me… and I just wasn't in the mood, so I decided to walk home. I came in the front door, but I heard this sound from the kitchen… it was almost like a kitten mewling… so I went in and… Oh, God, Lucinda…

"Cathy was on the floor and she was gone. Cathy was gone. The sound was coming from Preston. He was standing a few feet away and the back door was open. He had this look on his face… I've never seen anyone look so anguished. He was sobbing and making that terrible noise.

258

Oh, Lucinda, his heart was broken. When he saw I was there, he walked toward me and stepped in the... oh, dear... stepped in the blood. I told him to stop and then I came around and held him. He kept saying, "Who would do this... who would hurt my sister?"

"He didn't do it, he would never have hurt Cathy... he loved her so much!" She glanced around the room imploringly.

Lucinda looked at Preston. His face was buried in his hands and he was sobbing quietly. "Oh, dear God." Tears were rolling down her own cheeks unheeded. "You've carried this secret around all these years? Oh, Preston, I know you didn't hurt Cathy. I've always known that." She opened her arms, and Eric stepped aside. "You're my son and I loved you from the first moment I saw you."

Preston raised his eyes and looked at her with an expression of disbelief, then stumbled to the bed and let Lucinda hold him and stroke his hair as if he was a small child. They both wept openly.

Helene, smiled a sad smile, and went on to tell the group what had happened next, prompted by Eric for specific details.

"When Preston calmed down, I had him take off his shoes, because of the... ah... blood, and I told him to put on the old pair of sneakers he kept in the gardening shed. Then I told him to go back to the party and stay there. He was still upset... so upset that he fell in the pool on his way... I think maybe he had been drinking, too... or something... you know how young people are. Anyway, after he was gone, I cleaned up his footprints and wiped off the doorknob and whatever I thought he might have touched. I left everything else the way it was, though. "

Eric shook his head and Lucinda knew he was getting ready to jump into cop mode, but Helene put her hands on her hips and looked him square in the eye. "You have to understand! There weren't any footprints until I got there. There was no blood on his clothes! Preston didn't do it… there's no way he could have. But he was a typical teenager back then, doing and saying a lot of stupid things… and if his father had even suspected that…"

Eric started to interrupt, but Lucinda stopped him. "She's right. It was bad enough that Preston knew his father didn't want him, but if he was even suspected of killing Cathy, his life would have been made a living hell. Calvin really wanted someone to blame… that's why he went after the police department with such a vengeance."

Lentz nodded, but said nothing.

"So, after that I walked back to the church and I dropped the shoes into a dumpster a few blocks away. They hadn't even missed me! The pastor's wife was still blathering on about something, so I stayed to help clean up and when I came home again, the police where there. And when I walked in, Preston, you were such a wreck…" The tears she had held back began to flow.

Preston held out his hand to the woman who had dedicated her life to his upbringing and she hurried to him. Lucinda opened her heart and her arms to both. She grieved the love they had lost on this heartbreaking secret, but she felt a sense of ease enter the room, a sense of healing. She also felt a surge of power, the knowledge that there were no more secrets and that everyone present was now focused on finding and stopping the monster that had killed her daughter and had tried to do the same to her. Lucy looked out through her eyes and said, "Bring it on, you coward… bring it on."

Chapter Fifty One

"This… is your *little* cabin?" Molly looked around in awe. "Understate much?"

Quinn took in the room, feeling suddenly sheepish. It really was enormous, even by his standards. The great room, living up to its name, was cavernous, offering a number of cozy seating arrangements around the huge stone fireplace… he referred to it jokingly as a walk-in fireplace… or near the cathedral wall of glass that looked down over a small private lake. Those walls that weren't showcasing hunting trophies were adorned with original western paintings or antique Navajo rugs. There was a full-sized concert grand piano in one corner and it looked almost small, compared to its surroundings. Honestly, he hadn't paid much attention to the casual opulence of the place, but now, looking at it through Molly's eyes, he was embarrassed.

"Not mine. It belongs to a friend from University. And it comes with a housekeeper who can whip up a mean dessert… not a bad deal, really." Quinn was trying to lure Molly into a change of subject by guiding her towards the kitchen and the scent of warm peach cobbler.

She wasn't quite finished being awestruck, though. "You know, I could fit my whole house and my yard into this room, and still have space to add on." She shook her head. "Your friend probably uses the place two, maybe three, weeks a year. What a shame, really. You could house several families here and still have plenty of privacy." She sighed, but finally allowed herself to be gently nudged to the kitchen.

"Wow, there's more granite here than in the cemetery down the road."

Quinn laughed, "Yes, but compared to the cemetery, this is party central." He dished up two servings of warm peach cobbler, poured a dollop of cream on top of each and handed one to Molly. When he asked her how she took her tea, she answered "with milk" and he was pleasantly surprised, since few Americans understood the British art of tea. They sat at the breakfast bar and ate in companionable silence.

"You know," said Molly, as she warmed her hands around the teacup. "I actually feel sorry for Preston. I mean, can you imagine growing up like that?"

"Not really," answered Quinn, after some thought. "But I believe that people should take responsibility for their own actions... and their own behavior, regardless of the circumstances of their upbringing."

"That's true... Ok, speaking of responsibility for one's own actions, I need to tell you something about my past." Molly sat up straight and looked Quinn right in the eye.

"Ah, the mysteries of Molly at last... let's hear it, Lass."

She took a deep breath and said, "Well, when I was still in school..."

At that moment, Lentz walked through the door, heading straight for the peach cobbler. After he had dished up a healthy serving, he made himself at home next to Quinn, who sighed at the interruption, but poured him a cup of coffee.

Lentz had stayed at the hospital after they left to follow up with Locke and Helene Blanchard, and, Quinn suspected, to make sure that Lucinda was okay with everything.

262

"Well, I still don't know who it is, but I have a better idea of who it isn't. The kid didn't do it, unless he's the best actor in the world and, honestly, he's just not that smart. And the Blanchard woman was just trying to protect him. I don't agree with what they did, but I guess I understand... Lucinda helped me understand."

He poured himself another cup of coffee. "Still a couple of loose ends, though... Miss Blanchard insists she didn't wash the paring knife we found on the counter. She said it was clean when she got there and she didn't touch it. Also, just before I left Lucinda mentioned that Cathy had been wearing a necklace that night, a pearl necklace that her old man gave her for her birthday. She said she just assumed it was damaged or destroyed in the attack, so she didn't say anything about it. Said she dreamed about it before she came out of her coma. Anyway, we didn't find a necklace or any loose pearls, so I'm thinkin' that the killer took a memento." He paused. "We find that necklace, and maybe we find the killer."

"Oh, the pearl necklace... I had a dream about Cathy; she was wearing it and she told me to ask her mother about it. How strange is that?" Molly got an odd look from both men, but just shrugged and added, "Hey, don't knock women's intuition."

Lentz laughed. "I, for one, have a healthy respect for women's intuition." Quinn leaned forward and asked, "What about Jeff Golden? Did you ask Locke about that?"

"Oh, yeah, Locke knew that Jeff Golden had a thing about his sister, but didn't think much of it. Said he had never talked to Cathy about it, though. On the night of the party he said Jeff and his brother got into a big fight and he thought it was about a girl, but it never crossed his mind that it might have been about Cathy. So Jeff and his brother go at it, almost a knock-down-drag-out, but then it was over and Jeff proceeded to drink himself into a stupor. Locke said he passed out on a lawn chair by the pool and didn't remember him moving all night. It was news to the Blanchard woman, though. She just kept saying, 'What is the world coming to' or something like that."

Quinn gave some thought to what he had just heard. "Looks like we're running out of people to intimidate with our good cop, bad cop routine."

"Not yet, old buddy, not yet. We're still tracking down some of the party goers, probably want to have a chat with Jeff Golden's brother, Curt, and don't forget the dead girl's missing boyfriend."

"Looks like you boys have a busy day tomorrow, so I think it's time to head back to the hotel and catch up on some work. I could use a ride…" She looked hopefully at Quinn.

Quinn stood up, but Lentz insisted that he would do the honors since he wanted to stop by the hospital one more time, and then maybe the police department. Molly gave him a helpless shrug and mouthed "later" as she followed Lentz out the door.

Not even a peck on the cheek… and the secrets of Molly remain as mysterious as the moon. Quinn was disappointed. *But not for long… not for long.*

Chapter Fifty Two

There was a light blanket of white on the ground when Molly woke and she stood at her upstairs window for a long time, watching the morning traffic attempting to negotiate the treacherous roads that come with the season's first snow. Nothing serious, but there were a couple of near misses, one minor fender bender, lots of horn honking, and a couple of pratfalls on the slippery sidewalk below.

After returning to her hotel room last night, she worked for a few hours, and managed to get caught up on her documentation and her correspondence. Still nothing from the "mega-client" about the consulting position, but she wasn't really surprised. It was not unusual for corporations to take weeks, or even months, to make a decision. Sometimes they would decide not to decide, and put a project back on the shelf. She had learned long ago not to get too emotionally invested until the ink was dry on a contract.

She also called her boys, carefully broaching the subject of selling the house. Alex didn't seem particularly surprised, saying that he didn't like to think of her all alone in that big house. Alex had few friends left in Monroe and he had been something of a loner in high school, so he had no vested interest in her staying there. Jack's response was more complicated, though, since he was more strongly connected to Monroe. But he did agree that the house was too big for Molly by herself, and suggested she look for a cottage in the pretty resort town of Jennings, between Monroe and Hickok. It seemed like the perfect compromise for Jack, since the town offered skiing in the winter and white water rafting in the summer, and it was close enough for him to see his friends in Monroe and visit his grandmother in Hickok. "Wow," thought Molly, immediately liking the idea.

Having had enough of the traffic melodrama, she moved away from the window, but soon found herself pacing restlessly around the room, feeling edgy and unsettled. Her mother didn't have a therapy session today and Quinn and Lentz were off doing some investigating of their own, so she had the morning to herself, but she couldn't seem to concentrate on anything. Finally, she bundled herself up against the sudden, bitter cold and carefully made her way on foot to Strange Brew.

It was pandemonium when Molly walked through the door. She immediately recognized one of the "pratfall" victims, a middle-aged woman, wearing a brightly-colored warm-up suit... sequined butterflies flitting all over it... sitting near the door and having a very loud, very heated argument with, Molly assumed, her husband who couldn't seem to stop laughing. She was complaining about her tailbone, but he insisted that since her tailbone was so well padded, only her pride had been damaged. The woman got up, gathered her things and stormed out, slamming the door behind her. The husband, still laughing, paid for their coffee, and followed her outside.

Most of the other tables were occupied, but the atmosphere was so thick with tension that Molly thought she could cut it with a knife. She heard murmurings of wet shoes, frozen pipes, dead batteries, and kids late for school. "Whoa... I guess the change in weather brings out the worst in people."

"No, really?" Lissy answered with a perfect deadpan. "Here, throw this apron on, tie back that mop of yours, and make yourself useful until all these cranky folks go away."

Molly soon found herself taking orders, diplomatically avoiding arguments, and humming cheerfully as she whipped up a huge batch of gingerbread. It was just what she needed. During a brief lull, she filled Lissy in on what had happened at the hospital with Helene Blanchard and Preston Locke, but it soon got busy again and Molly found herself running to keep up.

The only really happy customer was a large fellow sitting by himself near the back. He said his name was Ed, and he owned his own towing company... said the first snow was his favorite day of the year. Molly brought him a cookie just because he was smiling and he thanked her kindly, but his eyes, she noticed, were on Lissy.

"So, your boss..." he asked casually, still gazing towards the counter "She married... got a boyfriend?"

"Uh... well, no. She's about as single as it gets, but you should probably be having this conversation with her."

"Didn't mean to put you on the spot, little lady... just think she's one fine figure of a woman." His beeper went off. "Well, looks like I'm needed for a mishap down the road, but I think I might be comin' back."

He left a generous tip on the table, and ambled up to the counter to pay his bill. He gave Lissy a beatific smile and looked her right in the eye. Molly was surprised to see Lissy so flustered that she miscounted the change, not once but twice, and they both laughed. He leaned in and said something to her, then winked as he went through the door; leaving Lissy in serious danger of falling off her stool. Molly gave her the thumbs up and her friend quickly recovered, firing back a rude gesture in her direction, but she couldn't hide the fact that she was blushing.

Later, when things had calmed down, the two sat at the counter with warm gingerbread and coffee. "So, looks like you have an admirer."

"Well, he did say he liked the way I was put together… don't think I've ever heard that line before. Almost makes me forget about Ryan Seacrest." Lissy couldn't keep her mouth from twitching into a smile. "He said he'd be back here at 7:00 tonight in case I might want to wander over to the Full Rack with him for a steak."

"Said he loved good food and good coffee, and was looking for a good woman who knew her way around both… I'm already mentally baking my wedding cake." Lissy grinned, but Molly thought she was only half-kidding. "Well, you go, girl! Finally you meet a man that can appreciate your many talents."

"We'll see how well he likes my smart mouth… can't seem to help putting my foot right in it. But, hey steak sounds pretty good." She thought for a moment. "Do you think you can close up for me if there are still customers at 7:00?"

"No problem, Hot Mama," answered Molly. Yes, this was exactly what she needed.

Chapter Fifty Three

Glancing around the tastefully-elegant home of Curt Golden, Quinn was surprised. He was not sure what he expected, but this wasn't it. Returning from the kitchen carrying an ornate tray with coffee and cookies, Golden seemed to read his thoughts.

"You can thank my mother for the decorating. I inherited the house when she passed away a few years ago and didn't have the heart to make changes. Sometimes I forget that she's not reading in the next room or giving the cook a hard time about using too much salt or not enough pepper." He laughed to himself as he poured the coffee into delicate porcelain cups and passed them to his visitors. He gestured to an assortment of butter cookies stacked artistically on a small plate. "Please help yourselves. So, gentlemen, to what do I owe the honor?"

Lentz declined a cookie and seemed ill-at-ease with the cup and saucer perched precariously on his knee. Quinn couldn't help but notice that he waited until Quinn had wrapped his fingers around the tiny handle and taken a sip, before following suit. Just to rub it in, he took a cookie and daintily dipped it in his coffee, ignoring the smirk from Lentz.

"Well, we were hoping you could tell us something about the relationship between your brother and Cathy Locke." Lentz removed a copy of the note from his pocket and slid it across the table.

Quinn watched carefully as Golden unfolded the note and held it up to his face. His eyes widened as he read it. "Whoa, that's a blast from the past. Definitely my brother's handwriting... I can tell from the spelling, or lack thereof." He set it down on the table, and shook his head sadly.

"So he was serious... I thought that he just messing with Preston about his sister. Jeff would think something was funny but he would always take it too far. The night that Cathy was... er... killed, he said he was going to go to her house and that they were thinking of running away together. I told him to knock it off; said it wasn't funny."

"We heard it was more like a fight, with shoving and threats."

"You knew Jeff, back then, Mr. Lentz. It always turned into shoving and threats. If you disagreed with my brother, you paid the price. Remember the kid he almost killed? And there were other times, too..."

Golden was lost in thought for a few moments, and Quinn glanced around the room. There were family pictures on the wall and one portrait, in particular, showed an interesting dynamic. The elder Mr. Golden was a solid, beefy man, with dark hair, a florid complexion and piercing blue eyes. His younger son had inherited those eyes. His expression said, at least to Quinn who had known similar men, 'I'm better than you, and don't you ever forget it.' The mother was thin, blonde, and perfect, not a hair out of place. She was beautiful, but had the glassy-eyed look of a china doll. The older brother, Jeff, was tall and solidly built, with his father's dark hair. He leaned slightly towards his father; arms crossed, and had the hint of a sneer as he looked straight into the camera. Curt stood between Jeff and his mother, wearing a slightly ridiculous bowtie and an exaggerated smile. Except for the eyes, Curt favored his mother. Quinn could tell right away who had the power in that family and he felt a wave of sympathy for the man sitting across from him.

Lentz broke the silence. "So you and your brother had an altercation. Then what happened?"

Golden shook his head. "Jeff stormed around for a while, shouting and breaking things, and then he got some tequila from Dad's bar and drank himself into a stupor. I think he was passed out by the pool most of the night, but I didn't stay out there the whole time. Never was much of a party animal..."

Lentz nodded, "What about Preston Locke? Do you remember seeing him leave the party at all?"

"Well, I don't remember him leaving, but I seem to remember him coming back... from somewhere, anyway. I thought it was funny because his clothes were wet and he was barefoot... carrying his shoes. He looked pretty freaked. Somebody gave him some pot and he got really wasted, even more wasted than he was. I always felt sorry for Preston; his old man was such a jerk. I never understood why he chose to hang around with Jeff... my brother treated him like garbage, but he still followed him around like a puppy. After Jeff got... well anyway, we're good friends now."

"Like I said, I was in the house... up in my room, actually... so I can't be sure of all the comings and goings in the back yard. My room faced the street and I was kind of watching out for my parents to come home. They were at the same charity event as Preston's folks, and I wanted to give everyone a heads up so they could take off before my Dad read them the riot act. We weren't supposed to be having a party, but Jeff just kept inviting people and it turned into this big thing. But my parents

didn't get home until really, really late. I guess my Mom had one of her...
ah... episodes."

Lentz cocked his head. "You said you were upstairs in your room off
and on, and the window faced the street? You can see the Locke house
from there, right? Did you notice anyone coming or going that night?
Maybe something out of the ordinary?"

Golden thought for a moment. "Well, I saw the police cars and
the ambulance... that's for sure, but before that, just the housekeeper,
Miss Blanchard; I saw her a few times."

"You saw her twice, right? Once before Preston Locke returned to
the party and then later after the police arrived?"

"Well, yeah, I saw her then, but she was also at the house before. It
was right after Jeff and I had our... uh... argument, and I was upstairs
changing my shirt. I remember thinking that maybe she had forgotten
something, because it looked like she was hurrying. When she got to
the door, she looked up and down the street, and then went into the
house. I didn't see her leave, though, because I went down to the party."

"Mr. Golden, why didn't you tell this to the police before?" Lentz set
the coffee cup back on the table and leaned forward. "Sounds pretty
important, don't ya think?"

Golden's face lost color and he lowered his eyes. "My Dad told me to
keep my mouth shut, and Jeff went kind of crazy after he found out about
Cathy. This was a bad place to be, then." He met Lentz's gaze. "I probably
should have said something, but I didn't think it meant anything... I
mean, Miss Blanchard? She's like Mrs. Claus!"

Lentz blew out a breath and got up to leave. "Sorry, I just get frustrated. Anyway, you think of anything else, give me a call." He handed him his contact information.

Quinn thanked him for his hospitality and headed into the foyer.

Golden picked up the copy of the note and handed it back to Lentz. "By the way, where did you get this? I suspect if the police had seen it back then, there would have been a lot more attention paid to my brother."

Lentz smiled wryly, "Well, this is a mystery that wants to be solved... ironically, the killer found it for us."

Golden looked bewildered, but Lentz just shrugged and walked through the door.

When they got to the car, Lentz said, "Well, what do you think old buddy?"

Quinn smiled. "I think we head over to Santa's workshop and have a chat with Mrs. Claus."

Chapter Fifty Four

Cheryl was giving her a manicure, not exactly professional but certainly with the best of intentions. The nurse had been so very attentive after her near death experience, protective even, that she reminded Lucinda of the bulldog mix that had guarded her fiercely throughout most of her youth. 'Taffy' was the dog's name, a funny-looking puppy her father brought home not long after her mother died. She lived to the ripe old age of 14, refusing to be parted from her mistress even at the end, when she curled up at Lucy's feet and quietly died. She regretted that Cathy had not experienced the pure love and devotion of a dog, but Cal refused to even discuss the matter. Lucinda mentally added 'find new dog' to her growing to-do list.

"Excuse me, Dahling... but could you pencil me in for a facial and pedicure?" Molly was in the doorway, striking a posh pose.

Cheryl laughed, but was quick to reply. "Booked up, but there is a cancellation for a deluxe colon cleanse..."

"Eeuww," said Molly, looking rather horrified.

"I know... eeuww... but I hear some people pay big bucks for a professional colon cleanse.

"That must mean they are full of..."

"Now, ladies," interrupted Lucinda, laughing so hard she had trouble catching her breath. "No-one likes a potty-mouth." But that elicited another round of giggles and it was several minutes before Cheryl could safely resume the manicure.

Molly came over and plopped down in the chair next to Cheryl. "So what's with the day spa?"

"I don't have to clock in for a few hours yet, and I got bored. I had a friend, but she ditched me for a rich, tall boyfriend and now I'm all alone with nothing to do." Cheryl tried to pull a pout, but it wasn't very convincing.

"Oh, yes, the rich, tall boyfriend... I want to hear everything!" Lucinda looked at Molly expectantly.

"I can tell you he was just at my house, along with your Eric."

Three pairs of eyes turned to the doorway, where Helene Blanchard stood, wearing rubber shoe covers and dusting snow from her well-worn woolen coat.

"Helene, come on in and join the party!" Lucinda waved her over. Molly hopped up and offered her a chair, then grabbed a spare and sat on the other side of the bed.

The older woman took off her coat and rubber boots, and then settled in next to Cheryl. "My, oh, my... I didn't think winter would ever come but it looks like the weather has been making up for lost time. I swear it snowed at least an inch on my way over here." She removed her scarf and patted her fluffy white hair back into shape. "Lucinda, you look so much better. It's nothing short of a miracle, you know. We were all so worried and poor Preston..." She leaned over and peered at her friend's face. "You have color back in your cheeks, but I'm willing to bet that has a lot to do with your handsome Eric." Helene's eyes twinkled and she looked almost impish.

Lucinda laughed, but she couldn't hide the blush that deepened her color even more. "Well, let's just say that I suddenly have a lot more reason to hope for a long and healthy life."

Helene smiled at her and Lucinda studied her friend. She looked like the sitcom version of everyone's granny; she had for a long time, actually, because of premature graying, but this was a complex woman and there was a lot more to her than met the eye.

"It's so nice to see you again, Miss Blanchard. I don't know how to thank you for your kindness when Lucinda was so... ah... sick."

"Call me Helene, dear. I'm just happy I could help. And, to be honest, I was glad you all were there... safety in numbers, you know."

Lucinda blinked at the odd statement, but decided to let it go.

"And, Molly dear, your... ah... friend is such a gentleman. So very polite and proper, and that accent... Why, if I were younger, you might have yourself some competition!" They all laughed at that, but Lucinda thought the woman looked a bit wistful.

"Helene," Lucinda asked. "What on earth were Quinn and Eric doing at your house?"

"Oh, my, yes. Well it seems that somebody... they wouldn't say who, but I'm willing to bet it was that awful Clara Leech who lived on the corner and was always spying on her neighbors, although I think she moved in with her daughter who lives in Fremont, or maybe that strange boy from down the street... well, anyway 'somebody' told them that I returned to the house shortly after I left for the church. And, you know, I had forgotten all about it." She paused to take a breath. "Marjory Purvis... you know, Lucinda... she used to always win the baking competitions at the fair... well she asked for my cherry preserve recipe and, of course, I was surprised that Marjory, who could cook like an angel, wanted one of my recipes. She was helping out at the church that night and I was going to take it to her, but forgot all about it until I got a couple of blocks away. So I hurried back, got the recipe, and then left again. You know she used my recipe and won a prize at the fair... I'm still not sure how I feel about that, but anyway..."

"So, Helene," Lucinda asked gently. "Did you talk to Cathy when you went back?"

"Oh, well, yes... I talked to her, but I didn't see her. She called down from upstairs to see who was home. I told her I had forgotten something and was on my way out again. Now that I think about it, she did sound odd, but I remember thinking she was thirteen and just wanted her own space." She looked meaningfully at Molly, then at Cheryl and added. "I may not have children of my own, but that doesn't mean I haven't raised some."

Lucinda smiled at her friend. "Helene, you're as much a mother as I ever was. You were the best thing to happen to Preston, to all of us, really..."

Helene waved away the compliment, tut-tutting, but her cheeks burned bright pink.

"You know, dear," she said, addressing Lucinda. "When Eric said that our Cathy had a love note from that horrid Golden boy... well, I couldn't have been more shocked. The boy had no respect, whatsoever... he and that strange brother of his used to call me Mrs. Claus when I walked past their house... and they would make very personal and inappropriate suggestions about what I could do with Santa." Her lips pursed and she blew out a sharp breath. "I mean, really, what is the world coming to?"

Molly, Cheryl, and Lucinda all nodded in solemn agreement, but it was obvious that Molly was having trouble keeping a smile off her face.

Lucinda looked thoughtfully at her friend. "You know, when I first read the note I thought it was harmless, but the more I think about it the more unsettled I become. Those poor boys didn't have a chance, what with their parents being the way they were. Their father and Calvin were peas in a pod and the mother... well; let's just say she wasn't really there for them."

Helene snorted, "Lucinda, you were always so politically correct. He was a bully and she was a lush. She was passed out in the bushes right next to my church one Sunday morning and we had to step over her legs to get up the steps. The police came and got her, but... really!"

"True, Helene... but I still felt sorry for her, living with that man. The older son, Jeff, was in Preston's class so he must have been seventeen or eighteen at the time. He was at the house a few times, and he made me nervous but I was just so happy that Preston finally had some friends," Lucinda said, "but I can't help thinking that what *could* have happened might have been terrible in a different way."

Helene got up and took Lucinda's hand and they were quiet for a few moments. Feeling the need to visit with her old friend alone, Lucinda whispered to Molly, who quickly helped Cheryl put away her manicure kit, and then gently guided her to the door, saying she had promised to help a friend.

"Hey, I still have two hours before I clock in. Want a manicure?" Cheryl asked hopefully.

"Nope, but I know someone going on a first date tonight that needs all the help she can get. Grab all the beauty products you can find and meet me at Strange Brew."

Cheryl looked shocked. "Lissy on a date? You think Lissy's gonna let us get anywhere near her with lipstick and nail polish? I think I'd better look around for my tranquilizer gun..." They laughed as they went through the door.

Lucinda, who had never met Lissy, laughed, too, and called after them, "You girls have fun... and stick together." *Remember, there's safety in numbers.*

Chapter Fifty Five

Lissy was a mess… no that was an understatement, but Molly just couldn't think of a word to describe what she was seeing. "Girl, it looks like a bomb went off in here and you were ground zero!"

"When I get nervous, I bake… can't help it." Lissy waved at the truly awesome collection of cookies, cakes and pastries that crowded the counter space. Her hair was dusted with either flour or powdered sugar, and she had an impressive glop of what Molly hoped was frosting on her chin.

"Well, if the way to a man's heart is indeed through his stomach, you got that covered… but, Lissy, it doesn't hurt to give him something nice to look at along the way. You know you have flour in your eyelashes, right?"

Lissy blustered and gave back some lip, but her bravado was short-lived. "I haven't had a real date in so long I can't remember… except that I seem to recall I wasn't very good at it. Maybe, I should go get cleaned up…"

"Ya think?" Molly tied her hair back, put on an apron and handed one to Cheryl. "We'll take over here. You get yourself presentable… run upstairs and change clothes, and if you don't behave Cheryl and I will tie you down and give you a full makeover… don't think we won't!"

Lissy reluctantly took off her apron and headed through the kitchen, and up the back stairs leading to her apartment, leaving a cloud of powdered sugar in her wake.

When Molly was sure she was out of ear-shot, she looked at Cheryl and they both burst into laughter. "This looks just like the food-fight scene in that chick flick." Molly was laughing so hard, she had to cross her legs. "But instead of fettuccine, it's frosting!" She handed Cheryl a rag and she grabbed a broom and got busy.

They were a good team and it didn't take long to put the café back into some semblance of order. As Molly was removing a smear of caramel syrup from the front of the microwave, she thought she glimpsed Lissy peeking around the corner. "Front and center, woman. You know, I think I could get used to this bossy/brassy attitude... after all," she added, eying Lissy. "I learned from the expert."

Lissy stepped around the corner looking uncharacteristically skittish, but she also looked... well... great.

"Woo, woo," hooted Cheryl. "Girl, you clean up nice!"

Molly gave her the once over. She wore an off-white tee over a pair of black jeans, finishing it off with a loose-fitting swing jacket in soft plaid. She complemented the look with short heeled black boots, and black hoop earrings. Her light brown hair, which was normally pulled away from her face into a severe pony tail, was loosely held back with black barrettes. And Molly was pretty sure she detected just a hint of mascara and possibly some lip gloss.

"Oh, Lissy, you're an absolute knockout! When the single guys in Hickok get a load of you tonight, you'll have to fight 'em off with a stick!"

"Cut the crap," muttered Lissy, but Molly could tell she was pleased. "Just because I don't get gussied up, doesn't mean I don't know how." She looked at the clock. "Still three hours before closing, so I guess I'll have to change back into work clothes. But, I'm kinda glad you were here for the dress rehearsal."

But before she went back upstairs, Quinn and Lentz arrived. Lentz stopped dead, gaping at the "new and improved" Lissy. Quinn raised his eyebrows and whistled in appreciation.

"You can put your eyes back in your head anytime now, Crew Cut. Just didn't want to waste my good looks on the likes of you."

"Well, coffee lady, I am speechless. Must be a special guy for you to get so prettied up… if he gets fresh, try not to hurt him too badly. Speaking of fresh… any chance you could throw out that slop you sell and fix me up a cup of decent coffee?"

The look on Lissy's face, actually made Lentz back up a step or two, but then she laughed and said, "Nice try, you old bag of bones. I'm actually in a good mood for a change, and I'm not about to let you get me all worked up." She poured him a steaming mug and then went upstairs to change back into her work clothes.

Cheryl looked at her watch and squawked. "Yikes… time flies when you're having fun… I shoulda clocked in five minutes ago… " She grabbed the bagful of cookies Lissy had prepared for her and ran for the door.

Quinn, still standing, walked over to Molly and planted a gentle kiss on her forehead. "We still have a couple of things to check out, but I wondered if you wanted to catch an early dinner with me, and then I could come over and help you close the café for Lissy."

282

Molly felt a tremor of excitement run through her. *This is just like high school... Oh, damn... I still haven't told him about high school.* Suddenly more nervous than excited, she took a deep breath and answered, "You're on... we have an important conversation to finish."

Quinn bowed, kissed Molly's hand and guided a puzzled-looking Lentz out the door. As Molly waited for the java queen to come back downstairs, she nibbled a cookie and smiled to herself. Lissy's response to her past had shocked her, but it had also made her realize that as awful as her indiscretions had seemed at the time, they weren't even a blip on the radar of other people's lives. Well, maybe a blip to Barbette, but she suspected the woman kept a large blip collection in order to use them against others. But Quinn... well, she knew she had to hand him the secret she had kept buried all this time. What he chose to do with it was up to him, and she hoped for the best. But the truth was, that in giving the secret to him, she would finally be able to let it go herself and if, heaven forbid, Quinn walked away from her, she would still be a better person for having done so.

After Lissy returned to the counter and Molly assured her she would be back before 7:00, she walked outside into the late afternoon snow. She was in danger... on some level she was aware of that, but in the midst of the darkness that gathered around her, she felt curiously light and free.

Chapter Fifty Six

Quinn flipped up his collar against the chill and slipped his hands into the pockets of his wool coat as he and Lentz walked down the tree lined street to Curt Golden's house. The interview with Helene Blanchard had answered their most pressing questions, but they just wanted to make one more pass at the timeline and they hoped Mr. Golden might be able to fill in some of the gaps. A cold wind was blowing and a light, dry snow had begun to fall. Quinn glanced enviously at Lentz's stocking cap and quilted parka and wished he had thought to bring a wool scarf and winter hat. *Man up, partner.* Strangely enough, the voice in his head was beginning to sound less like his father and more like his new friend, and Quinn decided that was a good thing.

While walking, they discussed results of the rush request for background checks on Helene Blanchard, Preston Locke, and Curt Golden that Quinn had just received. Helene's had come in squeaky clean, just as he had expected. She lived on a modest investment income, paid her taxes on time, and was quite active in the Lutheran church. The oldest of five daughters born to a poor farmer and his wife in upstate New York, she easily found work as an assistant nanny for one of New York's wealthiest families. Being very efficient and unlikely to tolerate nonsense, she was soon promoted and became known for her successes with difficult children. When Preston appeared on the scene, she was paid generously by the Locke family to accompany him to join his father in Hickok. It was assumed that she would return to New York, but she made the choice to stay with her charge. By all accounts, she liked the community and was, in turn, well-liked.

Curt Golden also had a clean record, despite the many tragedies in his life. His brother Jeff had been killed in an auto accident shortly before his nineteenth birthday. Curt had been seventeen at the time. His father, a prominent local physician, died four years later of a massive stroke. His mother inherited the entire estate, but soon, because of mental and physical issues, signed over control to her only remaining son, who quit medical school in his fourth year, and moved home to take care of her. Since then he had managed their investments conservatively, growing the estate into a tidy fortune. His mother had died of alcohol poisoning six years ago while he was away on a business trip. The police reported that he seemed very distraught and, even with the woman's long history of alcohol abuse, appeared to feel responsible. Other than that, Golden was active in local organizations, and known to be quite philanthropic. He was not considered a leader, though not exactly a follower either, and was respected in local business circles.

Preston Locke, on the other hand had lived a very big and very messy life. He had struggled with substance abuse throughout the years, having gone through treatment a number of times. The only part of his college career that could be called successful, was that which involved sex, drugs, and rock and roll. He managed to land in jail several times back in those days and barely dodged a sex-offender designation for taking off his clothes at a rock concert. While his father was still alive, he was given a comfortable allowance and after the old man died, Lucinda made sure he received half the estate. But he managed to squander a large chunk of it, before she intervened and helped him stabilize his assets. That had been fifteen years ago and his portfolio now allowed him to live a lifestyle that most people in Hickok would envy.

Interestingly enough, not one of the three had ever married, nor had there been any record of a "significant other." Preston Locke liked to be seen with beautiful women but apparently, none had made the cut.

Having reached their destination, Lentz rang the bell and they waited. They were just turning to leave when they heard footsteps.

When Golden opened the door he initially looked surprised, then genuinely happy to see them and quickly led the way into the living room, after first helping them out of their coats. Quinn wondered if the man had any real friends, but then remembered his association with Preston Locke.

After they were settled in front of a nice fire, Golden insisted on fixing them something warm to drink and hurried to the kitchen.

"So," said Lentz quietly, glancing towards the doorway. "Miss Blanchard did go back to the house early on, because she had forgotten something. She didn't see Cathy, but heard her from upstairs. Said the girl sounded strange, but thought it was just because she wanted the house to herself. What if Cathy wasn't alone? We need to find out from our new best friend here, if he remembers anything else that might help us."

"When we asked that question, he only remembered Miss Blanchard, but that was something he failed to mention to the police at the time… so, who knows?" Quinn shrugged.

"Right, old buddy, I have a gut feeling we're close… there's just some detail we're missing to make everything fall into place."

Golden bustled in with a tray of frosted sugar cookies. "Be back in a minute with drinks..."

Quinn was quiet until he was out of earshot. "You know, even though it seems unlikely, I keep coming back to Preston. Miss Blanchard did find him standing over Cathy's body, and everyone agrees he was high as a kite. Maybe we should ask..."

Golden returned to the room with another tray. "Thought you gents could use some hot cocoa and I took the liberty, since its early evening, of adding just a touch of peppermint schnapps. And I couldn't decide between whipped cream and marshmallows... you know those tiny ones, but I went for the whipped cream. Oh, I hope that's okay..."

Golden's worried expression made Quinn smile, and Lentz just looked relieved that he had been given a mug this time, rather than a delicate china cup. They both assured him it was "just what the doctor ordered," as they sipped their steaming drinks. Lentz dipped his cookie into the hot drink and it was Quinn's turn to smirk.

He looked relieved, and sat primly on an antique side-chair. "You probably think I'm crazy, but I just don't get too many visitors. So, how can I help you?"

"Well, we had a visit with Miss Blanchard and she corroborates your story, but we just wanted to ask a couple of follow-up questions."

"Well, of course... I'll do anything I can to help. That was such a terrible time and if I can help give Mrs. Locke some closure, well then it's worth having to remember it all." He took a sugar cookie, broke it in half and nibbled a piece.

"I know it's been a long time, but do you remember what time it was when you saw Miss Blanchard first return to the house."

Golden closed his eyes for a moment. "I was going to say no, but now that you ask I remember that it must have been just past 7:00 pm because the "Flower Power Music Hour" had just started." He turned to Quinn to explain. "That was a radio show and it was the only rock and roll we got back in those days. It was an hour a day, Monday through Saturday, from 7:00 to 8:00. The rest was country and western. I got so sick of country and western!" He looked suddenly embarrassed. "Anyway, it must have been just past 7:00."

Lentz looked impressed. "You should have been a cop, Mr. Golden... you have great attention to detail."

Golden looked down and blew on his drink. "Not sure I have what it takes to be a cop, but thanks, Mr. Lentz."

"Also, you said that you didn't know when Preston Locke left but that you saw him return and that he was pretty messed up. Was there a time when you realized he was missing? Do you remember the last time you saw him before he returned?"

"Oh, my, that might be hard. Let's see... Well, actually, after my brother and I had our 'altercation' I remember looking for Preston but he wasn't anywhere. I thought that was weird because, like I said before, he usually followed Jeff around like a puppy, even if my brother was mean to him. I wanted to assure him that Jeff was just kidding about his sister. But now that you bring it up, I don't remember seeing him for maybe an hour."

He was silent for a moment and then Golden got a strange expression on his face, and he quickly said, "This sounds like I think that Preston could have hurt his sister, but I'm not saying that at all. Preston is my

288

friend. Like I said before, I was in and out of the house a lot so I probably just missed seeing him... that's all."

"Did Preston ever talk about Cathy," Quinn asked gently.

"Well, sure. She was his kid sister and he called her a pest, things like that. It was just normal stuff... mostly."

"What do you mean mostly?"

"Well, once he said, 'Daddy's little angel needs to go to heaven' or something like that. We thought it was funny, but I know he didn't mean anything by it. Just family stuff... you know." Golden looked suddenly uncomfortable.

Lentz leaned forward and said kindly, "Hell, I'd still be in jail if I actually did all the things I threatened to do to my brother."

Golden visibly relaxed. "Well, like I said, I don't get a lot of visitors, so I'd like to send a bag of cookies with you, and I won't take no for an answer. If I don't give them away, I'll just have to eat them myself, so you would be doing me a favor. You two finish your drinks and I'll be right back."

"Well, when you put it like that," Quinn laughed and Golden headed back into the kitchen. When he was sure the man was out of range he leaned towards Lentz and asked, "What are you thinking?"

Lentz was frowning. "I think that someone is lying, has been lying all along, and I now have a pretty good idea who that someone might be. As soon as we leave here, I'll make one phone call and then I think we'll have our answers."

Feeling suddenly elated, Quinn held up his mug and said, "Well, then here's to the end of a mystery."

"Finally, after all these years," Lentz murmured and they finished their drinks.

Chapter Fifty Seven

Molly glanced at the big clock behind the bar again, and it was exactly five minutes later than the last time she looked. She had been waiting at the Full Rack for almost an hour and she was beginning to get a very bad feeling. She was also fighting off the irrational irritation that threatened to flare into real anger at the thought of being stood up… as any woman knew, being stood up was about as close to unforgiveable as it got. But that didn't sound like the Quinn she had come to know. Something must have come up… something that might shed some light on the questions they were trying to answer.

She hadn't ordered any food, and the waitress eventually got tired of asking and left her alone. With a sigh, she gathered up her things and headed toward the door, stopping first to introduce herself to the elderly cowboy at the bar who had given her a friendly nod when he entered. "Evening Ma'am," he said, lifting his hat to reveal a shiny bald pate.

"Evening," she replied, sitting down next to the old gent. "I just wanted to introduce myself since we keep crossing paths. My name is Molly, Molly Noble. I used to live in Hickok… my mother is still here."

"Would that be Shirley Noble? Your mama used to come out to the ranch and help us with calving when she was still in school. She was a pretty thing back then, with a lot of spunk. My wife used to laugh and say that girl was gonna give some fella a run for his money…" The old man smiled at the memory, then added, "You take after your daddy, Miss Noble, but I can see some of your mama in there, too."

She sat at the bar with him for a few minutes. His name was Will Jimmerson and he asked her to give his regards to her mother next time she saw her. She promised she would and, much to his surprise gave him hug before she left.

"Oh," Molly added before she walked through the door. "If you see the very tall and very late Mr. Quinn, could you tell him I'm over at Strange Brew?"

"Will do, Ma'am," said the old cowboy, nodding farewell.

"What the... get yourself upstairs and get cleaned up stat!" If it was possible, Lissy was more of a wreck than before. "It's a good thing I'm early, or you would be late for your date!" Molly noticed two trays of homemade cookies and a batch of fudge that had not been there before.

"I told you, I bake when I get nervous, and anyway, it's not really a date... it's just a dinner that I happen to be eating with someone else. I'll probably be back before the second course."

"Yeah... somebody that looks at you like he's starving and you're an ice cream sundae, so get upstairs and get that flour out of your hair. But," added Molly with a smirk, "You could invite him back here for dessert, if you know what I mean."

Lissy answered her with a rude gesture, but she couldn't quite wipe the smile off her face as she headed to the back stairs.

Molly laughed softly, put on an apron and, once again, grabbed a broom and began sweeping up after her friend. As she finished tidying

292

up the counter area, three women, loaded down with shopping bags, staggered in and ordered a round of hot cocoas. Molly, although not as efficient as Lissy, managed to fill their orders and, as a bonus, brought them a plate featuring a variety of the newly baked goodies.

"Hey, you're smarter than you look," Lissy stood in the doorway and was watching as the women abandoned all self-control and attacked the plate with relish. "Give them a lot of choices because, of course, they have to try each one and bite-sized pieces so they can believe they are getting fewer calories. Brilliant, really!"

Lissy was flour-free and looked lovely, if not a bit nervous. When Molly saw her looking at the mixing bowls and rolling pin longingly she guided her to a table near the counter and told her to stay put as she poured her a cup of coffee and plunked it down in front of her.

The table of shoppers looked content for the time being, though one of them was licking frosting off her fingers and eyeing the rest of the cake at the counter. Molly poured herself a cup and sat down across from Lissy. "You look absolutely beautiful! Poor Ed doesn't have a chance."

"Knock it off! I haven't been this nervous since... well I'm not sure I've ever been this nervous. Just let me throw together a batch of bread pudding. I promise I'll be careful."

"Sit and chill," laughed Molly. "You don't have a thing to be nervous about. Honest! Unbelievable as it sounds, that guy seems to like everything about you. So just be yourself."

"Thanks, Mom." Lissy settled back into her chair. "Hey, where's the big fella? I thought he was signed up to help you close."

"Good question. Quinn stood me up for dinner and I can either be seriously miffed or seriously worried, but to be honest I'm leaning towards worried. When I saw him earlier he said that he and Lentz had a couple of things to check out and then wanted to meet for an early dinner, but he never showed up. I haven't known him for long, but that just doesn't feel like something he would do."

"Are you nuts? The guy worships the ground you walk on and I can guarantee he would never miss a chance to be with you. Guess I'd better cancel my... ah... date, so we can get to the bottom of it." Lissy looked almost relieved.

"Nice try, but you are going to have dinner with Ed if I have to carry you over there myself. I'm sure it's nothing."

At that moment, the door opened and in walked the subject of their conversation. He looked at Molly, glanced at Lissy and then walked toward the counter. All of a sudden, he stopped, turned and looked again at Lissy. "Well, if I'd known I was gonna have dinner with a movie star, I woulda worn my tux." He whistled appreciatively and walked over to the table. He had obviously made an effort to clean up himself, looking surprisingly good in a wool shirt, denim jacket and jeans. He shook his head sadly. "Now I'm gonna have to stop by my truck and get a crowbar so I can fight off all the fellas that'll try to steal you away."

Lissy laughed nervously and stood up, almost spilling her coffee. She looked ready to bolt, but Molly gently nudged her towards Ed, who took her hand and guided her to the door. Lissy was almost as tall as Ed, and Molly thought they made a very cute couple.

Just as they were leaving, two high-school girls entered, followed a moment later by Curt Golden. Lissy stopped at the door to remind her of all the tasks necessary for closing, but Molly just waved them off.

As he closed the door, Ed called, "Don't wait up," earning him a punch in the arm from Lissy, but they were both smiling.

Molly was smiling, too; she was so happy for her friend. But duty called so she quickly ducked behind the counter and went into "java queen in training" mode. The girls had trouble making up their minds, so she waited on Curt Golden first. He asked for a complicated coffee drink, and as she prepared it he wandered off, looking at the artwork and pottery on sale.

As he paid for it, he gave her a big smile and a big tip. "It's too bad, Ms. Noble, that we haven't spent more time together. It's ironic... I don't have a traditional job yet my days are so full I hardly have a spare moment to myself."

"I know exactly what you mean," agreed Molly. The girls were suddenly anxious to order, so she gave him his change, expecting him to take his drink and go, but he stood there for a moment.

"Your friend, Quinn, and Mr. Lentz were just at my house. They seemed quite excited about something when they left. I do so hope they can put this business to rest and give poor Mrs. Locke some closure."

"Well, yes... did they happen to say where they were going?"

Golden thought for a moment. "Hmmm... they had just talked to Miss Blanchard before they came to the house and I think they might have been going to visit Preston. I can't be sure because I was in the kitchen off and on, but I think that's where they might have gone." He suddenly seemed to become aware of the fidgeting females behind him and quickly picked up his drink. "Goodnight, Ms. Noble. Hope to see you again soon." He gave her a jaunty wave and left.

Feeling slightly unsettled, Molly waited on the girls, gave them each a cookie, and then closed and locked the door behind them. As she flipped the sign to "closed" she assured herself that the counter area was clean enough, and then turned off the lights and headed into the kitchen to finish tidying up Lissy's baking mess.

She worked quickly, humming to herself, and when she was satisfied, she turned off the lights and went out the back door, carefully locking it. As she turned towards the alley, she came face to face with the barrel of a gun. Molly froze, but her blood ran even colder when a familiar voice said,

"Well, Miss Molly... looks like you've saved the last dance for me."

Chapter Fifty Eight

Quinn reluctantly opened his eyes, and then quickly closed them again, groaning. The room, whatever room it was, was spinning and it was all he could do to keep his stomach from heaving.

"It helps to pick one thing and focus on it. The dizziness will go away... but this headache... well that might take a while."

All Quinn wanted to do was to go back to that nice dark place where he had been a few minutes ago, but he was pretty sure Lentz wouldn't let that happen. With an effort he opened his eyes and searched frantically for something to focus on. He chose a doorknob across the room and stared at it as hard as he could. Lentz was right; after a few moments, the spinning stopped and Quinn was able to glance around the room. It looked strangely familiar, but he was pretty sure he had never been there before. It was a kitchen... oh hell, it was the kitchen where Cathy Locke had died.

He turned his head, and was rewarded with a bolt of pain that made his eyes water. "Holy mother of..."

"You can say that again, good buddy." Lentz was sitting to his left on a kitchen chair, and was liberally swathed in grey duct tape.

Quinn risked a glance down to see that he was in the same position. Someone had wanted to make very sure that neither of them could move and no duct tape had been spared in the process. Their mouths weren't covered, though, making him realize that there probably wasn't much danger of them talking their way of this one.

"Not sure how long we've been out, but I think we're getting short on time... maybe in more ways than one. The bastard's not through with us yet, or we'd already be dead. Not much we can do, taped up like this, but we need to shake off the effects of whatever drug was used so we can take advantage of any opportunity that might come our way." Lentz looked pale, but he had a firm set to his jaw and Quinn knew he wasn't about to go down without a fight.

Quinn took a deep breath and tried to slow his pounding heart. He, for one, wasn't used to being drugged and taped to a chair. "Okay, the last thing I remember is sitting in Curt Golden's living room. You said you needed to make one more phone call and that you thought you had the whole thing solved. We made a toast and after that it's all a blank."

"That's about the whole of it..."

But anger was beginning to creep up on him, and Quinn went on. "Whoever this guy thinks he is, he's in for more than he bargained for... you have police connections and abducting me will have international repercussions. I don't know what he hopes to accomplish with these shenanigans!"

Lentz was silent, and when Quinn looked over at him, he was staring back with his mouth open. "Please tell me you didn't just say shenanigans... and I was almost startin' to like you."

In spite of their dire circumstances, they both laughed.

Lentz shook his head. "When we first got to Golden's, there was something that was nagging at me, but it was just out of reach. But, after we sat there for a while it dawned on me that Curt Golden dropped out of medical school. That's the closest thing to a medical connection we have, and I'd be willing to bet he's also our friendly neighborhood dope dealer. Talk about hiding in plain sight. You know, I always felt sorry for the kid, but at the same time there was something about him that just wasn't right… could never put my finger on it."

Quinn answered, thoughtfully. "Even though we're both taped to kitchen chairs after having been drugged, I still have trouble believing that Curt Golden has been behind the whole thing. I mean, if you looked in the dictionary, he'd be the definition of normal. But I'll tell you one thing… for claiming that he didn't want to drop his best friend in the fire, he did a pretty good job of it."

"Exactly what I was thinking… Preston Locke is no angel, that's for sure, but he's also no killer."

"So, what was that one phone call you wanted to make?" Quinn chanced to look around the room.

"Well, I wanted to call an old friend in the department who had done some follow-up work after Jeff Golden's accident. Back then, he wasn't sure it was an accident at all… said there was evidence that the brake lines had been tampered with, but nobody wanted to hear it. Everyone else was relieved the kid was no longer around. Also, the kid's old man was a powder keg ready to go off, and after the fiasco with Cathy's murder the department was trying to keep a low profile. My friend even took it to the chief, who asked him if it was worth his job to keep making waves. That was the end of it, but he always thought it was a bad call… said he had proof and he kept the brake lines for evidence. By that time, I was on my way out, and didn't give it much thought. And even if it was true, I guess I figured half the town would have had a motive. It never once crossed my mind that Curt could have murdered his brother... until this evening, that is."

Lentz gave Quinn the once over and added, wryly, "Don't know about you, old buddy, but I think we've found our killer."

"Yes, but we may never find out why." Quinn felt strangely calm in the face of their situation.

"Oh, I wouldn't be too sure about that... people like Golden like to prove how smart they are. I'm sure he won't have any problem explaining how he beat us..."

At that moment the back door opened and Molly stumbled into the room, followed by Golden, who had a handful of her hair and a gun pressed into her back. He marched her to the center of the room, then pulled out a kitchen chair and pushed her into it. Picking up the duct tape from the counter, he quickly bound Molly to the chair, and then stood back, admiring his work. He carefully arranged Molly's chair so that it faced the two men, as if they were having a meeting, then stood back once more, nodding approval.

"Oh, how lovely... I know you're all anxious to get this show on the road, but we're still waiting for the guest of honor. Just talk amongst yourselves and I'll be back before you know it." He gave them all a dazzling smile and then danced through the kitchen doorway to the living room.

When he was gone, Quinn looked at Molly. A wave of anger rolled through him, to see her in such danger. More than anything he wanted to protect her and reassure her that everything would be okay. He wanted to take care of this woman, but with all the money and power in the world he was helpless, and the frustration was killing him. "Molly, are you okay? Did he hurt you? Molly, please say something…"

She looked pale and frightened, but he noticed that her chin stuck out ever so slightly and she returned his gaze evenly. "You are in deep trouble, Mister. You stood me up!"

Chapter Fifty Nine

Molly wasn't really feeling the bravado that she hoped she was displaying to Quinn and Lentz. Although Golden had not touched her, except with the barrel of his gun, he chatted about this and that all the way to Lucinda's house, in a strange sing-song voice. That frightened her more than if he had roughed her up and shouted. Sometime between him singing 'Tiptoe Through The Tulips' in the car and his awkward Gene Kelly dance number to the back door, Molly came to the sad realization that he wasn't angry, or jealous, or even greedy. He was crazy and she had no idea how to deal with that.

After her comment about being stood up, the look on Quinn's face might have made her laugh out loud, but given the circumstances she just shrugged as best she could while taped to a chair. "As usual, my timing sucks… I was just kidding about being stood up. Well, I really do hate being stood up… not that it happens a lot, of course… but it looks like you had a pretty good excuse. Next time, though… Oh, I hope there is a next time." Molly paused and took a breath. "Sorry about the babbling… just freaked, I guess."

"That's understandable, given our current situation." Quinn gave her a sad smile.

Lentz glanced at the doorway to the living room, from which they could hear Golden humming tunelessly. "The good news is that it won't take long for someone to figure out we're missing. I suspect the security folks you hired to watch Miss Molly here are hyperventilating and Lucinda's bound to be worried. She knows if I miss a visit it'll be over my dead body... uh sorry, bad choice of words. Anyway, if we can keep him talking long enough, we might get lucky."

Quinn glanced at his friend. "I feel better already. Now what's the bad news?"

"Bad news is I don't know how long "long enough" is, and this guy's on a short fuse."

Molly looked at Quinn with an expression of resolve, and then said, "If I don't tell you this, I might not get the chance and I'll never be free of it."

Quinn wanted to interrupt, to tell Molly that they had all the time in the world, but the look on her face told him this was important, so he just nodded. "Bring it on, Molly love... I want to know everything."

So she told him the secret that she had carried around her entire adult life, and he grew angrier at each detail. It didn't take long, there wasn't really much to tell in Quinn's opinion, and when she was finished a single tear rolled down her cheek and she looked expectantly at the two men across from her.

Quinn couldn't trust himself to speak right away, so remained silent, as did Lentz.

"Oh," a gasp escaped Molly, when she saw the expression on Quinn's face. "I was hoping you wouldn't hate me, but I guess I don't blame you if you do. I'm sorry... so sorry. I hurt a lot of people and now it looks like I hurt you, too."

"Molly, stop. What happened to you was terrible, but it wasn't your fault, and I think on some level you must know that. Someone in a position of authority took advantage of your naiveté and your trusting nature. You were a victim of the system and what happened to you in Hickok was a prime example of human nature at its very worst. You became the scapegoat, were given no support, even from your family, and the real culprit got away."

"Oh, I wouldn't say that," said Lentz, mildly. "You need to know Miss Molly that you weren't the guy's first rodeo… so to speak."

"What do you mean?" Quinn noticed that Molly's tears had stopped and the defiant look was creeping back.

"Well, little lady, when that happened I wasn't with the force, but I did some investigating on my own. Turns out the guy had been chased out of two other school districts before he ended up in Hickok. Same reason both times, and the second time, some girl's daddy ran him out of town with a shotgun." Lentz smiled. "After he left here, I had my friends keep tabs on him and make sure his reputation preceded him. Never worked in a school again, but opened a photography business back East. He got busted about ten years ago for statutory rape and child pornography… still in jail, if I'm not mistaken."

"Why, that sorry son of a… I hope he's the belle of the ball in prison!" Molly appeared to have forgotten all about being duct-taped to a kitchen chair by a killer.

Quinn was just beginning to enjoy himself when the sudden sound of a slamming door reminded him of their predicament.

Lentz leaned forward and whispered, "Okay, keep him talking as long as possible. Haven't quite figured out a plan, but I'm workin' on it."

Chapter Sixty

Eric had not stopped by, nor had he called, and Lucinda had a bad feeling... very bad indeed. When Cheryl checked on her after she clocked in a few hours ago, she told her all about Lissy's adventures in cooking and how wonderful she looked when she fixed herself up. She added that Quinn was taking Molly out to dinner and then they would close Strange Brew together. Lucinda found herself wishing that she had been there, and looked forward to a time in the near future when that would be possible.

But, as time passed and she had no word from Eric, she began to worry. Feeling foolish, although she knew that in these modern times it was perfectly acceptable she tried to call his cell phone, but it went straight to voice mail. She wasn't sure what to do next. She couldn't exactly call the police and tell them that she had a really bad feeling. She picked up the phone and tried Preston's number. No answer, although that wasn't really unusual. Next she tried Helene and her friend answered on the second ring.

"Lucinda, what a coincidence... I was just getting ready to call you. You know, tonight was choir rehearsal at the church... you must think I'm crazy to be in the choir, since everyone knows I can't carry a tune in a bucket... well actually, I suppose they're crazy to keep me, but I do always bring cookies and..."

"So, Helene, dear, why were you going to call me?" Lucinda interrupted gently.

"Oh yes, well, anyway, I was walking home after choir practice and I decided to go past your house, because the streetlights are much brighter and there aren't so many of those awful potholes in the sidewalk. You know, I almost took a spill right in front of my house the other day, that first day when it snowed. But I can assure you I called the mayor's office right away and reported the condition of the sidewalks. I mean, really, what is the world coming to?"

"Helene? The reason you wanted to call me?"

"Oh, yes. I was walking, like I told you, and then I saw Preston's car drive past. I thought he might offer me a ride, although I know that walking is good for me, but I don't think he saw me. Well, he drove right past me and parked in front of your house. I waved and yoo-hooed, but he just jumped out of the car, ran up to your door and went in. The strange thing was that the lights were already on at your house… the porch light, and the front room, and when I walked past I could see the kitchen lights were on, too. He seemed upset, Lucinda, but I can't imagine why."

"Helene, this is important. When was this? How long ago did this happen?"

"Oh my… well, let's see, I just got home so it was only about five minutes ago. But I'll have to call you later, dear… maybe tomorrow, because my program is just about to begin and it's a mid-season finale or something like that so I'm sure it will be very exciting. I'll stop by and tell you all about it!"

Lucinda hung up and immediately pushed the call button. When Cheryl came running in, she said, "Something is wrong. I need you to try to find Molly and Quinn and Eric… Maybe their friend Lissy might know something. If you can't find any of them in the next few minutes, then I'll call the police and tell them that someone has broken into my house and they need to check it out. Cheryl, please hurry I have a feeling this is a matter of life and death."

Without a moment's hesitation, Cheryl pulled out her cell phone and dialed Molly's number. No answer, then voicemail. Cheryl paused for a moment, and then dialed the number for the Full Rack.

As they waited for Lissy to be dragged, kicking and screaming to the phone, Lucinda thought about Eric and her new friends. She thought about second chances and she thought about all the time she had wasted by not taking chances. With an effort she threw back the bedclothes and swung her legs over. If risks were being taken, she wanted to take her share… *This is for you baby girl, sorry it took so long.*

Chapter Sixty One

Preston Locke walked into the kitchen and then stopped short with a look of bewilderment. "Curt, you said you had new information about Cathy. What's going on here?"

"Surprise! It's a party and you're the guest of honor." He slipped the gun out from beneath his jacket and aimed it at Preston. "Why don't you pull over a couple of chairs so we can have a nice chat before we play the party games?"

Preston looked stunned and didn't move until he was poked in the ribs with the gun, and then he pulled two chairs into the center of the room. Golden gestured with the gun and Preston sat down next to Molly.

"Curt, I don't understand. I thought we were friends…"

"Cut the crap, Preston. I'm a lot of things, but I'm not stupid. Before Jeff died you never gave me the time of day. And we both know that the only reason you tolerate me now is because you're afraid I'll out you about leaving the party the night Cathy died." Golden paused and looked at the others, obviously hoping for a reaction to his revelation.

"Sorry to disappoint you, son, but Preston told us all about it some time ago." Lentz seemed more than happy to burst Golden's bubble.

Golden's face went slack for a moment and then he beamed at Preston and clapped his hands. "Little Preston, you finally grew a set… your mother must be so proud!"

Preston looked at the three people taped to their chairs and then back at Golden. "You killed Cathy? You? I thought it could have been Jeff, but Curt, why would you do that? What did she ever do to you?"

Golden laughed; not just a chuckle, but a huge braying laugh. Preston cringed away from him, and Molly felt the knot of fear in her stomach growing into full-scale panic. He laughed and laughed and Molly thought it was the most disturbing sound she had ever heard.

He finally got himself under control, wiped a tear from his eye and said, "Oh dear that was priceless." He looked at the faces of his captive audience and sighed. "Well I suppose it won't hurt to tell you a story... one I'm sure you'll all find very interesting."

He settled into the chair, still aiming the gun at Preston, and began. "What I am about to tell you is not a sad story of an unhappy childhood. No siree, Bob. It's a story of triumph over hardship. It's a story of hard work, perseverance, and patience. It's a modern day Cinderella story!" He struck a pose, which Molly thought looked ridiculous.

"Ah, but I digress. I had the typical American family... you know, an overweight, pompous, tyrant of a father; a selfish, shallow, drunk of a mother; and a stupid, sadistic, bully of a brother... same old, same old. And there I was, the normal one, just trying to hold everything together. Do you have any idea what it's like to be normal when you live in the freak tent at the circus? I managed to blend in, though... I became the family clown."

Molly felt a jolt of shock and recognition at those words. Sitting across from her was the embodiment of the clown wall-hanging that had terrorized her childhood and the rodeo clown that stalked her dreams. In hindsight she couldn't believe she hadn't seen it.

Golden paused for dramatic effect, and then continued. "So, in my brother's last year of high school, he decides he's in love with the girl next door and they plan to run off together! Isn't that just the most romantic thing you've ever heard? The only problem is that my brother is eighteen and the girl is, oh, thirteen. Of course, he's not smart enough to do the math, but I am. He wasn't even bright enough to pick a girl who could be intimidated... one whose family could be paid off. No, he picks the only girl in town whose dear old Dad could... and would... destroy us."

He looked at Preston. "Don't get me wrong, your sister was quite the cutie pie, although I really couldn't understand what she saw in Jeff. I tried to talk to my brother, tried to reason with him on the night of the party... which, by the way, was his idea of a going-away bash for him and his girlfriend... but he called me a creepy nobody and bloodied my nose. I really won the jackpot on brothers. So, I pretended to give in, and brought him some of Dad's tequila to celebrate, but I had spiked it with my mother's tranquilizers and he was out like a light the rest of the night."

He sat back, looking thoughtful. "So, what to do... what to do? I took care of Jeff, but only for a while, because once he got something into his head, he never let it go. So, I decided to have a talk with Cathy, hoping that she was smart enough to be reasonable. I crossed the street and then went down the alley, stopping to pick a few flowers on the way, and knocked on the back door. No one answered, so I let myself in. I heard music upstairs, and followed the sounds. There she was standing in front of her bedroom mirror, singing "Holly Holy" and holding a hairbrush like it was a microphone. She had this cute outfit on and was doing a sexy dance... it got me hot. But then she saw me and I'll never forget the way she jumped and the terrified look on her face." He leaned over, and with a wry grin said, "To tell you the truth, that got me even hotter."

A moan escaped Preston, and his eyes were beginning to well up.

"Oh, don't be a party-pooper. I haven't even gotten to the best part yet! Well, I acted all embarrassed and told her that Jeff had sent me with a message. I apologized for coming upstairs, and I told her I had knocked, but that Jeff said it was a matter of life and death. I gave her the flowers and told her they were from my brother and she believed me. But right then, Miss Blanchard comes in... the old biddy forgot something... and Cathy was afraid she'd come upstairs and find me in her bedroom."

Preston moaned again. "Stop, Curt, please stop." The tears were now falling freely.

"No, we all need to hear this," said Lentz. "We need to know what happened."

Golden chuckled, "I have to admit I've been dying to tell this story for years. And I couldn't ask for a better audience."

"So, let's see, where was I? Oh, yes, after the old woman left, Cathy ran downstairs to put the flowers in water and I followed her. I was thinking she was really cute and I wondered why I had never noticed it before."

He looked at Molly. "You remind me of her... in fact, it gave me quite a shock when I first met you."

"She asked me what the message was, and I told her that Jeff wouldn't be able to make it and that he thought it would be a good idea if they cooled things off for a while, at least until she was older. I expected her to cry or something, but instead she told me that she thought the same thing. That she was too young to be making such big decisions and that she was going to talk to her mother about it, but now she didn't have to because it was all settled. She was so matter-of-fact, just like an adult. Preston, she was just too cute!"

"But then, I told her that I was available and she just looked at me like she didn't understand what I was saying. So I repeated that I was available and maybe I could be her boyfriend. She was quiet for a long time and then she laughed. She laughed at me and, well, that was just too much. I hit her… honestly I didn't think I had it in me… but I hit her hard enough that she fell to the floor. She landed face first, and I put my foot in the small of her back and grabbed her hair so I could see her face. She looked so afraid…" Golden smiled as he said this.

"I picked up a paring knife that was on the counter and held it at her neck. She was wearing this nice pearl necklace and I told her that if she gave it to me, I would let her go. I can't believe she fell for it. People are so stupid! But she took it off and handed it to me. She was trembling and made these funny hiccupping noises. I put it in my pocket, politely thanked her, and then slit her throat."

He was silent and the only sound to be heard was Preston's sobbing. "Baby sister, baby sister," he murmured.

Golden hummed an odd little tune and then said, "So who wants to play some party games? I won't take no for an answer." With a flourish he pulled a string of pearls out of his pocket, leaned over and fastened them around Molly's neck. "Ah, the symmetry… it comes full circle."

"Oh, and remember when I said I was dying to tell my story? Thank you all, I feel so much better for the telling." He stood up and aimed the gun at Molly. "But, unfortunately hearing my story will be the death of you."

Chapter Sixty Two

Quinn calmed himself. He knew it was a real possibility that this wouldn't end well, but he couldn't allow Molly to be hurt. He looked at Golden and said, in his best corporate executive voice, "I was hoping to hear why you murdered your brother."

The gun swung towards him. "Oh, don't be absurd… I didn't murder my dear brother!" Then Golden laughed. "Actually, it was a mercy killing. I just nicked his brake lines; made sure he had a good supply of dope and booze and waited. I can be very patient, you know. It was almost too easy. After Cathy died, Jeff just wasn't much fun. Always moping around… I found him crying once, can you believe it? It's one thing to have a brother that everyone's afraid of, but when people felt sorry for him… that was simply not acceptable."

"C'mon, Golden, who else? I know there had to have been more… you like it too much." It was Lentz's turn to face the barrel of the gun.

"Well, now that you mention it, I did keep my hand in it over the years… didn't want to lose my touch. But I was very careful… a junkie here and a drifter there. Remember those prostitutes that disappeared in the city a few years ago… moi!"

Golden became quite animated, waving his gun around as if to music in his head. "But, except for your lovely sister, Preston, my all-time favorite was my dear father. Remember back in the good old days when

I was in medical school? Well, I found I had quite an aptitude for pharmacology. When I was home for Thanksgiving break, I added a special little homemade concoction to my dad's prescription blood pressure medication. Just one magic little pill, and I shook the bottle so it wouldn't happen until after I had gone back to school. The old man had almost finished the whole bottle by the time he got to my present. What are the odds of that? His blood pressure shot up, he stroked out, and bye-bye." Golden sighed. "I only regret that I couldn't watch the old tyrant die."

"What about Lucinda? Why didn't you just kill her?" Lentz continued.

Quinn noticed that Lentz was beginning to rock in his chair, ever so slightly and he followed suit. He glanced at Preston, noting that the tears had stopped and that his expression had changed from anguish to anger. He nodded slightly in his direction and Preston nodded back. Molly's chin was out and she had her "bring it on" look.

"Oh, come on... you can't begrudge me my fun. I mean, I'm good at what I do... really good, but where's the challenge? And also, it was just too close to home, so I had to be careful and take my time. Remember, I'm very patient. You have to admit, though, it was brilliant, and I would have got away with it if it hadn't been for our friend, here." The gun swung back to Molly.

"So, here's how it will all play out. Preston, of course, murdered his bratty sister so he could have all of his Daddy's money... guess that didn't work out, but who knew? Then the white-trash Cathy look-alike cozies up to Lucinda and gets involved in the family secrets. She stirs things up so much that Preston, always unstable, finally goes berserk, kills the girl and her friends and then, sadly, takes his own life. All tied up with a bow for Hickok's fine police force." Golden stood up and did a dance step.

In the distance he could hear sirens, and Quinn felt just the tiniest glimmer of hope.

Golden obviously heard the sirens, too. "Oops, it sounds like the party's over… just a few loose ends to tie up." He looked at Molly, "Looks like you get to go first." He raised the gun and she closed her eyes.

Almost as if on cue, Lentz and Quinn rocked their chairs over, causing Golden to swing around. At that moment, Preston leaped on him, knocked him to the floor and tried to wrestle the gun from him. It went off, and Golden managed to elbow Preston in the face and get away. There was a sudden crash from behind, but Quinn couldn't be sure what it was. As Golden scrambled to his feet he turned the gun on Preston, but before he could pull the trigger, he was hit from behind.

To Quinn, who was on the floor still taped to a chair, it seemed like slow motion. Golden stood swaying for a moment, with a puzzled look on his face, and slowly dropped to his knees. Then his eyes rolled back in his head and he toppled like a tree.

Lissy stepped into his range of vision, with a crowbar in her hands, and there was a large man right behind her. "What? The asshole ruined my date and I went postal!"

The man behind her said, "Ruined? Hell, this is the best date ever…"

Quinn laughed, but something on Lissy's face stopped him and he followed her gaze.

Molly was still upright in her chair. She was looking at him and there was a ghost of a smile on her face, but she was very pale. Quinn smiled back. *Something's not right.* He looked down and there was a small pool of blood on the floor under Molly's chair and, for a moment, he didn't understand what he was seeing. Golden's wild shot had hit Molly and as he watched she closed her eyes and sagged in the chair.

"No!" he shouted, helpless even to move. The room was suddenly filled with policemen and emergency personnel. Someone righted his chair and did the same for Lentz, but there was a crowd around Molly and he couldn't see what was happening. He called to her and banged his feet in frustration until someone knelt down and began cutting away the duct tape with scissors. It was Lucinda.

"Hush, Quinn, hush," she said, as if to a child. "Cheryl came with me and she's with Molly now. She's going to be okay. She has to be okay. This story is damn well gonna have happy ending."

Chapter Sixty Three

"Hey, I know you."

Molly was disoriented. She could tell she was sitting, but she was cold and everything seemed so dark. She searched for the source of the voice until she noticed a smudge of light a few feet away and as she concentrated a young girl came into focus. It was Cathy, wearing the same pink fuzzy sweater she had worn in Molly's dream. The girl smiled at her and then stepped closer.

"It's Molly, right?" She came closer, peered into her face, and then looked her up and down. "Wow, you do look like me. That must have really freaked *him* out!" Cathy smiled at the thought.

"Cathy?" whispered Molly. "Am I dead?" She glanced down to see that she was sitting on one of Lucinda's straight backed kitchen chairs, minus the duct-tape. She reached out to touch Cathy, but the girl stepped back out of her reach.

"Not yet..."

"Not yet dead?" Not yet... what?" Molly could hear the edge in her voice.

"Not yet time to go where you need to go," was the enigmatic answer. "I have to go, too... and soon, but I wanted to thank you for saving my mother. I wasn't the greatest daughter, but she was the best

318

mother in the world. Not once in my life... not once... did I ever feel unloved. Can you tell her that when you see her?"

"Of course I'll tell her. And I feel the same way about Lucinda. I've never known anyone so caring."

"And none of this was her fault. Please don't let her think that for a moment. He would have killed her and he would have kept on hurting people... innocent people... for a long time. He's angry right now, very angry, but he still thinks he can fool people. I'm afraid he's going to be disappointed. And," Cathy added conspiratorially, "He won't last long in prison. That's one place where he won't be able to blend."

The girl moved in closer. "So, take chances, be happy, and follow your heart." She reached up to the pearl necklace around Molly's neck. "He was right about the symmetry... these look good on you. You should keep them." With one finger she gently touched the pearls.

Cathy began to fade, but there was a light in the darkness and it grew brighter and brighter until Molly had to turn away. From a great distance she could hear voices, a great many voices, but she couldn't understand what was being said. She finally focused on one voice, one that seemed to draw her...

"Hush, little baby, don't say a word, Mama's gonna buy you a mocking bird." Lucinda sang sweet and low.

Molly opened her eyes, blinking in the bright light. Still somewhat disoriented she glanced around the room. She was in a bed, a hospital bed, but everything seemed so familiar. It was the same room that her mother and Lucinda had shared not so long ago. *It really has come full circle.* Lucinda was sitting on one side of the bed and Quinn was standing on the other side, firmly holding Molly's hand. She thought she could see people milling around the doorway… Eric, Lissy, and Preston, but they were kept at bay by a vigilant Cheryl. Everyone was smiling or crying, or a combination of the two.

She tried to sit up, but was stopped by a pain that made her vision swim out of focus. Cheryl rushed over to the bed.

"Easy there, cowgirl, you got shot by the friendly neighborhood psychopath. I don't know who was looking out for you, but the bullet missed just about every vital organ and lodged in your hip without even breaking the bone. We got you into surgery right away, repaired a few nicks and removed the bullet. You're gonna be sore for a while, but you're gonna be just fine."

Cheryl settled her back in the bed and gave her a sip of water. "And think of the bragging rights… I mean, do you know anyone else who can say, 'Oh, the bullet wound? It's just a scratch?' Seriously, though, I really can't take you anywhere, can I?" Cheryl's eyes welled up and she whispered, "Glad you're back, that was a very close call."

She gave Molly an affectionate squeeze and then took off down the hall to the sound of her ever-present beeper. Quinn leaned down, kissed her hand and said, "Molly, love, don't ever leave me again." But before she could respond, she was mobbed by those who had been relegated to the hallway.

"Oh Lissy, thank you… you really saved the day!"

"Well," growled Lissy. "I couldn't a done it without Big Ed here. After Cheryl called us, we jumped into his truck to look for you. When we heard on the scanner that the cops were headed over to Lucinda's house, we were only a block or two away so Ed put the pedal to the metal. Front door was locked, so we came around back with a crowbar and looked in the window. Have to say I was surprised to see the weird goofy guy with a gun, but he looked pretty whacked out and was aiming at Molly... and then there was also that whole duct-tape thing. Chairs tipped and things got crazy, so Ed kicked open the door, and the next thing I knew I had the crowbar in my hands and the guy was on the floor. Like I said at the time, I went postal."

"I'll never again take my mail for granted," Preston vowed, and they all laughed. He was sporting the beginning of an impressive shiner where Golden had elbowed him. "But thank you for my life. I've never done anything brave or selfless before, and Preston the 'jerk' wanted to live long enough to brag about it."

Molly looked up at him. "Go ahead, joke about it, but you were a real hero, Preston. You made the difference between life and death." Preston blushed and Lucinda beamed proudly.

"Okay, okay, enough with the mutual admiration society. Everybody did good and I, for one, am just glad it's over. Come on Lucy; let's see if we can find someplace that serves decent coffee in this town."

Lentz took Lucinda's hand and led her toward the door, with Preston right behind them. Lissy huffed and turned to follow, but Molly grabbed her sleeve and pulled her close.

"Uh... Big Ed?"

"Oh, well..." Lissy actually giggled. "I don't know that for sure yet, but I have a good feeling. He even let me drive his tow truck!" She gave Molly a hug and took off after Lentz, muttering "decent coffee, my ass..."

And that left Quinn. He leaned over and gently kissed her forehead, then brushed her lips with the promise of passion.

"Molly, honey really!" Shirley Noble stood in the doorway and Dick stood behind her with a big grin on his face.

She marched up to Quinn and put her hands on her hips. "I think my Molly has had quite enough excitement for one day, thank you very much."

Quinn nodded solemnly and stepped back, but Molly could see he was having difficulty keeping a straight face.

"Well, dear, with everything that's happened I didn't want you to be concerned about me not having a ride to my therapy appointment. Dick volunteered to take me from now on, so you can just put that worry out of your mind."

The woman took a step towards the bed and looked closely at her daughter. "Well, you do look pale, but one of the nurses told me you'd be up and kicking in no time at all. I still don't understand how on earth you got shot... maybe, when you get out, you can explain it all to me." She looked at her watch. "Oh, dear, I suppose I had better go. Dick volunteered to take me grocery shopping and then we're having lunch at the house." She walked to the doorway, then stopped and turned around. "I love you, honey, and I'm glad you're okay."

"Love you too, Mom..." Molly whispered, as the woman walked briskly out the door. She was hit by a momentary wave of melancholy; the relationship with her mother was bittersweet at best.

But then Quinn, once again, was at her side. He took her hand and looked into her eyes. "Molly, my love, I want to ask you to..."

"Wait."

"But I was about to ask you…"

"I want you to wait, Quinn. I want a proper courtship with all the bells and whistles, and before I can answer your question, you need a thumbs-up from the two other men in my life."

Quinn looked shocked, and then laughed. "You're on, love… bells and whistles it is, with chocolate on top. And I can be very charming, so your boys can't help but like me. I'm quite spoiled, really, and always get what I want." He leaned over and kissed her with all the passion that was promised earlier. "And what I want, Molly Noble, is you."

Chapter Sixty Four

A few weeks later...

Suffering from an overdose of pumpkin pie, Molly sighed and pushed herself away from the table. She closed her eyes. There was chaos all around; raucous laughter from the kitchen, the sounds of a full scale video game battle filtering up from the game room, a rousing rendition of 'Heartbreak Hotel' from the living room, and an enormous barking dog on the porch who wanted to join the party in the worst way. She opened her eyes and smiled happily. It was heaven.

At that moment Quinn wandered up from the game room, obviously having reached his limit for video game humiliation. He planted a kiss on the top of her head and sat down. "Your children are without mercy... they remind me of me, but don't tell them I said so. And please don't tell them I came up here and whined to Mommy!" He grabbed a plate and served up a generous slice of pie and added whipped cream. "Too bad we're out of coffee," he said loudly.

"Keep your knickers on, greedy pig," Lissy called from the kitchen. Even though Molly had prepared the turkey and dressing, Lissy had brought side dishes and desserts that defied the imagination. She also, quite naturally, placed herself in charge of coffee, tea, mulled cider and whatever else she managed to dream up.

After a minute or two of gratuitous grumbling, she stomped into the dining room and plunked a full carafe and a plate of fudge on the table. Ed followed her in, grinning happily while munching a frosted sugar cookie cut into the shape of a turkey.

Molly groaned. "I can't believe I'm saying this, but I'm too full even for fudge. This is without a doubt the most amazing feast I've ever had. I'm so glad we're all together."

The jam session in the living room ended and Eric Lentz wandered past to let his dog Jasper join the party. He trotted in, looking more like a small horse than a dog, and went straight to Lucinda, who knelt down and rubbed his ears, causing the enormous animal to roll over like a puppy.

"So much for loyalty," laughed Eric, watching Lucinda and his dog. The look on his face pulled at Molly's heart. Lucinda, Lucy to him, had put her big house on the market and was staying with him at his cabin. She had hinted to Molly that there may be a wedding in the near future. Quinn kept hinting about the same thing, but Molly was in no hurry.

She looked around the room trying to commit it to memory. In two months she would be gone from here, moved into her new house in Jennings, halfway between Monroe and Hickok. Her house had gone under contract the day she officially put it on the market… there had never even been a 'for sale sign' on her front lawn. She looked forward to her move, she really did. She had found a sweet stone cottage on the outskirts of town, with a creek running through the property, but she had raised her children here and the place was full of memories. *Change is good, change is good.*

Soon her friends would be leaving to return to Hickok. Quinn would stay until she gently nudged him out the door. Her sons would take their video games and laundry and return to college, and Molly would have her life back… whatever that meant.

Before, her world was tidy, controlled and predictable… just the way she liked it, but through crazy circumstances, she had opened the door to chaos… to the insanity of relationships, and now there was no going back. Her boys wandered upstairs to raid Lissy's goody stash and she watched them interact with Quinn; lots of good-natured shoulder punching and macho name-calling. This felt so right. Order was overrated, she decided. Returning to the moment, she gathered up dirty dishes and followed Lissy into the kitchen.

Yes, life went on, but it was different.

Melinda Byrde lives with her husband in a quirky mountain community, cooks like a maniac, and sings the blues whenever she can.